W9-CCP-120

1/12

the

world

we

found

the
world
we
found

A Novel

THRITY UMRIGAR

HARPER

An Imprint of HarperCollins*Publishers*
www.harpercollins.com

HarperCollins books may be purchased for educational, business, or sales promotional use. For information, please write: Special Markets Department, HarperCollins Publishers, 10 East 53rd Street, New York, NY 10022.

FIRST EDITION

Library of Congress Cataloging-in-Publication Data is available upon request.

ISBN: 978-0-06-193834-4 (Hardcover)
ISBN: 978-0-06-213025-9 (International Edition)

12 13 14 15 16   OV/RRD   10 9 8 7 6 5 4 3 2 1

for

gulshan

hutokshi

perveen

always

"Suppose the world were only one of God's jokes, would you work any the less to make it a good joke instead of a bad one?"

—GEORGE BERNARD SHAW

BOOK ONE

1

The tooth broke three days after she received the awful news. There was no blood. No pain, even. For three days she had believed that it was her heart that had broken into tiny fragments, but turned out it was another part of her body that decided to mourn the news. No pain, no blood. Just a moment of puzzlement as she bit into the soft French toast she made for breakfast this morning and felt something hard and brittle in her mouth. She spat out two small pieces into her cupped hand. Adish stared at her for a stunned second and then said, "Oh, no. What happened?"

She stared back at him, unable to reply, transfixed by the rightness and wrongness of the broken tooth. On the one hand, she was not yet fifty and in the pink of health, as her mother would have said. Much too young to be losing teeth at breakfast. On the other hand, the evidence before her was appropriate, an outward manifestation of the brokenness she'd felt ever since the phone call from Armaiti. An uncharacteristic acceptance descended upon Laleh, in contrast to the denial she had felt since Armaiti called with news about her cancer. Then, she'd felt like a wild animal, lassoed by the tyranny of the telephone cord. No, no, no, she'd shaken her head as she got off the phone.

She rose from the table and headed into the bathroom. She

rinsed her mouth with cold water, and only then did she look up into the mirror. It was a side tooth and a stubble was still attached to her gums, and yet, how irrevocably it altered her appearance. For some absurd reason, it reminded Laleh of the New York skyline after the towers went missing, a gap that drew attention to what was absent. Until now, her teeth had been as sturdy and even as piano keys; but then, until now her oldest friend in the world had not been dying. It was right somehow, in this week of reminders of mortality, that she sacrifice something, too.

Still, she regretted the timing. She and Kavita were meeting in a few hours—not enough time to phone the dentist and get an emergency appointment—to go to Mrs. Lokhanwala's old address. They had not seen the woman in almost thirty years, and given the crucial nature of their mission, Laleh would've preferred looking her best. The broken tooth was already making her self-conscious. Laleh usually prided herself on not being vain, though the truth was, being beautiful, she could afford to give up on vanity. But now, she promised herself that she would simply not smile during her visit to Mrs. Lokhanwala's. If the woman—who would be, what? seventy-five? eighty?—was still alive, that is. She didn't allow herself to think of what they'd do if Nishta's mother had died or moved.

She heard Adish enter the bedroom and the next second he stood before her, leaning into the doorframe of the bathroom and gazing quizzically at her. "You okay, janu?"

She nodded, smiling with her mouth closed. "I'm fine."

"Sure you don't want me to go with you today? I could leave work for a few—"

"No need to. We'll manage. I'll call you if there's anything."

He ran his index finger gently over her lips. "Shall I call Sarosh to see if he can fit you in later this afternoon?"

"That would be great."

"Because you remember the party tonight, yes? I'm sure Sa-rosh can make you a temporary crown."

"Oh, shit. I totally forgot." She made a pleading face. "Can't you just go without me?"

In reply, he leaned forward and kissed her cheek. "Bye. Let me know what happens."

She grumbled lightly to herself as she got her things ready for her bath. Adish knew how much she hated his work par-ties, how lonely the empty prattle—the fake heartiness and fake humility—made her feel. They almost always fought on the way home from one of these affairs. And yet he persisted in asking her to go. Last week, after Kavita got held up at work, she had dragged Adish to a play, and in exchange he had extracted a promise to accompany him to Girish Chandani's party tonight.

Ah well, Laleh thought as she entered the shower. There were more important things to think about this morning. Nishta, for instance. They had to find Nishta. To relay to her Armaiti's fi-nal wish. Even though there had been years of silence between Armaiti and her. Even though such a wish may mean nothing to Nishta. Even though she had disappeared from all their lives, leaving only still air in her wake.

Kavita was driving, and, watching her steady, competent hands on the wheel, Laleh smiled to herself. She remembered Kavita as she'd been in college, a shy, dreamy girl who carried her gui-tar around everywhere. Hard to believe that that poetic, pensive girl was now one of the top architects in the city. Laleh sank into the leather seat and sighed inaudibly, feeling a lifetime removed from the young, impetuous, idealistic woman she'd been. From the time when Kavita-Armaiti-Nishta had been one word in her book, one beating heart. Where were they all now? One dying in America, one missing, and only Kavita still in her life.

"What?" said Kavita, ever attuned to Laleh's moods.

Laleh shook her head, unable to speak, her mind snagging on the memory of a certain golden afternoon. They had gotten together at Nishta's house to study, but what Laleh remembered now was the four of them lying on their backs on Nishta's bed, their knees bent at its edge, so that their feet touched the floor. "Those Were the Days" blasted on the stereo and they sang along lustily and loudly. "*La la la la, la la*," they sang at the top of their lungs, kicking their legs in time to the music. And suddenly, Armaiti had leapt out of bed and began to dance, dance with such loose, comic abandon—her hair flying about, tossing her head back and forth, flaying her rubber-jointed arms and legs—that the others rose to their feet and joined her. By the time the song ended, they were all laughing and sweating and exhausted. And then, as if she'd not been the agent of all this happy chaos, Armaiti said critically, "What a morbid song, yaar."

"What're you thinking?" Kavita asked.

"Nothing. Everything. About how young we were once."

Kavita looked rueful. "Know what's really sad? I used to think that everybody had that much fun in their teens. That everyone had the kind of friendships we did, felt as much passion and joy."

"I didn't," Laleh said promptly. "I always knew what we had was rare. Always. Even then. My own children don't have it, Ka. They have lots of friends, don't get me wrong. But it feels superficial to me. All they talk about are iPhones and designer jeans. And they want nothing to do with politics. It's crazy."

"It's a different time, Lal. They're growing up in a different India."

"Bull. That's what Adish says, also. But what's changed, Kavita? All the old struggles are still there, no? So they build a few dozen new malls for people like us. What does that change?"

How her father used to scoff at her and Armaiti when they would talk about building a better country. "A new India?" Rumi Madan would thunder at the dinner table after listening to the two teenagers talk matter-of-factly about the imminent revolution. "What do you girls think this is, a school play? What 'new India' are you two going to build? Darlings, if there is to be a new India, it will be built by the politicians and the businessmen. Above all, the businessmen. Not by a couple of little girls pretending to be revolutionaries."

Laleh blinked back the tears that rose unexpectedly. Ever since the phone call from Armaiti, the past had become more vivid than the present. She had sleepwalked through the past few days, unable to focus on anything.

And now, the past loomed again, in the form of Nishta's old apartment building. A thousand memories flooded Laleh's mind as Kavita searched for a parking space on the tree-lined street. And although she had felt a great urgency to locate Nishta's parents ever since Armaiti had called with the news, Laleh now felt herself moving slowly, as they exited the car and walked toward the building. When they reached the entrance, she and Kavita stood wordlessly for a second. Then Kavita exhaled loudly and they entered the familiar lobby. Their eyes scanned the large wooden board for the Lokhanwalas' flat number. "Look," Laleh said. "They're still here. Thank God."

"The lobby still smells the same," Kavita said, and Laleh nodded as they approached the elevator. "Yup. Like sandalwood."

They rang the doorbell twice before the servant girl answered. "Hello. Is memsahib home?" Kavita asked.

"Who is calling?"

Kavita hesitated. "Just tell her . . . it's some old friends."

The girl threw them a skeptical look before putting on the door chain.

"Yes?" A wizened face peered out at them a few seconds later from the slight opening in the door. "How can I help?"

"Auntie, it's us—Kavita and Laleh. Nishta's college friends. You remember us?"

There was a puzzled silence and then the old woman cried out softly. There was a rustling of the chain before she threw the door open. "Kavita. Laleh. I cannot believe. What brings you here? Come in, come in."

A minute later they were sitting across from Mrs. Lokhanwala in her large, airy living room, the three of them staring at each other, all of them too polite to comment on the changes time had wrought. "What will you take?" the old lady said at last. "Coffee? Tea?" And before they could answer she was calling out, "Deepa. Bring three cups of coffee. And some snacks."

"Auntie, please. Don't go to any trouble," Laleh said. Her mind was whirling, trying to reconcile the fact that the stylish, trim Mrs. Lokhanwala—had they ever known her first name?—was now an old lady. The living room itself looked frozen in time—the same cream-colored walls, the gray floor tile, the beautiful teak rocking chair.

"My God, you two look just the same," Mrs. Lokhanwala said. "I would've recognized you anywhere."

They smiled shyly. "You, too," Kavita lied. "And what news of Nishta?"

At the mention of her daughter's name, a curtain fell over the old woman's face. The smile vanished. Her eyes turned cloudy. "You don't know?" she whispered.

Laleh leaned forward. "Know what?" she said.

"We don't have any contact with her. My husband—he forbade any relations. She married a Muslim boy, you know."

Laleh realized that she'd been holding her breath. "Yes, we know," she said. "Iqbal was a friend of ours." She forced herself to keep her tone neutral. "We had hoped that after all this time, you know, that there might have been a reconciliation."

Despite her tact, the older woman recoiled, as if she'd been slapped. She stared out at the balcony for a minute before turning to face them again. "What brings you here today?" And before they could answer, "And whatever happened to that other Parsi girl—the fourth one? What was her name?"

"Armaiti," Kavita said.

"Ah, yes. So much I've thought about all of you over the years." Mrs. Lokhanwala smiled. "So lively our house used to be, with all of you here." Her face fell. "Now it's just me and my husband, you know. Our son—you remember Arun?—is settled in Australia. Anyway, how is Armaiti? You see her often?"

"Fine," Laleh said automatically and then she caught herself. "Actually, auntie, she's not fine. She lives in America, you know. And"—it was still hard to say the words, but she forced herself—"we just found out that she has a serious illness—a brain tumor."

"Arre, Ram—" Mrs. Lokhanwala's hand flew to her mouth. "How could that be? That sweet little girl?"

For a moment Laleh saw Armaiti as Mrs. Lokhanwala did— a teenager forever. She swallowed. "Yes, well . . . And that's why we're trying to find Nishta. Armaiti wants to reconnect with her, you see."

The woman's face was impassive. "I wish I could help you," she said.

Laleh suppressed the wave of anger that rose within her. "Does Nishta never try to contact you, either?" she asked evenly.

Mrs. Lokhanwala's eyes darted around the room. "Every year she sends me a birthday card," she said. "But my husband doesn't allow me to open. I just throw it away. Or return it."

Laleh stared at a spot over the old woman's left shoulder. She had saved every note her children had ever written her, from kindergarten on. She tried to imagine throwing away a birthday card from Ferzin or Farhad, asked herself what the children could ever do that would make her renounce them. She couldn't come up with one plausible scenario.

The servant girl came in with a tray and set it carefully down in front of them. Laleh grabbed Kavita's arm and pulled her to her feet as she stood up. "I'm sorry, but we have to go," she said. She wanted to get away from Mrs. Lokhanwala's presence before she said something that she would regret.

"At least have a cup of coffee," Mrs. Lokhanwala protested, but her voice was drained, flat, and there was a look of understanding on her face.

"I'm sorry, auntie," Laleh insisted. "We are already late." She would be damned if she took a sip of anything in this household.

Kavita took a few steps to where Mrs. Lokhanwala was sitting and put her hand on her shoulder. "It was nice seeing you again," she said softly. "Both of us have such good memories of this house."

Laleh felt a faint flush on her cheeks, reading a rebuke of her rude behavior in Kavita's thoughtfulness.

Mrs. Lokhanwala took Kavita's hand in both of hers. "I know it must seem strange," she began, but Kavita was already backing away.

They didn't say a word to each other as they rode the elevator five floors down. The silence held as they walked out of the building gate, crossed the two-lane street, and made their way toward the car. Finally, Kavita turned to Laleh. "I wish we'd never gone there," she said.

"I know. What kind of mother turns her back on her child?"

"I get the feeling it's the husband who's controlling the situation." She mimicked Mrs. Lokhanwala. " 'My husband doesn't allow me to open the card.' "

"Listen," Laleh said fiercely. "If Adish told me I couldn't talk to my children, I would pull his tongue out with pliers before I would comply."

Kavita sighed. "She's from a different generation, Laleh."

"Excuse, please," a soft voice said behind them. They turned around. It was the Lokhanwalas' servant girl. She was holding an envelope in her hand. "Memsahib wanted me to give you." She handed the envelope to Kavita, looked up toward the building, and then walked briskly away.

They followed the girl's line of vision in time to see a figure leaning over the fifth-floor balcony. But a second later the person had moved indoors. It was obviously Mrs. Lokhanwala, making sure that the servant had carried out her instructions.

Kavita turned the envelope around. It was addressed to Mrs. Lokhanwala and there was a return address, which someone had circled in red, with an arrow pointing toward it. And with the same red-ink pen Mrs. Lokhanwala had written in large, shaky letters, "Do not judge me. Please."

Kavita and Laleh looked at the piece of paper, and then each other. They glanced at the now-empty balcony, and then back at the envelope. When Laleh finally looked at Kavita again, her face was red. "I feel like a total piece of shit," she said.

2

Armaiti had been weeding for an hour, ignoring the waning light of the day, when she noticed the dead cardinals.

There were two of them and they lay facing each other, their eyes open, their beaks nearly touching, as if they had been kissing. Their bright-red feathers were bleached to a rusty brown, which told Armaiti that they had been dead for a few days.

Putting on the gardening gloves that she usually forgot to use, she lifted one of the birds gently, half-expecting it to stir and fly away. It felt impossibly light and bony, as if all that plumage was just dazzle, a sleight of hand to cover up a hollow core. The thought made her feel tenderly toward the dead bird. Turning it in her hand, she examined it for a wound, a mark where a cat or a larger bird may have attacked it, but saw nothing. She looked up at the June sky, as if expecting an answer. There was no overhead tree from which the pair could've fallen. Maybe the birds had simply tumbled out of the sky, she thought, the way whales sometimes beached themselves on the shore, for no apparent reason. The thought of these beautiful, red creatures falling to earth made her eyes fill with tears.

She was holding death in her hands. The thought unnerved her and she hastily set the bird down. But then she remembered, and she grimaced. She was holding death in more than just her hands—her entire goddamn body was playing host to it, throwing it a grand old party. To take her mind off the subject she checked her watch again. Still too early to hear from the others. The others. After all these years, that's still how she thought of them. Laleh, Kavita, and Nishta. Would they find Nishta? Find her in time? She so badly wanted to see the three of them again. But now, only now, while her body was still hers. Still hers, most of the time. Not later, when things would get ugly, when her diseased brain would be calling the shots.

Armaiti pushed herself off the ground and for a second the earth wobbled before righting itself again. But the next instant she was distracted by a sharp stab of pain in her knee as she rose. She usually thought of all pain as something to ignore, like a person with bad table manners. Today, she noticed. For the past two weeks, ever since the biopsy report had come back positive, she had been attentive to every whisper and whimper of her body.

She went into the wooden shed behind the garage and returned with a trowel to dig a hole to bury the birds. She laid them side by side in the small grave and then covered them with dirt. Later this week, she thought, she would plant some petunias over the spot.

It was getting too dark to stay out in the yard much longer. And Richard and Diane were indoors, putting together a dinner she knew she'd be too tired to eat. Still, she would try. For their sake. She had brought enough heartbreak into their lives, for the second time in five years. First the divorce, and now this. Diane, now a junior at Harvard, had still been in high school back then.

Why had she been so resolute to divorce Richard? Armaiti wondered as she put away the gardening tools. He had begged her not to go through with it, had sworn that Blossom Greer meant nothing to him. But what had sealed their fate was that Richard had no explanation for the affair. He looked as bewildered and incredulous as she felt. And that unnerved her. If there was no reason, no discontent that explained his infidelity, then it meant that something restless and untamable lived inside of Richard. Armaiti found it unacceptable, this mysterious threat to their life together, whose very ordinariness was their greatest triumph.

"What if it happens again?" she had said to him.

"It won't," he'd stammered.

"How do you know?"

"I . . . I . . . just . . ."

Two days later she called their lawyer.

But although Richard had been out of the house for five years, he still was what he had always been—her closest friend in the United States. Now it seemed to her as if they'd just been play-acting—the cheating husband, the outraged, unforgiving wife. How silly, how *unnecessary* it all seemed now. As she crossed the lawn and walked toward the house, Armaiti was struck by a thought: she had been afraid of the dangerous, unpredictable thing residing in Richard's heart, and it turned out that she had been carrying her own dangerous, unpredictable thing, nestled in her brain. As she pushed open the screen door, she marveled at the bleak irony of fate.

They had broken the news to Diane five days ago, and it had not gone well. They had waited until she came home from Harvard for the summer to tell her. And as if the shock of telling your only child that you're dying of a brain tumor—how lurid those words sounded, even now—and that you have six to eight months to live—like lines from a cheap movie—wasn't bad enough, she also had to break the news about her decision to refuse treatment.

Diane had remained calm, had kept her emotions under control as they told her about the unexplained headaches, the MRI, the biopsy. Her demeanor reminded Armaiti of the old days, when her four-year-old daughter would put on her lipstick and wear her shoes around the house, convinced that stepping into her mother's shoes made her a grown-up.

The trouble came a few minutes later. "When's your next appointment?" Diane said. "I wanna go with you to discuss treatment options."

"There isn't going to be any treatment, honey. I decided against it."

Diane looked puzzled. "Meaning . . . ?"

"Meaning I'm not going to get better. Even with treatment. It's a glioblastoma—a very aggressive tumor. Inoperable. Did I already tell you that?" Armaiti willed herself to go on, even though Diane looked as if with each word she was hammering a nail into her face. "I have six months or so, Diane. Maybe more. Who knows? You can't ever pin these doctors down. Not that they would know, either. How could they?" She heard the jittery quality in her voice and forced herself to slow down. "And I don't want to ruin that time with radiation and all that nonsense."

" 'All that nonsense'?" Diane's voice was shrill. "Mom? We're talking about something that could save or extend your life." She shifted in her chair to face Richard. "Dad? Say something. This is nuts."

Richard's face was blank. "I've spent all week arguing with her, honey. Her mind's made up."

Diane looked incredulous. "Are you guys frigging kidding me?"

"Watch your language," they both said automatically but Diane interrupted them. "Screw my language," she said, rising to her feet and looking around the room wildly. "This is bullshit. I can't believe—"

"Diane," Richard said. "Control yourself."

She flung her father a hostile look. "I can't believe you're letting her do this. That you'd just let her . . ."

"He's not doing anything." Armaiti's voice was more emphatic than she'd intended it to be. "It's *my* body. If I can't choose . . ." Her voice shook with outrage. But the next second her anger faded, as she took in her daughter's stricken face. "Listen. You don't know what I'd give to spare you this."

"Then start with the treatments. I'll take next semester off. I'll help you through it, I promise."

Armaiti reached out and pulled Diane back down on the chair next to hers. "I don't want to, honey," she said. "I—I watched my mother go through cancer treatment years ago. It was awful. And in the end it didn't make much difference."

"But that was more than twenty years ago," Diane said fiercely. "And it was in *India*. Things are so much more advanced now."

Armaiti nodded absently, remembering the small, dark bedroom in which her mother had died. After staying up half the night holding her mother's hand she had finally dozed off for a few minutes. When she awoke her mother's hand was cold and she was dead. Armaiti had sat holding that hand, taking in the bald head, the sunken eyes, the bony forearms whose papery skin was covered with bluish-black marks. She had not cried. Not then. Instead, she'd gone into the living room and phoned her Uncle Jamshed and asked him to call for the hearse. Then she'd padded into the other room and crawled into bed with her sleeping husband, letting some of his warmth seep into her. She had not awoken Richard until she'd heard the ambulance pull up outside the building. Then she shook him awake and he knew by her expression, and they stared at each other for a long moment before she rose to answer the doorbell.

"Mom? Are you listening?" Diane's voice had the streak of impatience that she'd first developed at thirteen and never lost. But now Armaiti heard something else in that voice—concern and fear, as if the fact that her mind had wandered for a second was proof of something more sinister, of the danger lurking in her cells. Get used to it, she told herself grimly. She had noticed that same thing in Richard already, a dual note, an undercurrent, a second melody that ran under the first one. Never again would she be allowed the old luxuries of forgetfulness or unpredictability. Now they would be measured against the backdrop of her illness.

"I am, darling," she replied. And then, realizing that Diane was waiting for a response: "I'll see. Let me think about it."

"Yeah, right," Diane said. "We all know what *that* means." She rose from her chair and looked down at them. "I'm going out for a while."

"When will you be back?" Armaiti asked automatically, hating herself even as she did.

Diane looked away. "I don't know. I need some air."

They heard the side door slam a few moments later. "I wish she had a boyfriend." Armaiti sighed. "It would make this so much easier for her."

"Armaiti," Richard said quietly. "We've just told the kid that her mother is . . . is . . . very sick. And refusing treatment, to boot. I don't think a boyfriend would lessen the shock."

Armaiti smiled ruefully. "You're right." She turned to face Richard. "I know you don't agree with me, either. But I need you to support me, okay? I'm not sure I can fight Diane by myself."

He made a small gesture with his right shoulder. "I'm here," he said simply.

Richard stayed with her until Diane came home, at nine that evening. There was a faint smell of alcohol on her breath. Armaiti fought against the lecture that percolated on her lips. Diane was a good kid, responsible. She'd probably had no more than a beer.

"Listen," Richard said as he rose to leave. "I have a meeting downtown tomorrow. Why don't you guys meet me at Roxy's for lunch?"

Armaiti turned toward Diane. "Hon?"

She shrugged. "Whatever."

It was another warm, breezy spring day the following afternoon, and despite Diane's sullenness and monosyllabic responses during the drive downtown, Armaiti felt her spirits lift as they walked toward the restaurant. But the momentary uplift was soon flattened by another, contradictory, emotion—for the first time since the diagnosis, a needle-sharp regret threaded through her. How lovely, how light, how pleasurable this afternoon would have been without the knowledge of what was to come, and of what already was lurking in her body. It would've been an afternoon like any other, an untroubled day in a long chain of such days. There would be none of this ticking awareness of how finite, how precious, this time with her daughter was; she wouldn't have been aware of the miraculous sun on her face, wouldn't have wanted to run her fingers lightly but greedily over the surface of the beautiful stone buildings they passed. She was storing memories, she realized, imprinting this day onto her mind, and for a moment Armaiti thought she could cry over what she had lost—the ability to live unselfconsciously, unreflexively. Involuntarily, her hand reached out for her daughter's, and, to her relief, Diane let her grip her hand.

"I love you," she said. "More than I can ever say."

Diane gave her hand a squeeze. As they reached the restaurant, they spotted Richard sitting at a table by the window and waved. He rose as they entered the restaurant and approached him. "How's my beautiful family today?" he said, and suddenly Armaiti felt beautiful. He'd always had this ability, Richard.

They were through with lunch and sharing a chocolate torte for dessert when Richard said, "Oh, by the way. Jordon called this morning." He wiped a piece of dark chocolate from his mouth before adding, "She wanted to know if we're going to Nantucket this year. I told her—under the circumstances—I don't suppose we will."

They had been to Nantucket every summer of Diane's life, to a cottage Richard and his sister had inherited from their parents. Armaiti swallowed her disappointment. "Guess not." She knew that Richard was just being sensible, of course. But a small part of her resented him for not asking her before telling his sister no.

"Do you feel like going *anywhere* this summer?" Diane asked and Armaiti thought she heard a plaintive note in her daughter's voice.

"Actually, I do," she said, surprising even herself. "I feel like traveling to Bombay. To see everybody . . . one last . . . again." She had no idea if she'd said this just to spite Richard for not consulting with her about Nantucket.

There was a short silence. "That will be hard, won't it, hon?" Richard said quietly. "I mean, it's a tough city even at the best of times."

Two things happened as Armaiti heard those words. One, she realized that she was posturing, that she had no real desire to navigate, in her present condition, the hot, humid, crowded city of her birth. But it was the second realization that took her breath away. It was a longing so acute, so piercing, that it felt like a living thing, something that dwelt in her heart silently, invisibly, and was now making its presence known.

Bombay! The cool, tranquil rooms of Jehangir Art Gallery. The crazy, colorful, exuberance of Fashion Street. The intoxicating freedom of walking down the seaside at Marine Drive in stormy weather. The gastronomical ecstasy of biting into a chicken roll at Paradise, the mayonnaise, golden as the sun, oozing off the side.

And, above all, the company of the other three. The four of them taking the train to Lonavala, leaning out of the open doorway, feeling the wind on their faces. Spending entire afternoons listening to music at Rhythm House. Watching reruns of *The Way We Were* and *Spartacus* at Sterling on Saturday mornings.

Laleh, Kavita, Nishta. The names blended into one and became a prayer, souvenirs from a paradise lost. "Babe? You okay?" Richard was asking, and Armaiti nodded, unable to speak.

She looked up, saw their puzzled faces, and pulled herself together. "I—I was just thinking of—old friends, and I suddenly . . ." But her words were so weak, her description of Lal, Ka, and Nishta as "friends" so inadequate and small, that Armaiti stopped. Jane Stillman was a friend, and so was Susan Jacobs. But it wasn't the same. She had never been on a demonstration with Jane; had never held hands and stared down a line of policemen with Susan. Laleh and the others had not just been friends, they had been comrades. And although the word had fallen into disrepair since the Wall came down, it suddenly felt alive and shiny to Armaiti, plump with meaning and significance, as luminous as love.

She had not known that she was crying until she heard Diane's voice, immeasurably mature and older than it had any right to be, say, "It's okay, Mom. You need to cry. It's good for the soul." Hearing the words she'd said to her daughter on numerous occasions made Armaiti want to laugh. She realized that they thought she was crying about the diagnosis but there was no way to explain that she was grieving not so much over her

aborted future as over her aborted past. The four years of college now seemed to have gone by too quickly. There was no real
explanation for why she had not stayed in closer touch after leaving for the U.S. Unless it was this: coming to America itself was
a kind of defeat—the inaudible but clear admission that their
days as young radicals had drawn to a close.

"Mom," Diane said, a new urgency in her voice. "Is there
anything you want to do? I mean . . . other than visiting India? And even that"—Diane turned to flash her father a defiant
look—"if you really, really wanna go, we should just do it. I'll
go with you. It'll be okay."

Armaiti smiled. Diane reminded her of Laleh in some ways—
the indignation, the puppy-dog fierceness, the relentless desire
to protect. It seemed preposterous that Laleh would never get
to know her daughter. And Ka. There was that unresolved thing
with Ka. She remembered how brittle Kavita had been around
Richard at the time of the wedding. What a shame.

Diane was waiting for an answer. "Your dad's right, honey,"
Armaiti said. "Traveling to India would be very difficult at this
time."

"So have them come here to see you."

Armaiti glanced at Richard. You can jump in at any moment,
her look said, but he stared back at her, his face impassive. She
sighed. "It's not that easy, darling," she said. "I'm sure they have
their own lives. Besides, I haven't spoken to Ka and Nishta in
donkey's years."

"Mom," Diane said. "These are your oldest friends. I heard
you talk about them all through my childhood. I'm sure if you
called and—I'm sure if they knew how sick you were, they'd
come see you." She scowled suddenly. "And maybe they can
knock some sense into your head. I certainly can't."

But there's so much you don't know, Armaiti thought to herself. Of how complicated things got, despite our love for each other.

"Mom?"

"I know you mean well, sweetie. But I haven't really kept up with the others. So it would strike me as a little selfish to ask them to disrupt their lives just because I'm . . ."—she forced herself to say the word—". . . dying. Don't you think?" All the while thinking, When did I become this sensible, practical, middle-aged schoolmarm?

Richard cleared his throat. "Now, that's ridiculous, Armaiti. First of all, you have no idea what their reaction will be. And, second, I've met your friends, remember? I suspect they'll be more than glad to do whatever they can."

"That was a long time ago, Richard. Times—and people—change."

Richard leaned back in his chair and gazed at her. "Well, all you can do is ask. We can cover all their expenses."

She opened her mouth to argue but just then saw Diane lean slightly toward her father. It was a sign she had come to recognize—and dread—over the years. It meant father and daughter had joined forces against her. "That's settled, then," Diane said, as if Armaiti had just acquiesced.

They had talked about it all the way home and there was no denying the dance her heart was doing at the thought of a reunion. Besides, even if they didn't come, it would be nice to be in touch with the others again. Maybe she could just talk to them on the phone every few weeks.

Still, she was nervous. Except for an occasional e-mail, she hadn't been in touch with Laleh for several years. And now, out of the blue, to lay this on her and Kavita. What she was asking for was preposterous, no question. "You're sure?" she'd asked Diane just before picking up the receiver the next morning.

"Mom," Diane groaned. "For Christ's sake. What's the worst that can happen? Just call."

"Okay. *Okay.*"

She dialed half of Laleh's number and then stopped, struck by a thought. "When should I ask them to come? Which month?" she asked Richard.

She caught the flash of pity in Richard's eyes before he looked away. "Soon," he said. "Soon."

———

Now, as she entered the kitchen, Armaiti was thankful for Diane's insistence. Laleh had immediately said yes. Kavita had phoned her two hours later. And the possibility of a visit had lightened the mood in the house. Not that Diane was any closer to accepting her decision to forgo treatment. She was still stomping around the house, making snide remarks, and generally making her opposition known. Let her, Armaiti thought. Let her hold on to her anger. It will get her through these next few months.

Diane was pouring boiled potatoes into a colander when she walked in. "Can I help?" Armaiti asked and Diane handed her the masher. "Can you mash? And don't skimp on the butter, either." She eyed her mother critically. "You're looking kinda skinny. Gotta fatten you up."

Armaiti smiled. "Yes, ma'am."

They decided to eat dinner on the screened-in porch. As they sat down, Armaiti removed her cell phone from her pocket and placed it on the table. Richard covered her hand with his. "It's not time yet," he said. "It's just mid-morning in Bombay, remember?"

She smiled. "I know. I'm just so nervous they won't find Nishta's parents."

"If it's meant to be, they will. Now, relax." He clicked his wineglass to her water glass. "Bon appétit."

Armaiti watched with something akin to awe as Diane wolfed down the grilled salmon dinner that Richard had cooked. Had she ever had an appetite like that? she wondered. She doubted it. No woman ate that heartily in the India she'd grown up in. And definitely not in her family. When Armaiti was a child, her mother's favorite word had been "ladylike." "That's not ladylike, deekra," she'd say if Armaiti asked for a second helping of cake at a birthday party, or, "That's not dainty, dear," if she blew her nose too vigorously. Her mother's life was ruled by one commandment and measured by one yardstick: What Will the Neighbors Say? And Armaiti, protective of her mousy, frail, widowed mother, had for the most part gone along. That is, until her best friend, Laleh Madan, had read *What If?* by Lenin and passed it on to her. Then Armaiti's life was guided by the opposite principle: Screw What the Neighbors Say. Damn their petit bourgeois neighbors and the hypocritical platitudes that came out of their mouths.

"So, are Auntie Laleh and Kavita coming for sure?" Diane asked with her mouth full.

"I think so," Armaiti said, thankful that they could talk normally about this subject at least. "They're trying to."

"And Auntie Nishta?"

"Don't know." She glanced at the cell phone, willing it to ring. "We should hear from Laleh in the next hour or so."

3

They had just called Armaiti with the good news about Mrs. Lokhanwala, and now Kavita was dropping Laleh off at the dentist's office. Adish, true to his word, had gotten her an emergency appointment.

"You sure you don't want me to wait with you?" Kavita asked again.

"No. Don't worry. Either Adish will come or one of the kids will pick me up."

"The kids. How are they?"

"Fine. Indestructible. Ferzin loves college—everything but the studying part, that is. And Farhad is . . . Farhad. Goofy, easygoing, not a care in the world. God knows what will become of him."

"He'll be just fine. Honestly, you don't know how lucky you are."

Laleh shot her a sidelong glance. "Yah, you and Farhad have always had a special bond." There was pleasure in her voice.

"It will be nice to meet Diane," Kavita said. "Finally."

"Yes."

"But can I tell you something, Laleh?"

"What?"

"I'm really upset that Armaiti won't try radiation. I don't

blame Diane for being furious. I mean, this is madness, no? To not try and fight?"

Laleh sighed heavily. "You know what Armaiti's like, Ka. She's always been like this. She's all mild-mannered and genteel, but made of steel on the inside. Stubborn as anything."

Kavita nodded. They were both quiet for a moment, and then Laleh said, so softly that Kavita was unsure that she'd heard her correctly, "I should've been the one who landed in the hospital."

Kavita took her eyes off the road for a second. "What do you mean? She's not in the hospital. She's home."

"Not now. Then."

"What?"

"Don't you remember? After the march? She was in the hospital with a concussion."

It took her a minute to realize what Laleh was referring to. "You mean in 1979? After the laathi charge?"

"Exactly."

"Huh." Kavita waited, wondering why Laleh was bringing up ancient history. When she realized that Laleh was not going to amplify, she asked, "What's making you think of this now?"

Laleh looked at her, a furtive expression on her face. "I'm just wondering if the tumor happened because . . . she had that awful concussion, remember? And the amnesia?"

As pragmatic as she is, Laleh can be so damn dramatic at times, Kavita thought. Thank God she married someone as even-tempered and easygoing as Adish. "That's crazy talk, Lal," she said.

"Is it?" Laleh said noncommittally. "In any case, if I'd been there that day, I could've protected her."

"Protected her? From those police goons? The bastards went crazy that day. Believe me, I know. I was there." An image of the dank jail cell and the humiliation that followed rose in Kavita's mind, but she pushed it away. She had spent a lifetime running away from the room of laughing men and she wasn't about to reenter it now.

"And I wasn't," Laleh was saying. "That's just it."

Why were they talking about an incident from thirty years ago? Now, when they had more urgent things to talk about? "Laleh, this is silly . . ." she began.

"I know. I know." Laleh shook her head. "Just forget it."

Kavita looked at her for a moment, puzzled. It's the shock about Armaiti, she told herself. She's not thinking straight. She cleared her throat. "Anyway. When do you want to go see Nishta?"

"As soon as possible."

"It's too bad they're not listed in the phone book," Kavita said. "This address sounds like it's out in the boonies. It will be maddening to go all the way there if she's not home."

"I know. But it can't be helped. I promised Armaiti we would try." Laleh stared out of the window for a moment. "I still can't believe we've lost touch with Nishta and Iqbal so completely. I didn't even know they'd moved from Mazgaon."

"Now, don't go blaming yourself for yet another thing." Kavita's tone was teasing but firm. "*They* pulled away from us. Remember how weird Iqbal acted at your house-warming party?" She entered the gates of the medical building, parked the car, and leaned over to give Laleh a kiss. "Today was a lucky day," she said. "We're going to see Nishta soon. Focus on that."

"You're right. Listen, how about if I call you tonight and we figure out a time to go see Nishta this week? I can go any day except Thursday—that's my day at the women's shelter."

"Righto. Call me before ten, okay?"

Laleh frowned. "Oh, wait. I just remembered, I have a stupid party to go to tonight. I'll call you tomorrow. First thing."

"Okay," Kavita nodded. "See you." She was anxious to get away now, to be alone in the car, to savor the memory of the brief phone call to Armaiti earlier today. How happy Armaiti had been at the news of Mrs. Lokhanwala's unexpected help. "Oh, thank you, Ka," she'd said, and Kavita had shivered, remembering in a flash the first time Armaiti had shortened her name and how it had felt like a feather brushed across her face. The four of them had gone to Juhu Beach for the day and she and Armaiti had lain on the hot sand, their hands occasionally touching each other's, staring up at the newly scrubbed sky. Kavita had felt languid, lulled into sleep by the heavy, salty sea air, and then singed into wakefulness every time Armaiti's hand brushed against hers. It was the most delicious combination of aliveness and dreaminess she had ever experienced. And just then, in response to something she'd said, Armaiti had rolled over on her side and propped her head on her elbow to look down at Kavita's face, inches from her own. "What you don't realize, Ka," she said, and then the rest of her sentence disappeared into the shimmering afternoon air, because the nickname had landed on her like a kiss and all she could see then was Armaiti's hair set on fire by the sun, the flecks of light in Armaiti's warm, brown eyes, Armaiti's golden face against the denim-blue sky, obscuring, no, taking the place of the sun.

Kavita waited until Laleh disappeared through the front door of the dentist's building, then pulled out of the gate and made a left turn onto the busy street.

Armaiti. Had she ever loved anyone as much? What she now had with Ingrid was so different. Kavita remembered the countless nights when she had lain alone in her single bed, pining away for Armaiti, trying to stop her hands from roaming her body, to intellectualize the slow heat climbing up her limbs, to explain away in anthropological terms the sexual desire that left her mouth dry, to not see the face that loomed before her tightly shut eyes, to not hear the name that threatened to escape from her parted lips. Armaiti. Armaiti—the steady eyes, the wry, wicked humor, the good, kind heart. And then the parts that Kavita saw in the not-seeing: the thin, sensual lips, the clear brown eyes, the pert breasts, just large enough to fill a woman's hand, the generous hips that would fit perfectly against her own.

It was India. It was the late 1970s. The West, with its women's movement and gay liberation movement and its permissiveness and promiscuity, was at least a planet away. It was India in the late 1970s, and the country was still coming to grips with the nightmare of the Emergency years, and corruption was endemic and food prices and college tuition were rising, and public services were breaking down. How could any moral individual worry about the clamoring of her own heart? It was India in the late 1970s and how would anyone even know what name to give this strange, unseemly obsession with another woman? Occasionally Kavita's mind would circle around the forbidden word, but then she'd remember what her older brother Rohit had once said: "Homosexuality is what men do to each other in prison." What did anything that ugly have to do with her and this tender, protective feeling that she felt around Armaiti? She could call it love, yes, but she loved Nishta and Laleh, too, though they were not the reason she looked forward to college every day. And since there was no word, no description for what she felt, it was easy—or at least possible—to subsume that desire, to channel the basic unjustness of her situation into a desire for justice for all the world's dispossessed. She didn't—couldn't—count herself as one of the dispossessed, not in the India of the late 1970s, not in a place where malnourished children and lepers with holes for noses haunted the streets, and most of her countrymen couldn't read or write their own names.

A car cut in front of her and Kavita slammed on her brakes, setting off a protest of car horns behind her. She barely noticed. Armaiti was dying, would probably be dead before she turned fifty.

Armaiti, almost fifty. It seemed impossible. She wondered what Armaiti looked like now, added twenty kilos to the slim, lanky girl she'd known to create a matronly figure, gave the sharp-faced girl a triple chin, made the lithe, nimble, movements slower and more deliberate.

It didn't work. She kept remembering Armaiti in the college cafeteria as the sun came in through the dirty windowpanes and lit up her face; Armaiti on piano and she on guitar as they learned the chords to a Moody Blues song; sitting beside her at Marine Drive as they watched the evening sky turn orange and gold; the two of them caught in a sudden downpour, soaking wet before they could even get their umbrella open, and laughing all the way home.

She had never told Armaiti about how she felt. Back then, they never discussed matters of the heart. The only boys they had talked about were named Lenin, Marx, and Mao. Of course, Adish and Iqbal had always buzzed around Laleh and Nishta, but the girls acted as if they barely noticed them. Nonchalance. That was their posture, their affect. How different they had been from the other teenage girls—passionate, yes, but about the political, not the personal. Broken hearts, broken fingernails, broken promises—all the things that their classmates fretted over, they dismissed. The four of them had been an odd bunch, eccentric and unconventional. They smoked, drank, swore. Claimed to believe in free love. But in many ways they were as virginal as nuns.

Why? Kavita now demanded of herself. Why were we so damn guarded? As close as we were, in some ways we were

almost shy around each other. Her mind flipped back to what
Laleh had said a few minutes earlier, the guilt that she felt
about being absent the day of the march. Had Laleh really been
carrying that burden all these years? And she? Why had she
never told the others about what the police inspector had done
to her in the lockup the night of the march? How his deputy
had penetrated her with his fingers, how the men in the room
had laughed at her humiliation? How the episode had nearly
unhinged her, how it was the first step in her journey away
from the political activism she'd once thought would be her
life?

The memory of one humiliation yielded another. And although this one was fainter, the memory of it still made sweat
form on her upper lip and Kavita lowered the car window to
let in fresh air. The year after Armaiti had left for America,
Kavita had mailed her a Valentine's Day card. She had debated
whether to do so for weeks and finally, unable to conceal or
reveal her true feelings, she had settled on a humorous card—
and then signed it, *Love you always.* It was the closest she could
come to letting Armaiti know. She had waited for weeks for an
acknowledgment, a reply, and when none came, hope turned
into shame and self-recrimination. Stupid, stupid, she chastised
herself. Finally, a powder-blue aerogram arrived in the mail—a
news-filled letter from Armaiti that talked about her classes,
the books she was reading, the Leonard Cohen concert she'd attended, droll commentary about life in Ronald Reagan's America, a board game called Risk that she was addicted to, and a
classmate named Richard.

After all these years Kavita could still remember the cold-
ness that had spread through her stomach when she'd read Richard's name. Because without knowing, she had known. Armaiti
would've never mentioned a boy's name unless she was serious

about him. And this was her way of gently rebuffing Kavita's declaration.

Kavita pushed down on the accelerator, absentmindedly running a red light as she came to a resolution. If they went to America—*when* they went to America, with or without Nishta—she would tell Armaiti. Not about the night in jail, perhaps. But about the other thing. About love. About how it had bloomed, unexpected and delicate, even in the inhospitable, barren soil of India in the 1970s.

4

A dish Engineer dipped two fingers into the silver bowl and dabbed his eyes with holy water from the Bhika Behram well. It felt cool against his tired eyes. He nodded to the few other Parsi worshippers gathered around the well and then made his way to a private corner where he could pray. He unbuttoned the lower buttons of his shirt so that he could reach for the kusti, the woven strings of sacred threads, that rested on his sudra, the thin undershirt that was a symbol of his faith. He untied the kusti from around his waist. "Ashem vahu," he prayed with his eyes closed.

Even more than the cool sanctuary of a fire temple, Adish liked coming here to pray. Unlike the cloistered, dark, exclusive cocoon of the fire temple, which only Parsis could enter, the Bhika Behram well stood in the center of a large, mosaic-tiled room that was open to the busy street. Adish loved the incongruity of being in this tranquil, airy space while all around him horns blared and vendors yelled and the Bombay office crowd moved at its usual frenetic pace. He liked concentrating on his prayers to the point of blocking out the sounds of the thriving metropolis around him. He relished the scent from the rose garlands and the rich smell of the oil lamps lit by his fellow worshippers. He enjoyed being in the company of the elderly, old-fashioned Parsi gentlemen who gathered here to pray, took pleasure in touching his forehead and saying a respectful "Sahibji" to them. It calmed him down, this place, took him away from the stress of business and family.

And he needed to get away from family—from Laleh, specifically—for an hour or so. Even though they'd made up before going to bed, some part of him was still fuming at how badly she'd behaved at the party last night, how brazenly she'd insulted Girish, their host. Sure, she had been in pain from the dental work. Sure, she was reeling from the heartbreaking news about Armaiti. But still and all, her behavior had been inexcusable.

The party was so big that they had been there for an hour and still not met their hosts. "How much longer do you want to stay?" Laleh yawned. "I'm tired."

"Remember how willingly I went to the theater with you last week?" Adish grinned. "Did I ask to leave during the intermission?"

"Don't you dare compare this wretched party to that heavenly experience."

"Shh. Keep your voice down." Adish tossed back the last of his scotch. "Okay. Let's go pay our respects to Girish before we leave."

"You go. I can't make any more small talk."

"Laleh." Adish took her hand and discreetly pulled his wife across the room to where Girish was holding court, his entourage around him. In his beige cotton shirt and blue jeans, Girish looked more like a young, hip movie director than what he was—a prominent real estate developer who was the heir to a textile fortune. "Nice to meet you, Mrs. Engineer," he said to Laleh, after Adish introduced them. "So glad you could come."

"Thanks," Laleh said. "Nice party." Her tone was flat, non-committal.

Girish bowed. "We try." He looked around. "Let me introduce you to my wife. This is my lovely Bindu."

At the mention of her name, Bindu turned slightly toward the Engineers, bestowed a haughty half-smile on them, and wordlessly turned back to her friends. Laleh arched an eyebrow and Girish said hastily, "Bindu's shy around strangers."

"So was my puppy. But we trained her."

Girish went pale. "I—beg pardon? You . . . ?"

"I'm sorry," Laleh began. "I didn't mean to—"

Adish stepped in. "Lal is so crazy about that puppy," he said smoothly. "I swear, I've heard her compare our children to that dog. "

"*We* have a puppy," Bindu said. Her voice was squeaky, childlike. "A Portuguese water dog. Just like the Obamas. Once they got one, bas, I had to have one also." She smiled. "My father-in-law had one sent to us from America."

A tiny pulse beat in Laleh's forehead. "You had a dog imported from America?"

Adish's head jerked up, alerted by a peculiar note in Laleh's voice, but before he could speak, Girish did. "Papa is crazy about Bindu. I'm always telling him, Papaji, don't spoil my wife so much." His entourage murmured approvingly. He looked at Laleh. "My father is Motilal Chandani, you know."

"Yes, I know your father."

Girish grinned. "Everybody knows my dad."

Adish felt Laleh shift next to him and his heart sank. Surely Laleh wouldn't. Girish was a new client. Surely Laleh knew better. He tried to catch her eye but she was staring directly at Girish.

"We used to picket outside his textile mills," he heard Laleh say. Her dark eyes searched Girish's face. "Your father refused his workers a twelve-paisa-an-hour raise. Can you imagine?"

Girish blanched. Then he laughed nervously. Bindu, who had gone back to talking to her friends, turned around to look at them curiously. "Your wife is a funny lady," Girish said to Adish.

"She is," Adish said grimly. He touched Laleh's elbow in warning, but she shook him away.

"In any case, my dad is now retired," Girish said. His voice was cheery, as if that fact explained away all past misdeeds.

"I know," Laleh said. "He made even more money developing the land the mills sat on than if he'd kept running the factories. That's where your high-rises are now being built."

"It was the bloody labor unions," Girish said. "Made it impossible for a businessman to earn a decent living."

Laleh let out a short laugh. "Oh, come on. Your dad did all right for himself," she said. "It's the workers who lost their jobs when your father closed the mills that we should worry about, no?"

Bindu spoke. "Hey, what are you?" she giggled. "A terrorist or something?"

There was a short silence. Then Girish said, "A Communist. Bindu means, 'Are you a Communist or something?'" He laughed, his eyes imploring his entourage to follow. They snickered dutifully.

Adish heard Laleh make a low growling sound and hastily put his arm around her shoulder and squeezed a warning. "I'm sorry. I apologize. My wife . . ." Girish was looking at him curiously. "We have to go. . . . She's not well. Had some dental work done today. Sorry. I'll phone you tomorrow, Girish. Okay?"

He hurried a protesting Laleh out of the roof-top apartment and into the elevator. He waited grim-faced until the doors shut behind them. Then he turned toward her. "What the hell was that performance about? What on earth is the matter with you?"

She was silent.

"Laleh. I want an answer. How dare you insult my client in this manner? What bhoot has gotten into you this evening?"

She looked up, her eyes flashing and dangerous. "I've told you a million times not to drag me to your work parties. You know how I get around these people."

"These people?" he snapped. "These people?" He grabbed her by her shoulder and spun her around so that they both faced the mirror in the back panel of the elevator. "Take a good look at yourself, Laleh. You—we—are these people. You have a maid and a chauffeur, you live in a huge flat at Cuffe Parade, you spend money as your heart desires. Who the hell do you think you are? The proletariat? You're no longer twenty years old, Laleh. You're no longer a rebel giving your old man conniptions. So give it up. Just give it up."

"It's not what you own, Adish. It's who you are. What values you have."

Adish banged his fist against the steel of the elevator. "Dammit, Laleh. Do you know how holier-than-thou you sound? What are you saying? That we're better people than the Chandanis? How dare you?"

"I should've known better than to expect you to understand." She was quiet for a second, and when she spoke again her voice was placating. "In any case, I was being semifacetious, when I compared his wife to our nonexistent dog."

He was about to say, *That's redundant. Either you are facetious or you're not*, but he stopped himself. He did not want to engage in his usual banter with Laleh tonight. He knew where it would lead—Laleh would say something impossibly witty and he would laugh, and his anger would fade. But she had crossed a line tonight and he wouldn't let her off the hook that easily. "You know what, Laleh?" he said. "You've done enough damage for one evening. So just shut up, okay?"

His anger thinned into melancholy as he drove home. It perplexed him, how Laleh could go from seeming like a soul mate to a stranger in the course of a single day. Several times he opened his mouth to speak but changed his mind, not wanting to disturb the silence. He pulled the car into their building's underground garage and then turned toward his wife. "Let me tell you something, Laleh," he began. "I know you're embarrassed by the life we live. I know you're even embarrassed by me——"

"That's not true," she interrupted.

"Don't lie. You are. But I want to say this—I'm not. I don't apologize for what I have, Lal. You would've been happy marrying some milquetoast social worker with ice water in his veins and TB in his lungs. Well, that's not me. I'm proud to provide my family with a good life. And we can do more to help others now than we ever could if we were piss-poor ourselves."

"You sound more and more like my father as you get older. This is exactly what he would've said."

"So? Your dad was a great man."

"That's not what I meant."

"You don't even know what you're saying."

"I'm saying that I'm not willing to throw in the towel, okay? I refuse to believe that what we once stood for was just wishful thinking, and that people like Girish were the smart ones all along."

Adish made an exasperated sound. "Why do you have to be so damn dramatic, Laleh? Why can't it be what it was—a moment in history? And then history changed and the moment passed." Absently, he flicked a piece of lint off his jacket. "Do you remember the day the Soviets invaded Afghanistan?" he asked abruptly.

"Of course I do. We were sitting in Kavita's living room when the news came over the radio."

"And do you remember what we all said? That the days of the American Empire were over, that the Soviet Union was the new imperial power." Adish's lips twisted into a smile. "Do you realize how wrong we all were? A few years later, the Soviet Union breaks into a thousand pieces, disappears like a child's dream. Just like that."

"So we were wrong. What does that prove?"

"You're right. In itself, it proves nothing. But, Lal, we also thought that liberalizing the economy would destroy India. Instead, look at what has happened. The economy is booming. Shit, there's so much construction going on in Bombay itself, my firm can't keep up with it."

"And in the meantime, farmers are killing themselves in record numbers," she snapped. "And there are food riots breaking out in the countryside."

"Laleh. It's a huge country. It will take time. But in the meantime, look at our own Farhad. Look at the pride he feels in his country. I asked him just last week if he wanted to go abroad to study. He said, 'Papa, why should I when I have so many opportunities here?' Now, isn't that a huge difference?"

"So what's the big deal? We could've all gone. We chose not to."

"True. But, Lal, we didn't go because of some twisted, misguided sense of loyalty to India. That's not why Farhad doesn't want to leave. He wants to stay—for his own sake. We stayed—for the sake of India. There's a difference."

It's no use, Adish now thought, flicking the strands of his kusti with more vigor than usual. She will never change. Laleh was the most exasperating, infuriating woman he knew. But she was also the most loyal, passionate, and fair. And he could not imagine his life without her. There you had it—a conundrum. When she smiled at him in that coy, flirty way of hers, his heart still flipped like a trained whale. After all these years.

He moved to the section with the burning oil lamps and decided to light one for Armaiti. She had always been kind to him in college, sticking up for him, protecting him from the lash of Laleh's sarcasm and advising him on how to win her affection. "Listen," she'd once told him. "I've known Laleh since the fourth standard. You know the best way to get her to pay attention to you? Ignore her."

He was smiling at the memory when he felt someone tap him on his shoulder. It was Maneck Sethna, the old man with the bad case of Parkinson's who prayed at the well every day.

"Sahibji, Maneckshaw," Adish said.

"Sukhi re, deekra, sukhi re," Maneck replied. "Be happy."

"Thank you. How are you?"

The old man's eyes filled with tears. "Chalta hai, deekra. Life goes on." Adish noticed how he labored to spit out those words. The Parkinson's seemed even worse than he remembered. He shifted his attention back to Maneck's words. "I'm worried about my son," he was saying.

"What's wrong?"

"He lost his job, deekra. Was working as an accountant for Kitar Enterprises. But business is bad, so they let him go. He has a wife and three children. Can't find a new job. I try to help, but on my pension, not much I can do."

Adish was relieved to be confronted by a solvable problem. Unlike the situation with Armaiti, this he could help with. "Do one thing, Maneckshaw," he said, as he dug through his shirt pocket for a business card. "Have your son call this number on Monday and speak to Ashok, my head accountant. I'm sure we can find a position for him in my company."

Maneck stared at him open-mouthed. "What are you saying, deekra?"

Adish laughed. "I'm saying that I will try to hire your son."

The old man gripped Adish's hand in both of his. "This is the miracle of this holy site," he said. "When I approached you, I had no idea. Many blessings on you, beta."

"Good," Adish said lightly. "I need all the blessings I can get." He extracted his hand from Maneck's trembling ones. "Good day, Maneckshaw. See you soon."

She had not showered. It was the first thing Adish noticed as he entered the apartment and walked into the bedroom. In all the years that they had been married he had never known Lal to wait this late in the day to shower. He found her sitting in the middle of the bed, her knees drawn up to her chest, rocking slightly. Her thick, dark hair had come loose, and when she looked up at Adish, her face was smudged, her eyes red and puffy.

And just like that, the residual anger over the incident from last night disappeared. "Oh, Lal," he breathed, making his way to her.

He forced himself to ignore the fact that she stiffened imperceptibly when he sat on the bed and put his arm around her. For a second he wondered if Laleh was still smarting from their argument from last night. "What's wrong, darling?" he asked.

"Armaiti called," she said. "It's the middle of the night there but she couldn't sleep." She twisted her head to face him. "Armaiti's dying. My oldest friend in the world is dying."

"I know. It's very sad." He bit down on the urge to point out that she and Armaiti had not been in close touch for years.

"It doesn't matter," Lal said, as if she was replying to his unspoken thought. "It doesn't matter that we didn't talk to each other a whole lot or stay in touch. Armaiti was—is—an aspect of me. The best, purest part of me."

Before he stubbed it out, Adish was singed by a jealousy that had its origins in an older time—the college years, when Laleh had seemed so attuned to Armaiti and so disinterested in him. "Love doesn't die when people do, janu," he said to her. "What you and Armaiti shared will always be alive."

It was the wrong thing to say. The look on Laleh's face told him this. "Don't try and pacify me with your spiritual mumbo-jumbo, Adish," Lal said. "It may work for you but it doesn't work for me. The fact is that Armaiti is dying and I've been a lousy friend to her. Nothing changes that."

He felt his face redden. "I—I was only trying to help," he said.

"You can't help, Adish. No one can. We both know why Armaiti is sick."

He looked at her blankly. "Because she has a brain tumor?" he said at last.

Laleh made a growling sound. "And what caused the brain tumor, stupid?" she said. "Why does a healthy woman who is not even fifty suddenly get a tumor?"

A bell was clanging inside Adish's head, and it was getting louder and louder. It was beginning to dawn on him what Laleh was talking about, but the thought was so preposterous, so far-fetched, that he let the clanging of the bell drown it out. He opened his mouth to speak but could only shake his head.

Laleh had an expression on her face that reminded him of another day from long ago. But he couldn't think of that now, because he was confused. And distracted. Because despite the disheveled hair, the eyes swollen with tears, the chewed-on lower lip, Laleh looked beautiful. Adish's eyes wandered to the spot where her long, dark neck met with the collar of a white shirt, worn over the black pants that she'd bought during their last trip to Thailand. The stone in Laleh's ring caught a flash of the sun and cast a fleeting rainbow on the wall. "Lal——" he ventured.

"It's happened, Adish," she said fiercely. "It took years and years to catch up with me, but it did. You know what I'm talking about. You were there."

He flinched, as if she had slapped him. He stared at her, at a loss for what to say. Despite her occasional penchant for drama, Laleh was the most pragmatic person he knew. Over the years he had learned to count on the coolness of her judgment on almost everything, from choosing the color of the upholstery to helping him decide to quit his job and start his own business. She had a way of clarifying the world, of reducing problems to their most basic roots, and then solving them, that he had always envied. He suspected it was one of the reasons she had always resisted the allures of the religious faith that he had found more and more compelling as he grew older—she was afraid that it would cloud the clear-eyed way in which she saw the world.

And now his wife was sitting on her bed telling him tearfully that she was responsible for Armaiti's fatal illness. He saw now that what he'd thought was grief and shock at hearing the devastating news was really guilt. The past coming back to haunt them. The past, which he had believed they had beaten down, like cotton stuffed inside a mattress.

"Laleh," he said. "You're not making any sense."

Her eyes were big and round. "It was the blow from the laathi, Adish," she whispered. "You remember when she was in the hospital? The bastard police officer had hit her right in the head. Don't you remember her amnesia?"

"It was thirty years ago." His voice was louder than he'd intended, and for a second he wondered where the children were. Then he remembered. Ferzin was at a friend's house. Farhad was at the gym. "And it was just a concussion. The amnesia was temporary."

"That's what Kavita said also. But I still remember how black-and-blue her forehead was. She probably bled internally. And there was probably scar-tissue buildup over the years. And that . . ."

He grabbed her wrist. "Laleh. Shut up. Shut up and listen to me. You're not making sense. You're not a doctor. This is just a coincidence—a very sad coincidence. You have to stop torturing yourself like this."

She said it so softly, he almost didn't hear her. "So is this how we absolve ourselves?"

He shot up from the edge of the bed and stood, towering over her. "What did you say?"

"Nothing." And then, with a defiant look in her eyes, she repeated what she'd said, louder this time.

Adish shook his head. "I won't let you do this. I won't let you drag me into whatever bullshit's swirling around in your head."

"That's up to you. You have to face your own conscience. I know that I made a Faustian bargain. And that I'm paying for it now."

He held back the tears that were lining his eyes. "So what are you saying? That you regret our life together?" His hand swept around the room and the life that they'd built. "That none of this matters?"

She pulled back, as if to see him fully, and then released her words, gently, languidly, like an archer knowing he was about to score a kill. "On the contrary, dear Adish. I'm saying that it all matters. Everything matters. Our virtues *and* our sins."

He was grateful for the out that she had given him. "Sins?" he yelled. "The woman who a few minutes ago gave me shit for my religious mumbo-jumbo is now talking about sin? What the hell, Lal? Suddenly you're a damn missionary? We were not even twenty years old, Lal. Younger than our Ferzin. There was no sin. Unless you're going to sit there and tell me that my loving you was a sin. And if you do, I swear I'll knock your teeth out. I'll lose you first before I'll have you call what I felt for you a sin."

"That's not what I meant." Laleh suddenly exhaled and looked deflated, like a sack emptied of its cargo. "I don't even know what we're talking about anymore," she mumbled. "I'm—I'm tired." She looked up. "I'm not trying to hurt you, Adish."

He stood looking at her, moving his weight from foot to foot, feeling the blood throbbing in his head. "Listen," he said finally. "I—I need to go to the office for a couple of hours. Catch up on some work. Okay?"

Laleh shrugged. "Whatever you want."

He couldn't say what irritated him more—the indifference or the defeat that he heard in her voice. But whatever it was, it made him grind his teeth. "Okay," he said shortly. "See you."

It took all the self-control he had to not slam the front door behind him. He walked to the elevator and punched the down button. He waited a few seconds and then jabbed at the button again. He glanced at the apartment door, afraid that Laleh would come out and coax him back in the house. He needed air, needed to walk, time to clear his head. Don't let Laleh open that door, he prayed to himself. But as soon as he got into the elevator and began his descent, another, contradictory, feeling came over him: disappointment that Laleh had not come out and apologized and led him back in.

The lift reached the ground-floor lobby and Adish lingered for a moment, trying to decide whether he wanted to walk or drive. Stepping out of the building with his head hung low, he didn't see Farhad coming toward him until he heard, "Hi, Papa."

He looked up and smiled involuntarily. "Hi, boss," he said. "How was your workout?"

Farhad shrugged. "Fine." He looked curiously at his dad. "Where're you going?"

"I'm not sure. For a walk, maybe."

"Yeah, right," Farhad drawled. "When's the last time you walked?"

Adish smacked his son lightly on the head. "Chup re, saala. Don't give your old man a hard time. Just remember, I may have put on a few kilos but I can still beat you at wrestling. And chess," he added.

Farhad grinned happily. He fell in step beside his father, walking in that loping, ungainly manner that warmed Adish's heart. "I'll go with you."

Adish stopped. "Actually, boss, I wanted to be alone for a little while." He hesitated, unsure of how much to say to Farhad. "I have a . . . business problem . . . that I need to solve."

Farhad reached into his jeans, took out a piece of gum, and popped it in his mouth. "Okay," he said simply. "When will you be home?"

"Are you allowed to chew gum with those braces on?" Adish asked.

Farhad grinned. "As long as Mom doesn't know, it won't hurt anything," he said.

The boy looked so much like a tall, gangly animal in his ridiculously large shoes and his baggy shirt, that Adish felt a gust of love sweep through him. He reached up and squeezed his son in a bear hug. "I won't be gone long," he said.

"Papa." Farhad sounded shocked. "What're you doing? My friends will see."

Adish wanted to hold his son forever. But Farhad was right. He forced himself to slacken his grip.

"Okay, bye," Farhad said.

"Farhad," Adish said. "Go upstairs directly, okay? No stopping for table tennis or anything. Mummy's really upset about Armaiti auntie."

Farhad stood blinking, and Adish could tell the boy was trying to decide whether to pretend to be blasé and indifferent or give in to his true, kindly nature. How hard we men make our own lives, Adish thought to himself. He put a hand on his son's shoulder. "Beta," he said. "No stupid jokes, okay?"

The boy nodded. "Don't worry," he said, and suddenly Adish was not worried.

Now if only the rest of his family was as simple as Farhad, he thought, as he left the gates of the apartment complex and turned left onto the street.

5

Yesterday's quarrel with Adish was fresh in Laleh's mind as the cab wound its way down the choking streets. She had apologized to him soon after he'd returned home, and he had accepted, but he had looked at her with guarded, cautious eyes this morning as he left for work, and Laleh knew that she'd scared Adish badly with her meltdown yesterday. She vowed to do better. Adish was a gem and deserved better than a wife who came unhinged because of a phone call from the past.

"I can't believe they live in this neighborhood," Kavita said, rolling up the window to keep out the stench. "Maybe Nishta was sending her mother a fake address."

"That makes no sense, Ka."

Years ago, Laleh had been envious of Nishta for marrying a Muslim, had seen her interfaith marriage as a badge of honor, and her estrangement from her parents as a heroic act. She'd said as much to Adish during their courtship. "I never thought I'd be dating a Parsi," she'd once told him, with her usual blend of irony and seriousness. "I'd always thought I'd be like Nishta—if I ever marry, that is."

"Add that to the list of what's wrong with me," he had grinned. "The fact that I'm a Parsi. And that your parents approve of me."

She'd smiled. "Too bad you're so good-looking. It would be so much easier to dump you if you weren't."

"Too bad you're so cute," he'd responded. "Otherwise, I'd have dumped you for being such a bitch."

They had laughed at the time. But now, looking out from the cab window, Laleh realized how immature she had been in her envy of Nishta. If her marriage had brought Nishta to this squalid neighborhood, she had paid a steep price. A lifelong Bombayite, Laleh had thought that she knew the city well, from its slums to its five-star hotels. But she had never been to this part of the city—this all-Muslim neighborhood—before.

The cab came to a halt and the driver turned around. "Too much crowding, ladies," he said. "Vegetable market starts here, you know. No place for my taxi to even turn around. You walk it up, please."

"Will you at least wait for us, bhaiya? We'll pay return fare plus extra."

The man tugged at his beard. "Arre, memsahib, where I'm going to wait? There's no room for an ant, let alone a taxi." He pointed out the window. "There's a taxi stand on the other side of the market. You walk there when you're done with your business here." He lowered his voice. "This is all-Muslim area, memsahib. Be careful."

"What does that have to do with anything, bhai?" Laleh felt compelled to say.

The old man looked at her as if they were sharing a secret. "Can't trust these beef-eaters, memsahib."

They paid the man and exited the cab hastily. Laleh shook her head. "A country of bigots. That's what we are," she said.

Kavita nodded. "Indeed."

The sidewalks were so crowded they were forced to walk on the street, dodging bicycles and cars. "Laleh," Kavita gasped after a few minutes. "Why on earth would they have moved into this area? I mean, I know their old flat was tiny, but surely it was better than living here?" She spread one hand out, and the gesture encompassed the street teeming with people and flies, the cubbyhole-sized shops that lined the road, the stench of the rotting vegetables and fish from the open-air market.

Laleh shrugged. "God knows. Maybe their place is really nice. After all these years of working at the bank, Iqbal must be drawing a good salary by now, no?"

Kavita looked dubious but remained silent. Spotting a young woman walking in their direction—one of the few women who wasn't wearing either a burkha or a head scarf— she stopped her. "Excuse me," she said. "Do you know where Mahani Manzil is?"

The woman frowned. "Mahani Manzil? That's a long ways down. There's a stationery shop opposite it."

They resumed walking. Laleh grimaced as her foot accidentally touched an overripe pumpkin that had been discarded on the road. "Shit." She looked around, ignoring the cries of the vendors squatting on the street.

"Is it my imagination or are we getting hostile looks?" Kavita murmured.

"I don't know about hostile. But we're definitely being stared at."

"Probably because we're the only women in slacks."

"And no head gear."

"Well, it can't be too far away now."

They stopped a young man who professed to know exactly where Mahani Manzil was and insisted on walking them to it. They were both aware of the fact that the young man was getting off on the fact that he was escorting two women dressed in Western clothes down the street. He strutted a bit; he solemnly told them to ignore the catcalls and wolf whistles coming from the other young men lounging on the street. But his dancing eyes gave away his pride and excitement.

At the entrance of the building, he stopped and reached over to pull the envelope out of Kavita's hands. "Who are you looking for?" he asked.

But Kavita held on to the piece of paper. "Thanks for your help," she said firmly. And when he didn't move, "Khuda Hafiz."

The boy's eyes widened at her easy use of the Muslim expression. "Khuda Hafiz," he responded. And then, in English, "Goodbye."

The building they entered was dark, damp, and moldy. A single bare lightbulb illuminated the stairwell, the walls of which were covered with paan stains. Laleh reached out to grab the dusty handrail on the old wooden stairs but then thought better of it. As they climbed the uneven, creaking, rickety stairs, she was genuinely afraid. The whole building looked like it could collapse under their weight. "Ka," she gasped. "This is a chawl. Surely there's some mistake. Nishta couldn't be living here."

Kavita held the envelope up to her face. "This is definitely the right address," she said.

They were gasping for breath by the time they reached the fourth floor. "I have become so spoiled," Laleh said. "I haven't climbed stairs in God knows how long." She turned to Kavita. "What's the apartment number?"

"It doesn't say. We'll have to ask."

A common balcony overlooking an inner courtyard ran around the building, which was laid out in a square. As they walked along the balcony, they could hear the shrieks of children playing in the courtyard. Many of the doors of the apartments they passed were open, so that they felt like voyeurs each time they accidentally peered in. They were debating whether to poke their heads inside one of the doors and ask for directions to Iqbal's apartment when they saw a woman walking toward them. "We'll ask her," Kavita said, gesturing toward the woman, who was wearing a light-blue burkha. Her face was covered and Laleh wondered how she could make her way in the dark.

The woman nodded at them in the dimly lit hallway and then brushed past them. "Excuse me," Laleh called. "Can you help us? We are looking for a Nishta Ibrahim?"

The woman stopped. There was a long pause. "Nobody here by that name," she said finally.

"Are you sure?" Kavita asked, even as Laleh turned to her and said, "See? I told you. I knew there was something wrong. They wouldn't be living here."

"But we have the address. . . ." Kavita said.

"So? She lied to her mother. Or her mother lied to us."

The woman in the long robe was still waiting. "Do you know an Iqbal?" Kavita said. "Iqbal Ibrahim?"

There was another pause, and then the woman said, "Yes. He is my husband."

They heard the smile in her voice before they recognized the voice itself. Laleh spoke first. "Nishta?" she said cautiously, cursing the dimness of the hallway.

The woman flipped up the hood of her burkha long enough for them to see her face. "No. I told you. Nishta is gone. I'm Zoha."

6

Kavita sat in Nishta's living room and wanted never to leave. Despite the dizzying revelations of the past hour—the fact that Nishta had converted to Islam, that Iqbal had insisted she adopt a Muslim name, that she was living in circumstances that were drastically different from the affluent life she had once known, that the Nishta who sat across from her was a plump, severe-looking, middle-aged woman, so different from the laughing, zestful, beautiful girl they used to know—being in this sparse, austere room made Kavita feel comfortable. She felt almost drowsy in her comfort, heavy-lidded and limpid. Happy.

They had found her. They had reunited with her. And she was happy to see them. The awkward stiffness of the last few times they'd seen her, was gone. Despite her ridiculous garb, the thick reading glasses, the lines on her face, this was Nishta restored.

"Look at her," she heard Laleh say. "She's grinning like an ass." She looked up to see the other two smiling at her, heard the pleasure in Laleh's voice. As if her joy gave Laleh joy.

"I can't help it," Kavita said. "This is so . . ." She groped for the right word and then she thought, but this is just it. I don't have to find the right word. They know what I mean, unspoken. "You know what I mean," she finished lamely.

Nishta—Zoha—nodded. "I know. I feel like all my prayers have been answered in one afternoon." She looked from one to the other. "When I sent Mummy those birthday cards—all these years, I never forgot her birthday once. Not once. Never knew whether she got them or not, whether she ever opened them. So many were sent back to me. But still, something made me. But never did I think I was sending *myself* a gift all these years. That the cards would lead the two of you to me. Funny, hah?"

They nodded. "So how is she?" Nishta asked. "My mummy?"

Kavita glanced quickly at Laleh, who was staring impassively ahead of her. "She seemed fine," she said. "We didn't really stay long. We wanted to come find you and—"

"I tried calling her a few times," Nishta interrupted. "During my first year of marriage. She would stay on the phone as long as I talked. But she never said a word. My father didn't want her to, you know. Finally, I gave up. For her sake. Wasn't fair, to keep calling."

Kavita swallowed and stared at the floor. When she finally forced herself to look up, she saw that Laleh's nose was dark as rust—a sure sign that she was fighting her tears.

But Nishta seemed oblivious to their discomfort. "But you can't destroy a mother's love, right?" she said happily. "And so she helped you find me." She sat back on the couch. "So what made you? Look me up, I mean, after all this time?"

Kavita looked at Laleh. You tell her, her eyes beseeched.

Laleh grimaced. "I am an idiot," she said. "All these years, living in the same city. You think I could've done this sooner, Nishta? But I didn't. What can I say? I guess I just got busy with my own stupid little life, you know?"

"Well, it's not as if I made it any easier," Nishta said. "I know we acted badly. Iqbal and I—well, it was very hard, you know? No support from my parents, and his weren't thrilled, either, him marrying a Hindu. I don't know, it just felt easier pulling away, withdrawing into our own world." She fell silent, twisting her hands in her lap. "I was also jealous, to be honest. I—all of you went on to graduate school. Armaiti making plans to go to America. Whereas me and Iqbal—we had nothing to talk about. I was only in my twenties and I was stuck at home giving French lessons to a handful of children. I felt so deadly dull."

Laleh stirred. "What nonsense," she said. "We used to admire you and Iqbal so much for the odds you overcame."

Nishta smiled. "Yeah, we were the model couple, right? Hindu girl marries Muslim boy, pioneers of a brave new world." She looked around her living room. "This is where the brave new world brought us."

"Anyway . . ." Kavita found herself saying. "We have some bad news, I'm afraid. Armaiti is sick. She has a glioblastoma. It's a kind of brain tumor." No matter how many times she said the words, they sounded lurid and melodramatic, as if she were reciting a line from a movie.

They waited for Nishta's reaction, but other than a muscle twitching in her jaw there was nothing. "She's very sick," Kavita repeated.

Nishta nodded. "I know. One of Iqbal's uncles was diagnosed with a tumor five years ago." She snapped her fingers. "Bas, three months and he was dead."

Kavita felt a stirring of anger. "Well, Armaiti has more time—has been given more time." Nishta's reaction was annoying her. They had just told her that their friend was dying and she was reacting as if she'd been told that Armaiti had a cold. Worse, she was comparing her to some stupid man who had died within three months.

"It's always like this," Nishta said softly.

"Excuse me? What is?" Kavita said. She didn't bother to keep the irritation out of her voice.

"This. Life. This meeting and parting. This winning and losing. Here I was this morning, barely able to get out of bed. Didn't have any reason to, you know? And this afternoon, I force myself to leave the house, to buy food for dinner tonight. It seemed like just another ordinary day. The kind that kills you by not killing you. Know what I mean? And then, the two of you walk into my life. Just like that. No warning, nothing. And I feel like someone peeled off twenty-five years of deadness and made me alive again. But then, it's life, right? So something has to be taken away. So you tell me that Armaiti has a brain tumor. Now, what do I do with this? Where do I place this, Ka? To me, Armaiti is the girl who used to balance on the seawall every time we went to Marine Drive. The girl who once ate nine bananas on a dare. That quiet, serene girl who—" And suddenly Nishta was crying, silently, wordlessly.

Laleh's nose was that dangerous rust color again, but Kavita remained dry-eyed. In all the years she'd been friends with the other two, she'd never seen them cry, she realized.

"She wants us to come see her," Laleh blurted out. "In America. Before she . . . gets too sick."

Nishta looked puzzled. "Wants who?"

"All of us. All three of us."

"But how?" The other two watched as a procession of emotions crossed Nishta's face. "I wish," she whispered finally. "But I can't."

"Why not?"

Nishta bit her lower lip. "I—we—we can't afford it, yaar. Iqbal works for his uncle at his electrical shop. We could never afford anything like a trip to America."

"He left the bank?" Laleh asked.

"The bank? Oh God, yes. Years ago."

"What if we paid for your ticket?" Kavita said.

Nishta lowered her eyes. "I couldn't accept that."

"Nishta. This isn't for you. It would be for Armaiti. To fulfill her wish to have all of us together."

"Even if I agreed, Iqbal would never let me."

"What the hell? How could he stop you?" Laleh demanded. "And why would he?"

In reply, Nishta rose from the couch. "Wait," she said and went into a room behind a curtain. When she returned a minute later she was holding a picture frame. "Who is this?" she asked.

It was a picture of a thin-faced man with salt-and-pepper hair and a short beard. He was wearing the traditional Muslim garb of a white skull cap and kurta and pajamas. "An imam," Laleh said. "So?"

Nishta laughed. "Look closely. It's Iqbal."

Iqbal? The Iqbal they knew wore bright floral shirts over tight jeans and usually had his sunglasses perched on top of a headful of long hair. Their Iqbal was a young man who cussed and joked easily, with a mouth that was forever curled into a teasing smile. The man in the picture looked so serious, as if he had not cracked a joke or said a cuss word in years.

But wait. There was the nose, straight and pointed. Iqbal's nose. And the thin lips. And something about the flat-footed way in which the man stood, his hip jutting out slightly.

When they looked up, they couldn't keep the wonder out of their eyes. "Wow," Laleh said.

Nishta nodded. "Wow. This is my husband."

There was an awkward silence. "So, does he always dress like this?" Kavita asked delicately.

Nishta's eyes were amused when they looked at her. But beneath the amusement was something else. "He's changed," she said finally. "He's not the boy you knew. He's become very religious. Goes to mosque regularly." Her mouth twisted. "And he dislikes Hindus. So of course, he couldn't have a Hindu wife. So I had to convert. He badgered and badgered me until I gave in."

"This is too much, yaar," Kavita said. "Iqbal was an atheist. He cared less about religion than any of us."

"You knew him many years ago, Ka," Nishta said gently. "People change."

And you? Kavita wanted to ask. Have you changed, Nishta?

As if she were anticipating her question, Nishta said, "As for me, I'm sure I've changed also." She patted her round belly. "In fact, the mirror tells me that everyday." She pulled a face. "How come the two of you still look so beautiful, yaar? What's the secret?"

"I certainly don't feel beautiful," Laleh said. She frowned. "Seriously, though, Nishta. How could Iqbal buy into all this religious bull?"

Nishta's face grew red and she blinked rapidly.

"I'm sorry," Laleh said. "I wasn't trying to be insulting. Honest."

"Don't. Don't apologize. I'm not insulted. Just the opposite. You don't know how long it's been since I've been with people who feel the same way I do. You don't know—I've spent years now with people whose lives are governed by religion. My mother-in-law, even Iqbal's young niece—they live in this building, you know. One floor up, only. Those are the only people I see all day. All God-fearing people. There was a time when Iqbal was my defender against them. When he used to laugh at his parents when they started on the virtues of Islam. Now the only member of his family I can really talk to is his sister, Mumtaz. But she's married and lives in Jogeshwari.

So I don't see her as much as I'd like. Mostly we chat on the phone."

Nishta got up again. "Something else I want to show you," she said. She crossed the room and rummaged through a file folder that rested on top of a small corner table. She returned with a business card that she handed to Laleh. "Ahmed Electronics. See? It's a little shop in Fountain. Iqbal works there with his uncle. They sell plugs, sockets, cables, that kind of thing." She flipped the card over. "But even on an ordinary business card they had to have a picture of a mosque." She sat back, an odd smile on her face. "That's the kind of family I've married into."

As the extent of Nishta's isolation and loneliness hit Kavita, the room that she'd felt so comfortable in earlier suddenly felt oppressive. She caught Laleh's eye and knew that she was feeling the same claustrophobia.

"Why didn't you put your foot down, Nishta?" Laleh asked. "When he first began flirting with all this stuff?"

Nishta smiled. "You don't have enough time to hear the answer to that, my Lal," she said gently. "It's a very long story."

Laleh flushed, as if she'd heard the deflection and the mild rebuke in Nishta's voice. "Sorry," she said. She looked sheepish for half a second but then let out a snort. "We can't leave you like this, Nishta. Not after having found you after all this time. Tell me, how can we help?"

"She's the same old Lal," Nishta said to Kavita. "Still wants to fix the world." She shrugged. "It's okay, really. I've probably made my life sound worse than it is. Iqbal's a decent man. And I don't usually feel sorry for myself. It's just that seeing both of you is reminding me of the gap between my life as it is and what I'd dreamed it would be."

Laleh leaned back on the sofa and closed her eyes. "But maddest of all—to see life as it is and not as it should be," she quoted softly. *Man of La Mancha* had been one of their favorite movies. They had often skipped classes to take in a rerun at the Strand.

The other two smiled in immediate recognition. "Too much sanity may be madness," Kavita recited.

"Perhaps to be too practical is madness," Nishta added. She paused. "God. I used to know the entire speech."

"He was a handsome man, that Peter O'Toole," Laleh said.

Nishta turned toward Laleh. "Speaking of handsome men, how's Adish?"

"Nice." Laleh grinned. "Smooth. Good transition. I'll tell him. He'll be flattered. He's fine. About ten kilos more than I'd like him to be, but fine."

"And you, Ka? Any man—anyone special in your life?"

Kavita caught the stumble in Nishta's voice. Nishta knows, she thought. Ingrid's warm, attentive face swam before her eyes briefly. "Nobody special, I'm afraid," she said, hating the quiver in her voice, hating herself for her dishonesty.

"Kavita's one of Bombay's top architects, you know," Laleh said. "She has no time for romance and all that stuff."

"And I look after my mother," Kavita added. "Rohit—you remember my older brother?—lives in town, but he's married. So of course the spinster daughter has to take care of Ma." She tried to keep her tone light but thought that it came out petulant.

Nishta's eyes darkened with an emotion Kavita couldn't read. "It sounds like a good life, Ka," she said vaguely.

There was a short, awkward silence, and then Nishta said, "So you're both going to see Armaiti?"

"We are," Laleh said. "And we're still hoping you'll go with us, Nishta. Surely Iqbal will understand." Her voice took on a new urgency. "She—she probably won't make it until the end of the year. She's hoping we can go while she's still feeling good."

"I've only been out of India once," Nishta said. "Imagine. Remember how we used to talk about traveling together to see the Pyramids and the Galapagos Islands and the Louvre? Well, he's only taken me out of the country once. And guess where? To Dubai. Only because his brother lives there and sent us tickets. It was awful. A totally artificial place. I hated it. Iqbal was very impressed. He's easily impressed, these days. Especially if it involves Islam."

This time, they heard the anger in her voice. "Perhaps we could travel a little bit around the U.S. after we see Armaiti," Kavita ventured. "If you came, that is."

Nishta made a dismissive sound. "It's no use, Kavita. He'll never let me go." Something flared in her eyes. "He'll be afraid I'd never come back if I went."

Kavita looked away, embarrassed by what she saw in Nishta's eyes. But Laleh looked her squarely in the face. "And would you? Come back, I mean?"

Nishta held her glance for a moment. "I don't know," she whispered. Then she recovered. "Of course I would. Where else could I go?" Her voice took on a forced gaiety. "After all, a woman's place is by her husband, as my dear mother-in-law reminds me at least once a day."

There was another short silence and then Nishta got up reluctantly from the couch. "You know, I could talk to you for a year and still my stomach wouldn't get full. But I have to go pick up Zenobia from her typing class." Seeing their blank faces, she said, "Iqbal's niece. Her parents are in Dubai, so she lives with my mother-in-law. She's sixteen. Iqbal doesn't like her to walk home alone, even during the day. So I have to go. I'm so sorry."

Kavita couldn't bear the thought of parting from Nishta so

soon. "How about if we hang out until you come back home?" she asked. "And then maybe we can go out for a chai or something?"

Nishta bit her lower lip. "I'm sorry, yaar," she mumbled. "Iqbal doesn't like me to leave the house once I pick up Zenobia. As it is, I'll have to stop and buy the groceries on our way back. And then I have to start cooking dinner for the family."

Laleh looked stricken but Kavita nudged her and rose to her feet in one graceful motion. "It's fine," she said smoothly, signaling Laleh with her eyes to also rise. "We understand. We'll just walk out with you, okay?"

Nishta hesitated. "If you don't mind, you two leave first. My mother-in-law sits at her balcony all day long. And even though she claims her eyesight is bad, she keeps an eye on all my goings and comings. And I—I haven't decided yet when I'll tell Iqbal about this visit."

Laleh looked like she was about to argue but Kavita spoke first. "No problem," she said. "But we'll see you soon, yes?"

"I'll give you my mobile number," Nishta said. "And let me have yours."

Ten minutes later, they were outdoors again, their eyes adjusting to the ferocious glare of the afternoon sun. "God," Laleh said as soon as they were on the street. "She's like a prisoner in her home." She dug through her purse for her sunglasses. "Could you believe that picture of Iqbal? What the hell?"

Kavita didn't reply, distracted as she was by one incessant thought. The small apartment they had just left reminded her of the jail cell where she and Nishta had spent the night after their arrest. She had never seen the inside of a jail again, had made sure that she never would. Whereas Nishta had apparently spent the rest of her life in one. And the bitterest irony was that it was Iqbal, *Iqbal*, who was her jailer.

Over the years, she had worked hard to suppress the memories of that horrific night. But now she remembered the suffocating, claustrophobic feeling. The panic and the desperation. We have to get Nishta out of this place, Kavita thought. It would be a repudiation of everything we once were, to abandon her now.

7

rmaiti stood in the middle of her lush backyard, feeling
the soft earth beneath her feet. Her eyes followed the
movement of a gray squirrel madly chasing another.
The sun felt like a warm, steady hand on her back. The morning silence was so deep, it felt audible to her, like those high-
frequency whistles only dogs could hear. This is the world, she
thought, and I am here in it. I am here. In this time. And then
she caught herself, caught the thoughts that tilted toward mor-
bidity and self-pity, saw the clichéd direction in which they were
headed—woman with six months to live finally learns to live
in the moment—and felt a rush of embarrassment and anger.
Whatever the tumor did to her, whatever it whittled her away
to, she would not allow it to reduce her to a cliché. There would
be no deathbed conversions, no New Age transformations, no
spiritual awakenings. She would not permit it. She would not.

She brought the little Rubbermaid stool from the garage
and placed it in front of the spot where she'd buried the two
dead cardinals. Sitting down, she began to weed near the area.
After a few minutes, as always, she felt her heartbeat slowing
down. Let the Christians have their Sunday mass and the Muslims their call to prayer. This was her church, her temple, her
religion, this soft soil that got under her fingernails, this thin

morning air, this single note that the robin struck over and over again. This large backyard with its looming trees and its merry flowers and trilling birds was the only taste of heaven she would ever need.

After fifteen minutes of weeding, she reached for the flat of petunias Diane had brought home last evening. She was eager to plant them over the grave.

She swiveled on the stool, ready to pop a plant out of its plastic container. She missed. Her right hand couldn't find its way to the bottom of the container. Her fingers missed their mark, clutching air for a few puzzling seconds. She frowned and tried again. And was unsuccessful. Her mind told her that her hand should be curling around the green box, but somehow her fingers remained a few millimeters removed from their destination. She turned her whole body around this time and, holding her right wrist in her left hand, tried again. There. Now her fingers were gripping the plastic.

She let go of the container, shaken by this abrupt refusal by her body to obey her commands. She sat still for a moment, waiting for whatever this thing was to pass. After a few seconds she reached for the box but struggled with coordinating the movement of her hands with what her eyes were telling her. Once again, she gripped one hand in the other before she could get hold of the box. And when she protruded her index finger to push the delicate plant out, she felt the same frustration as her finger kept missing the hole in the container. Finally, more by touch than sight, her finger found its target.

She spent ten minutes on this fruitless task before giving up. During that time Armaiti fought a rising terror. What was going on within her body? How would she manage if her coordination was this bad? And how could it have come on this suddenly? She wondered if she should call out for Diane, but dreaded facing a fresh bout of condemnation from her daughter. Maybe this thing is not related to the brain tumor, she told herself. Maybe I'm dizzy, maybe it's a touch of vertigo or sunstroke that will clear up as soon as I go indoors.

She rose cautiously from the stool and stood still for a minute before she risked taking a step. She almost cried out in relief when she realized that the strange thing that was affecting her hand didn't seem to be affecting her balance or her gait. Still, she was careful. She took another step toward the house, and then another. She was walking fine. Whatever was affecting her hand had spared her legs.

"Hey, Mom," Diane called as Armaiti walked into the house. "Want some brunch?"

"No thanks," Armaiti replied as she came up behind her daughter.

Diane turned around. "How about I make you a waffle?"

"I already ate. Hours ago."

Diane's blue eyes settled on Armaiti's face. "What did you eat?"

Armaiti looked away, flustered. The truth was she had not eaten a thing since she'd had some pasta last night. "What is this? An interrogation?"

"Damn straight." Diane's brow furrowed. "Mom, you gotta eat. You can't lose weight when—"

Armaiti smiled. She caught the indignant look on her daughter's face and tried to stop.

"What? You think everything is funny?"

"I'm sorry, darling," Armaiti said. "It's just that you sounded so much like I used to when you were a child that I'm—I guess I'm just laughing at the role reversal. You know what I mean?"

"What are you talking about? I never gave you a hard time about food."

"Are you kidding me? Do you know what you ate for dinner from the time you were two until you were four? A boiled egg. Every single night, I swear. I got to the point where just looking at a boiled egg made me sick. I couldn't even participate in those elaborate Easter egg hunts your dad used to plan each year."

Diane grinned. "Remember the time he accidentally hid a raw egg inside one of your shoes?"

"Do I remember? He had to take me shopping the very next day."

"Good old dad."

There was a sudden silence in the kitchen. Armaiti had heard the wistfulness in her daughter's voice and knew that Diane was thinking back to the years before the divorce. As far as she knew, Diane had never found out about Blossom.

The waffles popped up in the toaster and Diane moved to get them out. "Can you pass the butter?" she said, gesturing toward where the tub of Earth Balance sat on the kitchen counter.

"Sure," Armaiti said as she reached for the plastic pot. Her fingers missed the container. Mortification made her face flush as she tried a second time, focusing as hard as she could to pick up the box before her daughter noticed that anything was amiss.

Diane was staring at her with her mouth open. "Mom? What's wrong?"

Armaiti tried to keep her voice light. "Who the hell knows? I'm just clumsy this morning, I think."

Diane didn't bother to keep the panic out of her voice. "You can't pick that thing up?"

"Sure I can. Watch." And guiding her right hand with the other, Armaiti gripped the container. "Here. Butter your waffles before they get cold."

"What is going on, Mom?"

Armaiti eyed Diane's plate. "Your food is getting cold, honey," she repeated.

"I don't believe this. I don't believe you're talking to me about my waffles when you're—you're . . ."

"Diane. Calm yourself. I don't know what's wrong, okay? Chances are it's nothing, just, y'know, like a tic or something. Let's just wait and watch."

"Wait and watch?" Diane sounded incredulous. "You can't use your right hand and you're telling me to be calm?" The young face grew teary. "What's wrong, Mom? Don't you care about anything? I feel like you've just given up or something. It's hard enough that you're refusing treatment, but why do you have to be so—so—*cavalier* about this? Can't you see what this is doing to Dad and me?"

Armaiti took the two steps that separated her from Diane and put her arms around her daughter. Diane made to pull away but Armaiti merely tightened her grip until the girl relaxed. "I'm sorry, my darling," she murmured. "I know you don't understand my decision. I can't even explain it to you except to say I must live on my own terms. I must. As for this thing, it just happened, you know? I haven't even had a chance to figure it out. I'm scared, too. But I'm hoping it's temporary, you know?"

"Let me call Dr. Cassidy's office."

She was about to refuse when she saw the pleading look on her daughter's face. "Okay," she said wearily. "If you like."

8

You're doing this for Laleh's sake, Adish reminded himself as he pulled into a parking space. And Armaiti's. But his movements were sluggish as he reached into his leather briefcase and fished around for the business card Laleh had pressed into his hand this morning. After he found it, he sat studying it for a moment, adjusting the visor to keep the sun out of his eyes. Ahmed Electronics. Adish thought he knew the narrow little gully the store was located in.

He got out of the air-conditioned car with a sigh. The things a man does for love, he thought, smiling to himself. But then he remembered how Laleh had grown more agitated with each passing day that she had been unable to reach Nishta, and the smile turned into a grimace. Truth be told, he, too, was worried about the fact that Nishta had never answered her phone since the day of Laleh's visit. And there was that weird incident from last night. After dinner, Laleh had dialed Nishta's cell phone as she'd taken to doing several times a day. But this time, instead of a recording stating that the phone was turned off, a man had answered. "Please don't call this number again. Nishta isn't here anymore," he had said after Laleh had identified herself. It was Iqbal who had answered, Laleh surmised. She had spent the next two hours pacing the apartment, her face tight with worry as she parsed his words. "What does he mean she's not here?" she'd said. "Has he killed her or something?"

"Lal. Get a grip. You're not making sense," Adish had said.

But her agitation had not diminished. "Why won't he let her come to the phone? What is he afraid of? And why does she allow him to treat her like this?"

"I don't know," he'd said, putting his arm around her. "But if we're to get any sleep, you have to calm down, okay?"

He was aware of how she tossed in bed and muttered to herself all night long. So he wasn't too surprised when she placed the card in his hand the next morning with a request. "Go talk to him, janu. If anyone can knock some sense into Iqbal's head, it's you."

"Laleh, I can't," he'd protested. "I can't just barge into his life after all these years."

"If you don't go, I will."

"Don't you dare. In any case, Sarosh is expecting you in his office in two hours. You're getting the permanent crown put on the tooth today, remember?"

"I don't care about the bloody crown. . . ." Laleh snapped.

He was about to respond sharply when he stopped himself. Things had been so tense between them of late. First, the scene at Girish's party and then Laleh's ridiculous accusation that they, somehow, were responsible for Armaiti's illness. Maybe his meeting with Iqbal would appease her.

"Okay," he said. "Okay. I'll go see him later today. Satisfied?"

She eyed him suspiciously, not trusting his sudden capitulation. "You promise?"

He sighed. "Yes, dear. I promise."

And maybe he owed Laleh this much, Adish thought, as he sat sipping his tea, while Laleh bustled around in the kitchen making him breakfast. To make up for that day from his youth, when he had cracked under pressure from Rumi Madan, Laleh's imposing, patrician father. A day he had believed they had tucked away, like an old letter in a shoe box, until Laleh had dug it out again.

The morning of the march, Laleh had phoned him from Kavita's home and requested him to stop by her house on his way to the demonstration and pick up her migraine medicine. Adish had readily agreed. He was waiting in the living room for Laleh's mother to return with the pills when a glowering Rumi had strode in, waving a crumpled, discarded, hand-drawn map of Bombay University, and demanding to know what trouble his idiotic daughter was getting into now. "I know you youngsters are up to something," Rumi had thundered. "I won't rest until you tell me what you're plotting." Under Rumi's relentless questioning, Adish had revealed their plan—a march followed by a forced occupation of the university chancellor's office. He and the others had spent so much time perfecting their plan that it had lost its novelty. And so Adish was unprepared for the older man's reaction—Rumi's face had turned beet red, his eyes had bulged, and in the booming voice that had struck fear in many a criminal in the courtroom he had delivered his ultimatum— that Adish deliver Laleh safely home within the hour or accept the fact that he would never see her again. Adish went to the march, sick with worry at what he was about to do. But a small part of him was also relieved that Rumi uncle had given him an out. Two days earlier, Laleh had sheepishly admitted to him her terror of spending a night in jail, and this knowledge had haunted him, aroused his desire to protect her. Now he could.

He found Laleh in the throng of students beginning to gather for the protest and told her that her mother was ill and was asking for her. Laleh left the march with him. So that she was safe at home when Nishta and Kavita were arrested. And when Armaiti landed in the hospital after receiving a vicious blow on the head from a baton-wielding policeman. Laleh's outrage when she found out about Adish's perfidy appeared genuine. But he also sensed that part of her was relieved to have escaped jail. It made him think that he had not imagined the look that had passed between them when he'd told Laleh about her mother being ill, that she had half-known he was lying. It broke his heart to see the great, indomitable Laleh like this, caught between her honor and her fear, because he knew how important it was to Laleh to always do the principled thing. And the fact that she had wavered, just this once, made him love her even more.

What he had not counted on was the fact that after all these years Laleh had not forgiven either herself or him for that one moment of weakness, Adish mused as he handed a twenty-rupee note to the parking attendant. How absurd was that? He should've reminded Laleh that the only reason that Armaiti had escaped with just a concussion was because of him. He had returned to the march after taking Laleh home, and when the police had opened their laathi charge, he had fought off the two policemen who were attacking Armaiti. He had been too late to prevent the blow to her head, but he had grabbed Armaiti's arm and pulled her away from the dangerous, violent streets and toward safety. When they had finally stopped running and Armaiti had not recognized him, he'd assumed that she was joking, and then, when he realized that the amnesia was real, he panicked and called Laleh's father. Acting on the older man's advice, he'd taken Armaiti to the hospital. So it was bullshit, really, what Laleh had said a few days ago, about complicity and guilt and sin. And how far-fetched, how unscientific, to think that a blow to the head would flower into a brain tumor thirty years later.

And yet, here he was, walking under a blazing sun, looking for the store where Iqbal worked. Mr. Fixit, charged with a new mission. He had no idea what he would say to Iqbal or how Iqbal would feel about him showing up at his place of work after all these years.

Ahmed Electronics, when he found it, was exactly as he had pictured it—a long, dark, narrow strip of a shop that was crammed fuller than a magpie's nest. Customers stood on the pavement in front of it and called out their orders. Adish waited as the man ahead of him purchased two AAA batteries and paid for them. He peered inside the shop, searching for someone who looked like Iqbal. The burly, bearded shopkeeper who was handing the customer his change certainly wasn't him.

Now the shopkeeper was looking at him. "What can I get you, sir?" he asked.

Adish took a step forward. "I'm looking for someone. Iqbal Ibrahim. Is he in?"

"Iqbal? He's my nephew. A minute ago only he was here." The man turned around and yelled into the tunnel of the shop. "Iqbal? Hai kya? Someone looking for you."

A door slammed in the back and a thin, lithe figure dressed in all white shuffled out of the shadows and toward the front of the shop. "Kon hai?" the figure said.

Adish took in the salt-and-pepper hair and the almost-white beard and was disappointed. A part of him had been looking forward to seeing Iqbal after all these years, he realized. "I'm sorry . . ." he began.

The shopkeeper pointed at Adish with his chin. "This gent wanted you," he said. He looked from one man to the other.

The man in white stared at Adish blankly for a second and then a slow recognition spread across his face. The look was followed immediately by another, as if the man couldn't decide whether he was happy or angry at the sight of Adish. But it was that first expression of recognition that triggered a reciprocal recognition in Adish. "Iqbal?" he said incredulously. "Saala, is this really you?"

A look of annoyance flitted across Iqbal's face. "Hello, Adish," he said. "What brings you here?" He asked the last question as if he already knew the answer.

Iqbal's uncle was still staring at both men. "Can we go somewhere where we can talk? Maybe for lunch?" Adish asked quietly.

"I don't take lunch," Iqbal said. There was a chiding quality in his voice that irritated Adish. He remembered dimly that even in the old days, there had been something about Iqbal, a delicateness, a quality of self-righteousness, that had bugged the shit out of him.

Adish turned to face Iqbal's uncle, an amiable smile on his face. "What is your capacity?" he asked pleasantly.

"Sir?"

He gestured toward the shop. "Your capacity. Inventory. I'm a real estate contractor, you see. If I placed an order for, say, a thousand sockets, can you provide?"

The man's eyes widened. Adish surmised that the shop didn't sell this kind of quantity in a month. "I'm not for sure, sir," the man mumbled. "But I can find out, quickly-quickly."

Iqbal opened his mouth to say something but Adish spoke over him. "Great. I will phone you in a few days to get your quote." He smiled broadly. "In the meantime, can you spare this fellow for an hour or so? He's an old friend of mine."

Iqbal was shaking his head no but his uncle was on his feet.

"Of course, sir. This is family business, you see. He come and go as he wishes." He turned toward Iqbal. "Go. Go. Your old friend has come to see you." He gave the reluctant man a slight push. "For Allah's sake. What you standing here for?"

Despite the fact that Iqbal hadn't said a word since they had begun to walk, Adish could feel him seething with anger. He felt a sense of disappointment at Iqbal's obvious distaste for his presence. He could well understand his companion's outrage at having been tricked into accompanying him. But Iqbal had not displayed the slightest pleasure at seeing Adish after all these years—and that stung. It made him question the years when they had all been so close. He remembered the night of Nishta and Kavita's arrest, when a distraught Iqbal had knocked on his door and they had walked the nighttime streets for hours, both of them bound together by their love for women who barely acknowledged their presence in public. He remembered now that Iqbal had told him that night that he had asked Nishta to marry him and that he was willing to convert to Hinduism if it helped with her parents.

"Wow," Adish had said. "When was this? And what did she say?"

"She said she'd talk it over with her three friends. And let me know her answer at an appropriate time."

They had looked at each other for a moment and then burst out laughing. "Could we have found two more difficult women to fall in love with?" Adish had said.

But the man walking beside him retained no vestige of the openhearted, lovesick boy from that night. He had no idea how to talk to this man. Adish's heart sank at the realization.

Still, for Lal's sake, for Armaiti's sake, he had to try. "Iqbal?"

he said softly. "It's good to see you again, yaar. How long has it been?"

He had misjudged the depth of Iqbal's anger. He stopped walking and turned to face Adish. "What do you want? Why are you here? Why are you people interfering with my family?"

Adish felt his face flush. Mortifyingly, he felt his eyes fill with tears. He looked away, embarrassed. He had always prided himself on being more practical than the others. Over the years, he had come to think of their college days as a spot of sweetness, when their youth had burned as bright as their idealism, but as a period that inevitably had to end. He had not remained stuck in the past as he sometimes thought Laleh and Kavita were and was proud of the fact that he had grown up and changed with the times. He had never shared Laleh's romanticism about their socialist past, and as he'd grown older he felt he had a lot more in common with his father-in-law, the pragmatic, solid Rumi Madan, and less with Rumi's impetuous daughter. He was often impatient with Laleh's theatrics, the constant self-recriminations, her expressions of solidarity with the poor, even while she enjoyed the fruits of his success. He had come to believe that his way was cleaner, more honest, less hypocritical— yes, he had once believed in a different system, and then, when he'd seen the difficulty—the impossibility—of the path he had chosen, he had gotten off that path. When free-market reforms came to India, he had freed himself along with them, and when the old regulations loosened, he felt something loosen within himself. He didn't believe for a minute that he had made a pact with the devil or sold his soul in doing so. That was the essential difference between him and Laleh—when she thought back on their college days, she saw them as a template for the rest of her life; Adish looked back on those days as a lovely dream from which it was difficult, but essential, to wake up.

And yet. Standing in the middle of a busy street, being bumped and run into by passersby, blinking away the tears that had inexplicably filled his eyes, Adish had to confront a new truth—Iqbal's dismissal of him hurt more than it had any right to. Which meant that those college years and the friendship that had seen them through a thousand cups of tea and countless political discussions had meant something after all. That the years were not pieces of paper that one could ball up and throw away. And that Iqbal—Iqbal, whose faint air of superiority had always made him bristle—even Iqbal was dear to him, was a brother to him in ways that no other friend had been since—not his friends at the club, not his tennis partners, not the men who had sat on the same boards that he did. Laleh had known some essential truth about their lives that had eluded him until now.

"I wish you no harm, Iqbal," he heard himself say. "And I'm sorry if I—if we . . ." He shook his head impatiently. "Forget it. I told Laleh this was a stupid idea. Listen, you go back to work. I—I should get going, too." He held out his hand. "Nice seeing you, yaar."

To his surprise, Iqbal took his hand. And held on to it. "Think I'm going to release you from buying me lunch that easily?" And Iqbal smiled, and even though his teeth were more yellow than Adish remembered, the middle-aged man in the pious garb fell away and in his place stood the long-haired, impish boy with the ever-present grin.

Something tightened in Adish's chest. He understood that Iqbal had noticed his hurt reaction and was trying to correct the situation. He suddenly felt crazily, triumphantly happy. But Iqbal was a feral cat he didn't want to scare off with a sudden move. So his face was impassive and his voice neutral as he said, "Where would you like to go?"

Iqbal shrugged. "I don't care. Zoha usually packs my lunch. You decide."

Some instinct told Adish to steer clear of the expensive restaurants he normally patronized. "There's a small Irani joint around the corner from here," he said. "Shall we go there?"

"Wherever, yaar." Iqbal smiled again. "You're paying."

9

They had finished lunch and it had been surprisingly easy chatting with Iqbal. I'd forgotten how charming the fellow can be, Adish thought. Iqbal had listened attentively as Adish had described his business, and laughed at the appropriate moments when he'd described the antics of his gangly, clumsy son. So far, Adish had shied away from asking Iqbal too many personal questions and had tiptoed around the reason why he had come calling. But now, looking at the big clock that hung behind the cash register, he knew he didn't have much time.

He leaned back in his chair as he cast an appraising glance at Iqbal. "So, saala," he said. "What's with the beard and stuff?"

Iqbal stiffened for a second and then broke into a faint smile. "You haven't changed, Adish. As blunt as ever." He waved away Adish's apology. "No. It's okay. I don't mind. I've always liked that about you."

"Thanks." The dimples widened in Adish's face. He waited.

Just when he thought Iqbal had forgotten his question, he spoke. "In 1993, I became a Muslim. A real one, I mean. Devout." Iqbal waited, as if expecting Adish to react. When he didn't, he continued. "My religion calls for all good Muslims to grow a beard." He paused. "Muslim *men*, that is."

Adish smiled politely at the joke. He had the feeling that any wrong move on his part would shut Iqbal up, would make him withdraw into silence. But Iqbal didn't seem ready to say anything more.

Adish cleared his throat and started again. "So. I'm assuming that Nishta told you—"

"Zoha," Iqbal corrected.

"Pardon me. Zoha told you that Laleh had stopped by your house?"

"Of course." Iqbal's eyes were now shiny, attentive.

"And she told you why?"

"Yah. She wants my wife to accompany her to America." Iqbal's voice was flat.

Adish felt a small wave of irritation. "Well, you know why, right? It's because Armaiti is dying. And it's her wish to see her friends before . . ."

Iqbal raised his hand to cut him off. "Zoha can't go."

Adish waited for him to continue. When it became clear that he wouldn't, he said, "Bas? That's all? No explanation?" He didn't try to keep the incredulity out of his voice.

Neither did Iqbal. "I'm surprised by that question, Adish, I must say. 'No explanation?' I need to explain my family mammala to you, someone I haven't seen in, what? Over twenty-five years?"

"That's not what I meant, Iqbal," Adish said softly. Don't lose your temper, he told himself. It won't help anything. "I meant that Armaiti was a dear friend. And . . . and in six months' time she might be dead. I just thought that you'd respect that memory enough—that, you know, for old time's sake, you'd at least attempt to explain your position."

"I only explain my position to one person, Adish. And that is to Allah."

Adish felt his right hand twitching with anger. He bit down

on his lip and looked away, not wanting Iqbal to see the anger he was feeling. "You sound like a fanatic, yaar," he said finally. There was a dry, hollow feeling in his mouth, like he'd smoked too many cigarettes.

Iqbal's eyes narrowed. "Is that a sadra I see, Adish? Under your shirt?" He was referring to the thin, muslin-cloth undergarment that Adish wore as a sign of his Parsi faith.

"Yes."

"So you're no longer an atheist, either, right? But you don't hear me calling you a fanatic. Only us Muslims are fanatics in this world? Whereas you Parsis, why, you don't even allow a non-Parsi into your fire temples or to convert into your faith, but you're not fanatics, correct? I'm a fanatic because I wear my faith on my face. But you hide yours under a shirt."

"That's not what I'm saying, Iqbal." Adish realized with dismay that they were quarreling, that he had upset Iqbal, which was the last thing he'd planned on doing. Still, there was no stopping now. "I was referring to your dismissal of your own wife's wishes to see her dying friend."

"Did Zoha say that? That she wanted to visit America?"

"Not exactly," Adish stammered. "That is, I'm not sure. I wasn't there."

"She doesn't want to go," Iqbal said flatly. "She told me so herself."

"Then why doesn't she tell Laleh that herself? Why is she not allowed to come on the phone?"

Iqbal's face flushed. "You're poking your nose in my family business, Adish."

"I'm just explaining what I meant when I called you a fanatic, Iqbal. It has nothing to do with your religion. It has everything to do with how you're treating your wife, as if she's some nineteenth-century chattel."

Iqbal slammed his fist on the wooden tabletop. "Don't you lecture me about how I treat women," he said. "And don't judge me until you've lived my life, Adish. You and Laleh—your wealth has always protected you. You people . . . you think because you're Parsis you're a minority in this damned country. You try living as a Muslim for one day. And then you talk."

Adish watched in horror as Iqbal's eyes glittered with tears. "Listen," he said. "I'm not trying to insult you, Iqbal. I'm just saying—I've known you for years, yaar. I just don't know how to reconcile all this with who—"

"You don't know shit." Iqbal's eyes were wild. "That stupid boy that you used to know? Forget him. He died in 1993. He's finished."

"What happened in 1993?" Adish asked cautiously.

The waiter came up to them with the bill. In order to delay him, Adish said, "Two cups of chai." He glanced at Iqbal. "You'll have a cup of tea, yes, boss?"

They waited until the waiter returned a minute later with the milky tea. "So what happened?" Adish asked again after he'd left.

Iqbal looked around him. The café was almost empty. "The Hindu-Muslim riots happened. In 1993. You remember? Or were you living in your golden cage, then?"

Adish let the insult pass. "Of course I remember, Iqbal. You couldn't live in Bombay then and not be aware of it. It was horrible." A memory of that time stirred in his mind but he pushed it away.

Iqbal was watching him closely and with sudden interest. "Why? Did you know anyone who died in the riots?"

"No. Thank God."

"Anyone who was injured?"

Adish shook his head. "No."

"Anyone who lost their home? Their business? Their relatives?"

"No. Not personally."

"Then why do you say they were horrible?"

Adish threw his hands in the air. "Because they were. It was a blot on Bombay's reputation. The secular, easygoing city that I had known changed forever during that time."

"Ah, Adish. So it was all—what was that term we used to use?—all theoretical for you, right? Something to talk about over dinner."

"That's not fair."

"Not fair? Not *fair*? Let me tell you what's not fair, Adish. What's not fair is that my parents had to give up their beautiful flat and move to the shit-hole neighborhood that we now live in. You remember the apartment Zoha and I were renting? It was tiny but we loved it. We gave that up, too. We sold my parents' flat in a hurry for a pittance just so that we could live among our own people. Safety in numbers, in case those Hindu butchers decide again to spill more Muslim blood."

Adish's eyes widened. "They hurt you? Your family?"

Iqbal sat back in his chair and stared appraisingly at Adish, as if trying to decide how much to tell him. Then, he exhaled loudly. "Not exactly. That is, we got lucky. My parents' Hindu neighbors in the next building took us in. Mr. and Mrs. Sharma. Long-time family friends. They hid us in their apartment for a week. At night we watched Muslim-owned shops and houses burning up and down the road. But we were spared, praise God."

"So, then why paint all Hindus with a broad brush, Iqbal? You just said that a Hindu family saved your life."

Iqbal's hands shook as he lifted his cup. "You don't understand," he mumbled. He stared at the table for a full minute and then looked up. A small muscle worked compulsively in his jaw. "I'm going to tell you something I've not even told my own mother. Even Zoha doesn't know. You understand?"

Adish nodded reluctantly. "You don't have to tell me anything you don't wish to."

"You remember Mumtaz?" Iqbal interrupted. "My baby sister? No? Well, it doesn't matter. What matters is, Mumtaz was sixteen in 1993. Okay? Beautiful girl, sweet as sugar, innocent as an angel. Never even looked at boys." He chewed on his lower lip, still avoiding Adish's eyes. "So a week after the riots are over, we're back in our own flat. Mumtaz is coming home from school and she runs into the Sharmas' son. He's a grown man, in his thirties. I had known him for years. Used to play cricket with him when I was a kid. Anyway, he tells her that our mother has forgotten a piece of her jewelry she'd given the Sharmas for safekeeping during the riots. Could Mumtaz stop by and pick it up, please? Mumtaz, she's like a child. She's never seen a snake. She follows the bastard home. And he—he does—he makes her do things to him, Adish." And now Iqbal rested his head on the table and cried softly, his thin arms shaking with his sobs.

Adish stared transfixed at the man in front of him. "He—he raped her?" he whispered.

Iqbal raised his head. His eyes were bloodshot. "He made her suck him down, Adish. Can you believe? My pure, beautiful sister. She had never even received a boy's kiss, let alone . . ."

"What did you do? How did you find out?"

"She told me. Three months later. I knew something was wrong, Adish, but I didn't realize at first. We were all so shaken up by the riots, you see. Everyone we knew had lost someone or something. And I—married to a Hindu girl—I had always been so proud of what Zoha and I had done. And now I felt like everything I had ever believed in—socialism, secularism—everything felt like a joke. I had spent years arguing with my father and brother when they talked about how Hindus wanted to massacre Muslims so that they'd have India all to themselves. Now I didn't know what to believe. So I didn't see that Mumtaz was suffering at first. But little by little, I see something is wrong. We'd always been close. So one day I took her to her favorite restaurant for kulfi and she pushed the kulfi away. Then I knew. I said, 'Little sister, whatever is wrong, I will right.' Finally she tells me."

"What did you do?"

Iqbal's eyes were bottomless wells of grief. "Nothing. Not a damn thing. I should've killed that chootia with my hands. But I did nothing. Who would believe us? The police had stood and watched when they were burning Muslims alive. I was afraid if I said anything the wrath of the mob would come down on all of us. So, I talked my abba—he was alive then—and ammi into vacating. We sold the flat quickly for little money. And then, the only thing we could afford was the falling-down building we live in now."

A million questions pricked at Adish's mind. "You never told Nishta?" he asked. "And how is Mumtaz? Does she live with you?"

Iqbal stared through him, as if he'd not heard the question. After a long minute he said, "I was right not to have confronted that pig-eater. Ten years later it all happened again, didn't it? In Gujarat." He swallowed hard and then continued. "They say over twenty-five hundred Muslims died in the Gujarat genocide, Adish. The real number was probably twice that. Did anyone refer to that as India's 9/11? At least the Americans who died were killed by foreigners. But the Muslims in Gujarat were butchered by their own countrymen. Has anybody been brought to justice? Of course not. Because a Muslim death means nothing in this cursed country."

Adish nodded in agreement. "I know. Those bastard politicians should rot in hell for Gujarat." He stopped, not knowing where Iqbal was going with this, his mind still reeling from what Iqbal had told him about his baby sister. "Is Mumtaz all right?" he asked. "Where is she now?"

"I never told Zoha about Mumtaz," Iqbal said. "But I made my wife convert and change her name when we moved." He looked at Adish defiantly. "Forced her. Threatened her. I couldn't risk a Hindu wife in the new neighborhood. And I didn't *want* to be married to a Hindu by then. As for Mumtaz, I did the only thing I could. I married her off. I couldn't risk any of this getting out, you see. She would've never found a husband, ever."

"You married her off? At sixteen?"

Iqbal's face twisted. "Don't judge me, Adish. She's happy now. Has two beautiful children of her own."

Adish shook his head. "It's not my place to judge, Iqbal." He looked at the man in front of him. How far we've traveled, he marveled to himself. What different paths life has taken us down. He had a sudden insight that beneath Iqbal's bearded visage, beneath the religious garb, there lay a wreck. That he was gazing upon a broken, tormented man, whom secular society had failed completely. His eyes burned at the thought. "I'm so sorry, dost," he said. He felt he had never meant anything more.

Iqbal's eyes glittered with tears. "Religion gives me comfort, Adish," he said softly. "When I'm at the mosque, I feel safe. Like I am listening to beautiful music. Or swimming in the sea." He smiled mirthlessly. "I know Zoha thinks I'm using religion as a crutch. She even gave me a hard time when I became a trustee at my mosque."

Adish made a wry face. "I know what you mean." Seeing Iqbal's surprised look, "Same situation in my house, yaar. Laleh's still a confirmed atheist. Whereas me . . . I've come to believe in the power of prayer."

To his relief, Iqbal smiled. "Laleh," he said. There was a lifetime of wonder and awe and affection in that word.

Adish's voice was gentle as he spoke. "I promised Laleh I would try to convince you to let Nishta—Zoha—travel with them. What should I tell her?"

Iqbal looked Adish straight in the eye. "Tell her I said no, Adish. Tell her please to not interfere with the only beautiful thing I have left in my life. Tell her I said please."

10

After they shook hands outside the restaurant and said goodbye, Iqbal stood on the busy street corner and watched as Adish walked away. For a brief second, he felt the urge to run after Adish, to ask him not to disappear from his life as he had ordered him to do minutes earlier, but instead to walk down the crowded streets with him, as aimlessly and happily as they had done a thousand times in their youth. A lump formed in his throat as he caught sight of Adish's familiar head one more time in the crowd. He was convinced that if he yelled Adish's name loud enough, he would hear him, hear him above the roar of the traffic and the cries of the vendors, and would turn around and walk back toward him with a wide, guileless smile. Adish had never been able to hold a grudge, and the fact that he, Iqbal, had told him minutes ago to exit their lives and leave him and Zoha alone would be forgotten in an instant. Of this he was sure.

But what then? After they'd walked for an hour or two, after they'd stopped for another cup of tea, say, after they'd exhausted their supply of new jokes and old stories, after they'd reminisced about how torturous their pursuit of their respective wives had been, what then? What did the two of them possibly have in common other than the wisps of memories

that still had the power to caress and tantalize? He remembered how casually Adish had tempted Murad with the prospect of placing an order that was larger than the number of
items they would sell in months. A rich sahib toying with a
poor man, trading on his hope and aspirations, in order to get
his own way. He remembered how puzzled Adish had seemed
when he'd told him about marrying Mumtaz off. How could
someone like Adish possibly understand the claustrophobic
atmosphere of the basti, where everybody knew each other's
affairs and rumors ran like barefoot children from one flat
to another? And despite Adish's declaration of being devout
himself, Iqbal knew it wasn't the same—Adish probably still
drank alcohol, indulged all his senses, enjoyed every decadent
pleasure that the life of the rich offered. The piety, the disci-
pline, the purity of Islam—how could Adish know the joys of
sacrifice and self-restraint? What could he, Iqbal, have in common with a pampered, middle-aged man who had the spirit
and look of an overgrown baby, who had never known a day's
suffering or deprivation? All the while that he had sat across
from Adish in the restaurant, he had observed him—the expensive haircut, the big, gold watch, the soft, delicate hands,
hands that had never been empty, that had seldom curled into
a fist, clean, manicured hands, hands that had never known a
hard day's labor, that had never had to grasp, fight, claw.

Out of the blue, Iqbal remembered the old rivalry between
him and Adish about their grades. Despite their almost identi-
cal ranking at the top of their class, he had always believed that
Adish was the more gifted, the more naturally talented student.
Adish had always boasted about how he never did homework,
about how he would start studying a few days before their exams, that any more preparation was a waste of time. And Iqbal
was too embarrassed to admit that he actually began to study

for their final exams months earlier, thinking of this striving as some kind of an intellectual defect. But now, his lips twisted with bitterness as he thought back to the conditions in his home during his youth—all of his family crammed into a sunny but modest two-bedroom apartment, his mother insisting that Iqbal turn off the lights as soon as his father went to bed, so that there was no chance to pull an all-nighter like most of his classmates did, the constant quarrels between his parents about money, his guilty awareness of how much his mother endured so that he could go to college. Adish, on the other hand, had his own bedroom where he could read late into the night, a mother who woke up early each morning during the exams to prepare him a special drink made with almonds and saffron and milk, parents who groomed him for academic success as if he were a thoroughbred racehorse.

Why had it never occurred to him before, the unfair advantages that Adish had had over him? But even as he asked, he knew the answer: he had been deluded by all the bullshit talk of comradeship and equality. Just as he had almost been lulled, a few minutes ago, while watching Adish's retreating back, into believing that they still had something in common, that there was a possibility of friendship between them.

Iqbal shifted from one foot to the other in his agitation. Adish had disappeared into the crowd, had probably stopped thinking about him the minute he walked away, and still, here he was, rooted in the same spot. He glanced at his Timex. He had been away from work for over two hours. Murad would be phoning him any minute now. But the thought of returning to work, of facing his uncle's inquisitive questions, Murad's open curiosity as pungent as chili powder, produced a feeling of revulsion in him. Besides, he needed to think, to calculate what and how much to reveal to Zoha, to weigh whether he could trust Adish to keep his word. Reaching for his cell phone, he took shelter on the first step of the Irani restaurant they had recently exited, stepping away from the incessant wave of people rushing past. He dialed Murad's number.

"Where are you, yaar?" He could hear the annoyance in Murad's voice. "I gave you time to go to lunch, not to go on a damn honeymoon."

The feeling of distaste grew. He had not taken a day off in so long. The thought of returning to that crowded, narrow strip of a shop for the rest of the day depressed him. "Listen," he said. "I'm feeling sick. I think I ate something bad for lunch. I'm thinking of going home."

He held the phone away from his ear as his uncle went into this usual tirade of insults, threats, and ultimatums. "Murad bhai," he said finally. "I have to go. I have to use the bathroom again. See you tomorrow. I'll make up the time. I promise."

The feeling of freedom that he felt as soon as he hung up reminded him of the delirious feeling he used to get when he and Zoha used to skip classes to go to the seashore or to Hanging Gardens. It convinced him that he had made the right decision. The afternoon hung before him, an empty stocking that he could fill with the currency of his choosing. A movie? A short bus ride to the sea? Dropping by to visit a friend? Just the idea of choosing, of options swirling in his head, made him feel rich, a member of the leisure class. He reentered the Irani restaurant and was greeted by his waiter, a quizzical look on the man's face. "Kya hua, seth?" the waiter queried. "Forget something?"

Iqbal smiled expansively. "Nahi. Just wanted another taste of your excellent tea."

He sat sipping the tea, looking out at the bright, sunlit street. As he sat, his earlier resentment of Adish ebbed. Adish was a decent fellow, he decided. Trustworthy. And he had as good as confessed that Laleh had put him up to this. He remembered how single-minded Laleh could be and felt a shot of sympathy for Adish. Picking up his cup, he took another sip.

And felt something in his mouth. Something soft and furry. Stopping in mid-swallow, he reached for the saucer and spat out the liquid. Along with the dead fly.

His eyes filled with involuntary tears as he ran his tongue around his mouth. "Hey," he called, signaling to the nearby waiter, his voice shaking with outrage.

"Yes, sir?"

"What's this? A fly in my teacup?" he spluttered. "What kind of a third-rate joint do you run here?"

The waiter eyed the saucer. "Sorry, sir. You want a new cup? I bringing hot-pot."

He could still feel the sensation, the violation of something soft and furry in his mouth. "Are you mad? You think I would trust another cup in this cheap place?"

The owner of the restaurant, who until now had stared resolutely out of the open windows, now moved his bulk out from behind the cash register and shuffled over. "Su che? What's the problem? Ramdas, what happened?"

"This gent here says fly landed in his cup, sir."

The owner made a dismissive gesture with his beefy hand. "So? Flies are everywhere. I should give up my restaurant and become a fly-catcher instead? This is Mumbai, my friend. More flies than people here. How can I help if one decides to share your tea?"

Iqbal rose to his feet. "Listen, the insect was at the bottom of my cup. It didn't just fly into it."

The man frowned. "Impossible. We run the cleanest kitchen here." He snapped his fingers at the waiter. "Ramdas. Bring this customer another chai."

"That only I was offering, sir."

"I'd rather die than to drink your tea." Iqbal's words came out more aggressively than he'd intended.

The owner's eyes narrowed. "Sir, then you please leave. No insults tolerated in my restaurant. Otherwise, I'm not responsible."

Iqbal felt his cheeks burn. "Don't threaten me, you . . ."

The waiter placed himself in the middle of the two men. "Please, sir. You leave now. No charge for tea. Just please to go."

Iqbal allowed himself to be eased out of the restaurant. Out on the street, he glared at the owner one last time, but even as he did so, he could feel the anger and outrage leaking out of him. Instead, as he walked away, a feeling of defeat and melancholy gripped him. The promise of a golden afternoon flattened into humiliation.

They would've never treated Adish this way. Of this he was sure. He remembered how the owner of the restaurant had half-risen from his stool when Adish and he had entered, how the man had wandered up to them halfway through their meal and asked if their food was in tip-top shape. If it had been Adish who had found an insect in his tea, the owner would've practically prostrated on the ground in apology.

In fact, there would never have been a fly in Adish's tea. Iqbal slowed down as the thought struck him. Of course. It was a setup. They probably didn't want any Muslim customers. As long as he was there with Adish, he was tolerated. But the fact that he'd dared to reenter on his own . . . He stopped himself. Saala, you're going mad, he scolded himself. They probably serve a hundred Muslim customers a day. A real persecution complex you're developing.

He continued with this new narrative as he walked, pleased with himself for being fair-minded, tried to douse the flames of his outrage, even tried to interject some humor into the whole episode. But one thing he knew beyond dispute—Adish would've never been insulted by the owner as he had been. And that recognition caked his mood, dimmed the open-ended feeling of the day, made him feel failed and weak, as he did most days.

And another thought flew abruptly into his mind and darkened his mood: the fact that he had told Adish about Mumtaz's violation. Why this bothered him so, he didn't know. It was not as if he distrusted Adish or was afraid that he would gossip about this. He had no doubt that his secret was safe with him. Besides, they had no friends in common.

No, what bothered him, he realized, was himself. His own weakness. How easily he had been lulled, how easily he had stepped into the cradle of friendship and allowed himself to be rocked to sleep. He had always believed that he would go to his grave without telling another soul about what had happened to Mumtaz. He had wanted to confide in Zoha a million times, especially when she would make a scathing comment about how he'd married off his sister at sixteen, her voice sharp with contempt and indignation. But he had let Zoha believe the worst of him rather than betray Mumtaz's trust. His little sister had suffered enough—he wanted nothing to graze her skin now, not even the nibbles of Zoha's pity.

But Adish. Adish had managed to wrest his secret out of him. How had he done so? Not by bullying him or forcing him. Instead, Adish had merely touched the lance of his puzzlement to his heart, had let his bafflement—and maybe his disappointment—show in his eyes, and, bas, the words had tumbled out of his mouth. Was his ego really that fragile? His need to appease, to demonstrate that he was a man and not a monster, that strong? Did Adish's good opinion, after over twenty-five years of silence, still mean so much to him? Iqbal felt his body go stiff with anger and self-loathing at the thought. Saala, coward, he cursed himself.

And then his anger changed directions and he thought, Damn Zoha. Damn her for putting me in this position. If she had just told the others flat-out that she couldn't go with them to America. That would've been the end of the matter, bas, book closed, case khatam, finis, finito. But no. Whatever she had told the two women was enough to keep hope dripping in the back of their throats. And so they had sent Adish. What was that name they used to call him in college? Iqbal scratched the tip of his nose as he tried to recall. Mr. Finisher, or something like that. He remembered what Laleh's father had once said about Adish: "If this boy had been alive then, he could've made the British give India to Gandhi twenty years earlier. Hell, he could've even convinced Gandhi to give India back to the bloody British." No wonder they'd sent Adish, like a bloodhound, to find him, track him down, make him agree to their preposterous plan. Did they have any idea how Muslim women were being treated in America these days? What if some pink-faced officer decided to get fresh with his wife at customs or immigration? Every day at the mosque there was a new story of how Muslims were being harassed and humiliated in America. Not just at the airport, either. Laleh and Kavita in their Western clothes, their jeans and T-shirts, would be fine. But what about his Zoha? Did any of them even stop to think about this? Armaiti's dying was sad, yes— he had prayed to Allah, praised be His name, when he'd heard the news—but did that mean that his family had to die, also?

Without intending to, his feet had taken him to the train station from where he caught the train home every day. He felt a moment's sadness when he realized this. Arre, Feet, he said to himself, even you have betrayed me. So much for my plans to go to a movie or to the seashore. Chalo, I will heed your advice and go home to my wife.

By the time he climbed up the creaking stairs that led to his apartment, the failure of the afternoon had crystallized into rage. He noticed immediately that instead of looking happy at his early return, Zoha looked surprised and annoyed. "Kya hai, bibi?" he taunted. "Not happy to see your husband?"

She shrugged wordlessly and this provoked him more than any words could have.

"Expecting someone else? Have I interrupted your plans?"

Zoha turned to face him. "Iqbal, please. Don't start on me today. I have a headache."

He smiled mirthlessly. "Me, too. I had a headache, too. His name is Adish. But I got rid of him."

She looked at him closely this time. "What are you talking about?"

Finally, he had her. Her full attention. It made him feel a bit giddy. "He came," he said. "To see me. At the shop. About"—he waved his hand dismissively—"the whole Armaiti affair."

Did he imagine the light that flared in her eyes? He couldn't be sure.

"And?" Zoha said cautiously, after he fell silent.

Iqbal raised an eyebrow. "And? I explained things to him, naturally. Man to man. Made him understand the impossibility of the request. Bas, that's all."

He could see the emotions wrestling on Zoha's face, noticed how she tried to make her face turn neutral. How much she cares, he thought, and it took his breath away. "And?" she said finally.

"Again, *and*? And nothing. He agreed. Saw the error of his ways. Asked my forgiveness. Promised he would never trouble us again. Said he would handle his wife."

Zoha gave a short laugh. "As if."

"What?"

"As if Adish can handle Laleh."

He looked at her with contemptuous eyes. "Not all men let their wives sit on their heads like I've let you do."

She opened her mouth and then shut it. They stared at each other for a few seconds and then she said softly, "Do all men steal their wives' cell phones? Did you ask Adish that?"

His hand itched in sudden fury and he shoved it into the pocket of his pajama. He would not rise to her bait. He would not. Besides, it was done. He had won. Adish would never pester them again. He forced his mouth into a yawn. "What time will dinner be?"

Her eyes were dull. "Same time as every night."

A wave of pity and self-recrimination rose in him and he pushed it down. "Okay. I'll go visit with Ammi for a few hours."

"Iqbal."

"What?"

"Is this the way . . . is nothing else possible?"

He knew what she was asking, and for a moment he was tempted. She would only be gone for a few weeks, after all. And he knew that if he permitted himself to yield even a tiny bit, his body would be flooded with grief at the thought of Armaiti dying. Something in him softened, but then he remembered the fly in the tea, the restaurant owner's rudeness, Adish's easy lie to Murad, his betrayal of his sister's secret. Strong. He needed to be strong. His faith required him to resist temptation. And what Zoha was offering—the softening, the laying down of arms—was the most tempting thing of all.

He pretended to misunderstand the question. "You want to go out for dinner instead of cooking tonight?"

He saw the hurt in her eyes as she turned away. A sharp feel-

ing tore through his chest as he left the apartment, and he had
no idea if it was grief or satisfaction.

———————————

Laleh was waiting by the door when Adish got home that evening. "I tried calling you the whole day," she said as soon as he
walked in. "Why didn't you answer? What happened?"

"Hello, darling," he mimicked. "How was your day? Did you
have a hard day at the office? Should your loving wife make you
a cup of coffee? Or offer you a chilled beer?"

Laleh looked chastened. "Okay, sorry," she said. Then she
frowned. "But you don't know what's it been like, waiting all
day. Why the hell didn't you answer the phone?"

He shook his head in exasperation as he ducked past her and
headed toward the bedroom. "I swear, Laleh, you're worse than
the children ever were. Can a man not even change his clothes
before he faces the bloody Inquisition?"

"Of course," Laleh conceded but he noticed that she followed
him in. She perched on the bed and waited until he emerged
from the bathroom.

"So how does he look?" she asked eagerly.

Despite himself, he laughed. "You're a pit bull," he said.
"Relentless." Noticing the bright anticipation on his wife's face,
he sighed to himself. Laleh was not going to like what she was
about to hear.

"Listen," he said. "Do both of us a favor. Go pour me a beer.
And pour yourself a glass, too."

Her face tensed. "It's not good news?"

He exhaled sharply and grabbed her by her shoulders, forcing her to her feet and spinning her around. "Go. I'll be out in
a jiffy."

But in the bedroom, he lingered, trying to work out how

much to tell Laleh about what Iqbal had told him. He knew that without hearing the full story, she would not understand his promise to Iqbal to leave him alone. But Iqbal had said he had not shared the story of Mumtaz's humiliation even with his own wife. What right did he have to share Iqbal's secret with his?

When he entered the large living room, Laleh was sitting on the window seat overlooking the sea. She had turned off the lights, and under a darkening sky he could see the blue Philips neon light across the water. He went and sat down beside her, took a long gulp of his beer, set the glass down between them, and then took her hand in both of his. "Look," he said. "I'm sorry. The answer is no. He doesn't want her to go."

In a reflexive gesture, Laleh pulled her hand out of his. "He can't stop her. She wants to go, Adish. I told you. I could read it on her face. Maybe I can talk to him . . ."

"No." His voice was louder than he'd intended, more emphatic, and he modulated it before he spoke again. "No, Lal. That's not a good idea. Besides, I . . . I promised him that—"

"Promised him what?"

"That we would not trouble him again. That we would not interfere with his life."

She let out a small cry. "You can't. You can't speak for me." Laleh's eyes blazed in the dark. "Funny how you always make promises that involve me behind my back. An old habit of yours."

He felt a reciprocal anger flare in him. "Funny how you always twist everything. You're a great one for clinging to the past, Laleh. It's one of your least attractive traits."

"You had no right, Adish. You're not the one who has to face Armaiti and her disappointment." Her face contorted with emotion. "My God, what kind of a monster has Iqbal turned into?

To refuse a sick woman's final wish? Did you tell him—that Armaiti is dying?"

He felt a sudden stab of pity for Laleh. But then he remembered the anguish in Iqbal's eyes as he'd recounted the molestation of his baby sister. Laleh's pain would pass; Iqbal's would be lodged in him the rest of his life. Adish closed his eyes and imagined someone hurting his daughter, and just the thought of it made the blood rush to his head. To have actually lived through such a thing and to be too weak to do anything about it—to be too poor, too powerless—to not be able to march over, knock on the bastard's door and kill him with your own bare hands—was something he could not fathom. Iqbal had lost so much; he, Adish, couldn't ask him to give up anything else. Maybe if Laleh had not mentioned to him what Nishta had said about probably not returning if she left India. Maybe if he had not carried that knowledge to his meeting with Iqbal, he could've tried harder. Been more persuasive. But that knowledge had sat like curdled milk inside of him and made it impossible to deceive Iqbal into thinking he was parting with his wife for a mere few weeks.

"I want to tell you something," he said quietly. "And I need you to trust me. Trust my judgment." Seeing that Laleh was about to argue, he raised his hand to cut her off. "Wait. Let me finish. Please." He paused, his eyes searching her face, trying to find the right words. "Look, I know you're disappointed. And Armaiti—if you like, I'll give the news to her. But Iqbal—he's a broken man, Lal. That young, bright man who was our friend? Forget him. He's gone. He's had a very, very hard life since the time we were friends. Some terrible things, you know? And please, I can't say more. I promised. And yes, I also promised him we'd leave him alone. And I won't go back on my word, Laleh. Not even for you."

She emitted a sound he'd never heard before. "You're not even making sense. Why can't you tell me? Maybe we can help them. Why did he cut us off?"

"Laleh. Calm down. This thing—there's nothing we can do to help. Some things are too big even for you, sweetheart. You . . . I told you. You'll just have to trust me on this one. Don't you think I know how much this means to you? Don't you know me well enough by now? That if I could've made you happy, I would have?"

And suddenly, she was in his arms. "I'm sorry, Adish. I'm an ungrateful bitch. I'm so thankful you even tried to reason with him." She looked up at him tearfully. "Oh, but the thought of Nishta in that miserable house. It makes me want to throw up."

"I know, sweetie. I get it. I hate it, too." All the while thinking that misery was the connective tissue that bonded humans to each other. All the while tracing the path from the tragedy of the 1993 riots to the personal catastrophe that had engulfed Iqbal, and to its aftermath, Iqbal's religious conversion, and how that curtailed Nishta's life, to its most recent manifestation, the pain it was causing Laleh. And all because the despicable politicians had played one group against the other in order to shake down a few votes. And all because one bastard couldn't keep his prick in his trousers.

Adish tightened his grip on his wife. "So, did you get the tooth fixed today?" he murmured after a few moments. She nodded. "And? Are you in pain?"

"No. I'm okay."

He hugged her even tighter. "Do you want me to call Armaiti with the news about Nishta? I'll tell Kavita, too, if you want."

She shifted in his arms. "You've done enough. I'll tell them."

She looked up at him, her face small and pinched. "Maybe it'll be enough, after all, to have me and Kavita with her?"

"Of course it will." He swallowed the lump that had suddenly formed in his throat. After all these years, Laleh could still slay him with a look or a word. Just slay him.

11

I don't get it," Armaiti said. "Iqbal really said no?"

"I'm afraid so."

Armaiti picked at a piece of dry skin on her face. "Adish did tell him, right? About the reason—about my condition?"

"Yes, my darling. I'm so sorry."

"And she'd said she wanted to come? When you saw her?"

"I, I think so. I got the distinct impression that if Iqbal had—"

"Give me her phone number. I'll call her directly."

"You can't reach her. I told you. He doesn't want us to contact her anymore." Laleh sighed. "I just hope Adish showing up doesn't get her into trouble."

Armaiti forced herself to concentrate. Because she was having difficulty comprehending. "Trouble? With whom?"

"With Iqbal, of course. He obviously doesn't want her to have anything to do with us." Laleh made a mocking sound. "He's probably afraid that we would infect his begum with our godless, secular ways."

"I don't believe this. Why does Nishta put up with this? She has a degree in French from a good college, dammit. Surely that's worth something? Why doesn't she put it to use? With all these multinationals flocking to India, surely there's a need for translators?"

Even across the phone line, she heard the smile in Laleh's voice.

"You've lived away from India for too many years, my Armaiti. You've forgotten how hard it is to do anything in this damn country. There's probably ten million graduates with more skills than Nishta. And they're all unemployed. Besides, I told you—she's changed. There's something—I don't know—sluggish about her."

"Nishta? That's impossible."

"Anyway. Kavita checked her work schedule today. She can leave in about twenty days. Adish is working on booking our tickets. A lot depends on when they give us an appointment for our visa interviews. I'll keep you posted, okay?"

"Okay. I'll fax the letter from my doctor tomorrow. Hopefully, that should help with the visa."

"I'm not worried," Laleh said. "It's all going to work out." There was a brief pause, and then she said, "I feel like I've let you down, Armaiti. About Nishta, I mean."

"And it's raining here today. Feel guilty about that, too, would you?"

Laleh laughed. "Bitch."

"Better believe it."

She laughed again. "You're in a feisty mood today. You feeling better?"

Laleh had become the one person with whom she could talk freely about her health. "Not really. My hand-eye coordination is pretty bad. I'm fine with large movements. But if I try to break an egg on the rim of a cup, half of it might land on the counter."

"Are you in pain?"

"Not much. The steroids are helping with the headaches, thank God."

"Thank God," Laleh repeated. "You take care of yourself, okay, my darling?"

"Oh, I do." Armaiti was quiet for a moment, and then she chuckled. "You know what's funny? For years and years I told myself that if I ever found out I had six months to live, I'd have potato chips, French onion dip, and a Coke for breakfast every single day."

"So do it. What the hell."

"That's the funny part, Laleh. I tried doing it once. And I hated it. I've become more paranoid about eating healthy than I ever was. Isn't that strange? It's like I'm training for a marathon. Turns out even dying is hard work."

"Armaiti . . ."

"I've depressed you. Sorry."

After she hung up the phone, Armaiti remained on the couch, trying to process the incomprehensible news about Nishta. She remembered so clearly the morning Nishta and Iqbal had bounded into the college cafeteria and announced that they'd decided to get married soon after graduation. Despite the obstacles they all knew she faced, Nishta had looked so sure, so confident. As for Iqbal, he had kept whistling "I'm Getting Married in the Morning" until a groaning Adish had offered him a ten-rupee note to stop. How to reconcile that happy memory with what Laleh had just told her? Could time really alter things so much? If so, the devil that every religion taught people to fear and loathe was simply the passage of time.

She was lost in her thoughts when Diane entered the room and flopped down on the armchair across from her. "Okay, that's it, Mom," she said in that take-charge tone that set Armaiti's teeth on edge. "I'm going to confiscate the phone if you're gonna look so glum each time you talk to your friends in India. The whole idea was to cheer you up."

Confiscate the phone? Armaiti bristled. Was their role reversal really that complete? Already? She was thinking of a suitable response when Diane asked, "So, what's the word on Auntie Nishta? Were they able to reach her?"

Her disappointment about Nishta not coming was still too raw to discuss with Diane. "No," she said shortly.

"Why not? What's the problem?"

Armaiti couldn't keep the frustration out of her voice. "The problem is her husband. He won't let her come, it seems."

"Why not?"

Her words came out in a rush. "Because he's turned into a religious fanatic. He's become this pious, fundamentalist Muslim who apparently prays five times a day and—" She stopped, noticing the look on Diane's face. "What?"

"I can't believe you said that."

"Said what?"

"That you called him a fundamentalist, just because he's religious."

She loved Diane deeper than life, but right now Armaiti's fingers itched to slap the smug off that young face. "He used to be a *socialist*," she said. "He used to laugh at the person he's become. He's become a caricature of the person he used to scorn."

"So? He's not allowed to change?" Diane had that righteous look made Armaiti fume. "How come you're so contemptuous of people of faith, Mom? You're so dogmatic. Don't people have the right to believe whatever they wish to?"

Her daughter had never seemed as much of a stranger to her as she did right now. Diane had gone to a prestigious private school where political correctness was extolled, where tolerance and multiculturalism were buzzwords. She had grown up in a town that proudly—if inanely—labeled itself a nuclear-free zone, had gone to the nondenominational Unitarian church the few times her parents had bothered taking her to church, and now attended a university that was famously liberal. Diane had become exactly the person she and Richard had wanted her to be—progressive, broadminded, tolerant.

So why did she feel like she and her daughter were not speaking the same language? That there was something simplistic, even childlike, about her daughter's understanding of the world? That right now Diane seemed more like Richard's daughter— good-hearted, well-meaning Richard, whose American inno- cence had always felt endearing and dangerous to her—than her own? That the Diane who was looking at her with a slight frown on her face was truly the child of the American Midwest— sweet but bland—with not a trace of her mother's heritage of spice and vinegar?

And you, Armaiti asked herself, what language do you speak? A dead language. The language of a faraway time, of a world that no longer exists. Of a time when they had believed the prophet who claimed that religion was the opiate of the masses. They had not seen religion as a polite, innocuous, private issue, as Diane did, or a topic for cocktail-party conversation. Not for them the benign, New Age, crystals-and-angels view of religion shared by so many of her American friends. She and the others had seen religion as a ferocious beast to be tamed, as a weapon that the ruling class used to keep the masses in servitude. Or a demon- genie that the politicians let out of the bottle every time there was an election to be won. And then mobs of Hindus and Mus- lims and Sikhs bludgeoned each other to death, set houses and people and children—*children*—on fire. Or threw acid on the faces of young girls walking to college. Or rioted to ban books or movies or paintings that offended their religious sensibilities. Several times Armaiti and the others had gone on fact-finding missions after a riot or a massacre, traveled into the hinterlands of Bihar or Orrissa, witnessed the aftermath of religious fervor. It had turned her off religion, forever. Or, rather, it had given

her a new faith. She and the others had proudly called themselves secular humanists, the words honey in their mouth. The
only gospel they could believe in was one that preached food for
the hungry, clothes for the naked, and justice for the oppressed.

She looked now at her daughter, lovely and guileless, and was
torn with conflicting desires—the protective, motherly desire
to have Diane always remain this innocent, secure in her small
outrages over small grievances. But there was another part of
her that wanted her daughter to know—not just the world she
had grown up in but to know *her*, the wars she'd fought and lost,
the idealism that she wore like a tarnished shield. It felt like a
dereliction of duty somehow to die before passing on some of
this knowledge to her only child. Because she feared that the
world had changed too much, that this new, jittery world of
global capital and virtual friendships would never again nur-
ture the kind of community and optimism that she had known.
Diane would be a good person—she would put milk out for
stray kittens and remember to refill the bird-feeder, she would
send money to sponsor a child in Africa and she would give up
her Fridays to read to old people in a nursing home—but she
wouldn't know the meaning of a collective struggle, wouldn't
know the heart-pounding thrill of marching along with tens of
thousands of others, or the cold fear of facing down a police
barricade.

In short, Diane would lead the same happy but dull middle-
class life that she had for the last three decades. Armaiti sat up
in her chair at the realization.

She must've looked stricken because she heard Diane say,
"Hey, Mom, I'm sorry. I wasn't really angry at you or anything."

She struggled to respond but found it hard to concentrate on
what Diane was saying. Because she'd suddenly realized why it
was so important to her to see the others again. It was because

of Diane. They were the heirloom she would pass on to Diane. They would help explain her to her daughter.

She needed to be alone for a few minutes, needed some time to think. "Listen," she said. "You know what I have a real taste for? Some rum-and-raisin ice cream. But the only place around here that sells it is the market off Emory. You wouldn't want to go get some, would you?"

As she had predicted, Diane rose immediately. "For you, my dahling, anything." She blew her mother an exaggerated kiss. "Be back in a jiffy."

"Take your time."

It was a rare pleasure to have the house to herself. Ever since she'd received the diagnosis, Richard had practically moved back in, and Diane hovered and fussed over her more than her own mother ever had. Armaiti knew she should be grateful, but sometimes she forgot to be. They were making her feel more and more of an invalid with each passing day, and where they left off, her own stupid, unreliable body took over.

She sat luxuriating in the solitude for a few moments and then rose slowly to her feet and made her way to her bedroom. Cotton was sleeping on the bed and greeted Armaiti with a yawn and one outstretched paw. She patted his bony head absently as she moved toward the closet. Standing on her toes, she reached toward the stack of photo albums balanced precariously on the top shelf. But she misjudged the distance and her hand hit the bottom album so that three of the books fell down. She moved out of their way just in time. "Shit," she said out loud. "I've become a total klutz."

The cat cocked one ear back and remained motionless. But he got up to rub his face on the books as soon as Armaiti put them on the bed. "Move, Cotton," she said, pushing him away. "You're gonna get hair all over my wedding album."

Her wedding album. The first year after the divorce, she had caught Diane thumbing through its pages. How inconsolable the girl had been then. And now, a few years later, how hard she was trying to be the responsible one, making sure that Armaiti ate her meals on time, helping her with the yard work.

Her daughter would be home soon. Using her good hand to steer the other, Armaiti flipped through the album, past the pictures of Richard and her. She lingered a few times when she came across a picture of her mother at the wedding reception in Bombay. She peered closely, scanning her mother's face for any sign of the cancer that would eat at her body a few years later. But the older woman looked uncharacteristically happy in the picture, beaming as she looked up adoringly at her tall, handsome American son-in-law. "Probably was glad I didn't marry a black man," Armaiti muttered to herself, and then giggled at the thought of Diane's face if she'd said that out loud. Diane wouldn't know how to deal with the obsession that Indians had with skin color.

She had to focus while thumbing through the pages of the book, had to compensate for that fractional disconnect between the true position of things and what her brain told her. But at last she came across the photograph she was looking for, toward the middle of the album. A large picture of the four of them. Nishta, Kavita, Laleh, and her, at her wedding reception in Bombay. All of them dressed in expensive saris, all of them looking more grown-up and glamorous than she ever remembered them being. No one was being a cutup in the picture, no one was crossing her eyes or making a face. Just four young women staring straight into the camera's eye, their postures erect, their faces composed and steady.

They were beautiful, Armaiti realized. Even she, although she had always felt mousey compared to the three of them. Kavita was probably the least conventionally beautiful one among all of them, but Armaiti noticed the warm brown eyes under the bob cut, the even, white teeth, the slender waist. Kavita was standing with her arm around Laleh's shoulder. Laleh's thick, long hair framed her face, and Armaiti took in the straight, patrician nose, the arched eyebrows, and the thin, sensitive lips. Laleh wore a look of ironic bemusement that Armaiti recognized immediately, as if she were enjoying some private joke. Beside her stood a radiant-looking Nishta, her hair tied up on her head, her lips parted in a big smile, so that Armaiti could see the gap in between her teeth. Armaiti caught her breath. She had forgotten how gorgeous Nishta was.

She looked at herself, standing next to Nishta, ready to criticize her own appearance. But her two years in America must've agreed with her. Or maybe it was being in love with Richard. Or perhaps simply being back with the others. Whatever the reason, she looked good.

She heard Diane's car in the driveway as she pulled the picture out of the album. She flipped through the album faster, wanting to find a few more pictures of the others before she put it away. The side door slammed and she heard Diane come in. "Mom?" Diane yelled. "I'm back."

"Hi, darling. I'm up in my room," she yelled back.

"Be up in a minute."

"Put the ice cream in the freezer first."

She came across a picture of herself, with Richard and Kavita on either side of her. She peered closely at Kavita's face. It was as blank and expressionless as a winter sky. She felt a pang in her heart. How hard it must've been for Kavita to meet Richard. "I'm sorry, Ka," she whispered, running a finger across Kavita's face. She wondered whether to pull that one out of the album but decided against it.

She had shoved the wedding album under the bed—she'd get it out later, no point in risking upsetting Diane—and had fanned out the four pictures she'd pulled out onto the bedspread when Diane entered the room. "Hi, Mom," she said. "Whatcha doin'?" She noticed the photographs. "What's this?"

Armaiti picked up the one that had the four of them in it. As she lifted it gently, careful not to get her fingerprints on the photograph, and passed it on to Diane, she was aware of handing something precious to her daughter. She thought of the gold jewelry, family heirlooms, that her own mother had given to her at her wedding. She had protested, refused to accept it. But her mother had insisted. "This never belonged to me," she had whispered as she'd kissed Armaiti's bent head. "I was only holding it for you. Just as you will hold it for your daughter, until her wedding day."

She wouldn't be alive to see Diane married. Just last week she'd considered passing her mother's jewelry on to Diane. Now, while she was alive. But she'd decided against it, knowing how much it would upset her daughter. And Diane was a flower child, more interested in bead necklaces and costume jewelry. Despite their beautiful craftsmanship, the gold bracelets and ruby rings would not impress her, would never have the emotional weight of family history that they still had for Armaiti, no matter how much she chided herself for being so hopelessly bourgeois. So she had decided to leave her mother's things with Richard, with instructions to give them to Diane when the time came.

Diane's hair fell across her face as she studied the picture. "These are your friends? At your wedding?"

"Yes."

"They're so good-looking." She perched on the bed next to her mother and took Armaiti's hand in hers. "Of course you're the loveliest of them all."

"Isn't it pretty to think so." She made a face. "I was the ugly duckling of the group, I'm afraid."

"Are you kidding me? My God, Mom, you're beautiful. Jeez, have you seen how Dad looks at you, still? Like he—like he could just inhale you or something." Diane sucked her cheeks in.

Armaiti squeezed her daughter's hand. "You're funny. Anyway, it doesn't matter who was pretty and who wasn't. What matters is"—and here she hesitated, wanting to get it right the first time—"that . . . that these three women gave me something. A sense of belonging in the world, but more than that. A sense that the world belonged to me. Do you understand? A belief that it was my world—our world. To shape it as we wanted. That we never had to settle for things as they were, you know?"

Diane was looking at her intently, her big eyes searching her face, and Armaiti saw how perilously young her daughter still was. Something about that look broke her heart. "You still believe that, Mom? About changing the world?" Diane asked.

How simple, how lovely, it would be to answer with a direct, honest yes. But Diane was looking at her with such trust, looking at her with the same hungry eyes as she used to when Armaiti was breast-feeding her a lifetime ago. She hesitated. "I—I don't know." She looked around the room, trying to find the right words. "I don't know if the world we dreamed of is an illusion, a 'children's palace,' as Laleh's father used to call it." She looked at Diane sharply as a thought hit her. "But I do know this—that my desire for that world was true. It was the truest thing I've ever felt, as true as my love for you. And—and I'd like to believe that that means something. You know?"

Diane nodded. "I think so." She stared at the picture she was still cradling in her hand. "When are they coming?"

"I don't know exactly. I don't even know if—what shape I'll be in by the time they come. Kavita can't leave for a couple of weeks. But Diane, I want you to promise me something. I want you to get to know my friends. I so regret . . . it's important to me that you know them."

Diane threw her arms around Armaiti. "Of course, Mom. You don't have to make it sound like homework. I want to know them."

Armaiti laid her head on her daughter's shoulder. It's going to be okay, she thought. Diane's going to be okay. The others will make sure she is.

12

A week had gone by since Iqbal had come home early from work with murder and humiliation in his eyes and told her about Adish's unannounced visit to his store. Murder and humiliation but also something else, a kind of cunning, as if the ultimate triumph had been his.

At that time, she had wondered why Iqbal had told her about the visit. Not in a million years would she have suspected that Adish would call on Iqbal, after the years of silence. But then she'd decided that it actually made perfect sense. If she knew anything at all, she knew how persistent Laleh was. She must've hounded poor Adish until he capitulated and agreed to look up Iqbal. But did Adish really make that promise to Iqbal? What could her husband have said, what insult could he have leveled at Adish, to make him say those words?

Nishta was still thinking about this as she finished ladling the last of the daal into the stainless-steel bowl. "Chalo," she called. "Supper is ready."

"You're not eating?" Iqbal asked as soon as he entered the kitchen. He lowered himself onto the wooden chair and pulled the small dining table closer.

"I'm not hungry," she said shortly. An uneasy silence had

risen between them since that afternoon a week ago and she was not anxious to pierce it.

" 'I'm not hungry,' " he mimicked, a smirk on his face.

She felt distaste rise from her stomach and into her mouth. She struggled to control the urge to take the hot, steaming pot of daal and throw it across his lap. "The bhoot's still in you, eh, miya?" she said sarcastically, not trying to keep the anger from her eyes.

She saw his face flush before he quickly looked away from her and into his plate. She sat down to his right, sipping from a glass of limewater. "Did you send Ammi her dinner?" he mumbled after a few seconds.

Nishta sighed. "Yes, I did, Iqbal. Just like I have sent your mother dinner every sodden day of my life with you."

She jumped as Iqbal slammed his fist on the table, spilling some of the white rice. "Your life is that miserable?" he yelled. "I do everything for her but the Hindu princess is still unhappy?"

"Princess?" She snorted. "That's what you call a woman who you keep a prisoner in her own home? Who is not allowed to talk to her friends? Who cannot make a lousy phone call because her jailer has taken her cell phone? You're a Fascist, Iqbal. A pucca Fascist."

Iqbal's right hand flew up from the table and landed hard across her cheek. The impact of it knocked her into the back of her chair. Her mind went white and blank with shock and it took her a second to realize that Iqbal had struck her for the first time in their marriage. They stared at each other in stunned silence. Then, as the pain burned her face, Nishta's eyes filled with tears. Iqbal swallowed hard a few times, his eyes looking for a place to focus.

Nishta rubbed her cheek, her eyes still on him. Fear and outrage battled within her, and then the fear settled down into a simmer while the outrage boiled over. "You hit me?" she said. "This is what it's come to? How low you've fallen? You, who used to talk about women's rights? Have you no shame left, Iqbal?"

"Shut your mouth," he hissed. "Lower your voice."

"Why?" she said loudly. "So that the neighbors will think you're a pious, devout man who goes to masjid six days a week? Who does namaaz five times a day? I'll tell everyone. When they find out—"

He rose from the table, grabbed it by the edge, and toppled it. The rice flew upward before it descended like thick snowflakes even as the pot of daal erupted in midair before it landed on the tiled floor. A few hot drops of the liquid pricked at Nishta's bare feet.

She looked at Iqbal in fear. In all these years she had never seen him as out of control as he seemed at this moment. "Iqbal, have you gone mad? What are you doing?"

"You are the one who is responsible for this," he yelled. "One visit from Laleh and your head got turned with thoughts of going to America. So shallow you are. Here we were, living a simple, happy life, and then they had to come and spoil everything."

"It's a lie," Nishta said. She reached out for him but he jerked out of her grasp. "Iqbal, listen to me," she said urgently. "You may have been happy, but I was not. I haven't been happy for a long time. Not since you moved us to this suffocating place. Bas, just like that, you uprooted us. Did you even ask me, Iqbal, if I wanted this life? Hell, you didn't even consult your own parents. Just like when you gave up the bank job, on a whim."

"On a whim?" A vein throbbed in Iqbal's forehead. "Do you have any idea how much abuse I put up with from my manager? How much he humiliated me? Why? Because I was a Muslim. And he wasn't just a Hindu, he was a Brahmin. Never let me forget for a minute."

"That's bullshit." Nishta moved toward the sink to pat some cold water on her burning cheek. She turned around to face Iqbal again. "Mr. Agarwal was always nice to us. Remember when he'd invited us to his house for his son's birthday? I hadn't even wanted to go, but he was really sweet to us."

"Exactly. Exactly." Now, Iqbal seemed more weepy than dangerous. "You know why? Because he thought you were a Muslim, too. The next day at work he came up to me to praise you for knowing so much about Hindu culture. And without thinking, I laughed and told him that you were born and raised Hindu. You should've seen his face, Zoha. Like I'd told him I'd raped my grandmother. From that day on, he changed. Acted like he wanted to vomit every time he saw my face. Hounded me, hounded me, until I had to leave."

She eyed him suspiciously. "How come you never told me this?"

He made an exasperated sound. "My dear wife, if I'd told you about every insult that's come my way because of our marriage, you would've crumbled under its weight a long time ago."

Moved as she was by his words, something about the righteous way in which he said it irritated her. Iqbal always had a tendency toward self-pity. There was a time when it had endeared him to her, aroused her protective instincts. But she had since then learned how easily he crossed the line into manipulation. It was that same pleading, hurt look with which he had come to her years ago, begging her to wear a burkha when she went out in public in their new neighborhood. She had felt some part of her die when she finally acquiesced, unable to withstand the combined pressure from her husband and her in-laws. Mumtaz, then seventeen and already married, had been the only one who had asked her to resist. But Mumtaz, having mysteriously given in to her older brother's abrupt and relentless insistence that she drop out of college and marry, had not been in any position to back her up.

Now, remembering this, she steeled herself against the haunted look on Iqbal's face. "We could've helped each other, Iqbal," she said. "You had no right to keep this from me. We were partners. I didn't need your protection."

He looked at her with something akin to compassion. "Men and women cannot be partners, Zoha," he said, as if talking to a developmentally challenged child. "If you read the Koran for a day you'd know that. It is my duty to take care of you."

Nishta remembered Dilip, the homeless man who lived on the street across from her childhood home. Her father used to hire the man to do odd jobs and run errands during the day. But every evening, Dilip, an opium addict, would disappear for a few hours. When he returned, there was a glazed, beatific expression on his face. As a young girl, Nishta had always felt sad looking at Dilip in this condition.

Now it seemed to her that Iqbal wore the same expression. The look of an addict. She turned away to hide the pity in her eyes but it was too late. He had seen it.

"What?" he said, grabbing her hard by her arm. "What are you thinking?"

"Nothing. Stop it. You're hurting me."

"Hurting—you don't know what hurting is." Even in the dim light of the kitchen, she could see the glint in Iqbal's eyes. "Don't patronize me, Zoha. I can't take it."

For the first time in all the years she'd known him, Nishta was afraid of Iqbal. She had known for some time that beneath the serene, religious façade Iqbal presented to the world there lay a bed of seething resentments. But now she saw how close to the surface those resentments were, how fragile and tenuous the balance was. Something about the visit from Laleh and Kavita—a visit from the past, a mocking reminder of how far they'd fallen from the couple they'd once hoped to be—had unnerved him. And although he had withheld the details of his conversation with Adish from her—save for the fact that he had apparently convinced Adish never to contact them again—she had seen the turmoil in him when he had returned home.

She forced into her voice a lightness that she didn't feel when she spoke to him. "I'm not, Iqbal. Now relax, na. I don't know what you're so upset about. Now, you go sit down while I clean up." She noticed the cautious gratitude creeping into his face. No sudden moves, she said to herself. Slowly, she extracted her arm from his slackened grip, keeping her eyes on his face the whole time.

"Go," she repeated. "I'll clean up."

"Forgive me," he began, but she cut him off with a shake of her head.

"It's okay. No use crying over spilled rice." She attempted a tentative smile and then forced her face into a look of concern. "You are tired."

"That I am." He yawned. "I'll watch TV, then, okay?"

"Okay."

Her motions were mechanical as she got the broom and swept the rice into the pan. But her mind was fevered as she replayed the conversation they had just had. Why tell me now, after all these years, the reason he'd quit the bank? she wondered. If he had confided in her back then, she would've leapt to his defense, would've even valorized his resignation as striking a blow for some unnamed principle. But not now. Not after years of living with the consequences of Iqbal's hasty decision to join his Uncle Murad's business. Two months after Iqbal had quit the bank, she had suffered a miscarriage. And with their income cut in half, they were reduced to accepting help from Iqbal's older brother, who worked in Dubai and sent part of his salary home every month. Although no one ever spelled out the terms, it soon became obvious that this aid came with strings attached—taking care of Iqbal's parents and niece had soon become Nishta's responsibility.

By the time she had wetted a cloth and was rinsing the floor, Nishta had come to a resolution. No more. She could not live like this anymore. For years now she had made excuses for Iqbal. She made herself notice how, despite their modest income, he was forever giving money to neighbors and relatives in need; had appreciated how, despite his growing religiosity, Iqbal argued with the men in his mosque against the Muslim practice of taking multiple wives; had admired how generous he was toward his mother, how he postponed buying himself a new pair of glasses or shoes in order to buy Ammi a watch or a new appliance.

But this same man had just slapped her. Had forbidden her from talking to her dearest friends. Had hidden her phone. No more. Dear God, she couldn't live like this anymore.

She was already on the floor and so it wasn't much of a stretch to kneel and surreptitiously fold her hands. Help me, she prayed. Please. Help me. She had no idea to whom she was praying or what kind of help she was asking for. She tried to conjure up a picture of a deity but her unpracticed mind was rusty, confused. Who could she appeal to? Allah? The Hindu gods of her childhood? Aware of Iqbal's movements in the next room, knowing she didn't have much time, she closed her eyes and tried again. But the only picture that floated before her eyes was that of Laleh and Kavita sitting across from her in her living room.

13

Kavita propped a pillow against the headboard of the bed and sat up, listening to the sound of running water as Ingrid took a shower. She smiled drowsily as she pulled the white cotton sheet over her breasts. A few seconds later, she heard Ingrid shut the water off. She was about to turn on the television when she heard Ingrid singing to herself and the sound deepened the pleasure and contentment that she was feeling. Unconsciously, Kavita began to hum the same song. She stretched languidly, pulling her arms above her head, acknowledging the fact that her whole body was singing, humming its satisfaction.

She had known Ingrid for almost fifteen years now. In those years they had traveled around Europe together and collaborated on umpteen work projects. Whenever Kavita was in Hamburg, Ingrid practically moved in with her. She also knew that Ingrid found her sexy and funny. Once, when Ingrid was still married to Hans, and during one of his rare moments of jealousy—for the most part Hans had good-naturedly accepted the fact that his wife had an Indian girlfriend whom she saw a few times each year—she had even warned him not to make her choose between him and Kavita. Don't be so sure you'll win, she had said to him.

But until now, Kavita had not known that Ingrid loved her. Not when Ingrid had insisted that Kavita be the lead architect on the award-winning project they had submitted for the museum in Brisbane. Not when she called every single night when Kavita had been down with the flu a few years ago. Not even when, two years ago, she had taken Kavita's hand while sitting in a bar in Dublin and told her that she was leaving Hans. Kavita had been perturbed—she knew that Ingrid and Hans had been together for over twenty years, that despite her occasional grumblings, Ingrid cared deeply about him. "Why, Ing?" she'd asked. "You two have such a good life together."

Ingrid had shrugged. "He's getting too high-maintenance as he gets older. Clingy. Wants to be together all the time." She flung her arms out. "Whereas me—I want to be free. To travel. To make new friends. To live an open life, without complications. Free."

At the time, Kavita had assumed that Ingrid had meant that she wanted to be free of all encumbrances. She had prepared herself for a diminished role in Ingrid's life and had accepted this without rancor or resentment. After all, what could she expect? They lived on different continents, separated by a distance of five thousand miles. She, Kavita, lived with her mother, for God's sake, lived a closeted, cloistered existence. She may as well have been one of those nuns who worked in Mother Teresa's homes, for all the sexuality she emitted. She was sure that her mother and brother thought she was a virgin. And, indeed, if it wasn't for Ingrid and a job that thankfully provided her with regular opportunities for travel, their assumption would've probably been true—unless you counted the unsatisfying, silent encounters at the massage parlor at Cuffe Parade she used to patronize in the years before she'd met Ingrid.

Fifteen years ago, Rahul had bounded into her office one morning and announced that the merger with the German firm of
Stuggart and Associates had gone through. Kavita had been
measured in her response, knowing Rahul well enough by now
to be a little wary of his bouts of enthusiasm. Even though they
were the same age, Kavita always felt like the older sister around
Rahul. "What are the final terms?" she asked.

Rahul had shaken his head. "I don't believe this. Aren't you
the least bit excited, Kav? This is a big coup, I say."

But she hadn't been excited. Hadn't been until three months
later, when she and Rahul sat across a glass table in a confer-
ence room in Hamburg with three ruddy-faced Germans who
kept saying in their heavily accented English how "vunderfool"
it was to do ze business together. And then only because a
woman had walked—had strode—into the room and taken
her breath away. A woman almost as tall as the men and with
a manner as brisk and no-nonsense as theirs was obsequious.
Who wore a sea-blue silk shirt tucked into tight blue jeans and
red boots that came up to her knees. Whose inquisitive, mis-
chievous eyes belied the cut-through-the-bullshit efficiency
she otherwise radiated.

"Hello. I'm Ingrid," the woman said, offering her hand to
Rahul. "I feel like I know you from all our communications."
Unlike the others, her accent sounded clipped, more British to
Kavita's untrained ear. "Welcome to Hamburg."

Rahul rose slightly in his chair but Ingrid intercepted him.
"Please. Don't get up."

She turned to Kavita with her hand extended. And Ingrid
gasped, just the slightest intake of breath that only Kavita noticed. She forced herself not to blush. Still, there was an unin-
tended huskiness in her voice when she said, "I'm Kavita."

As the meeting proceeded, Kavita noticed that Rahul was

talking a mile a minute, the way he did when he was nervous, but the Germans did not seem to notice. Despite the fact that it was only noon and they had gotten a good night's rest after flying in the previous evening, she suddenly felt uncontrollably sleepy. She must've nodded off for a second because she heard Ingrid say, "I think it's time to break for lunch. We're being poor hosts, I'm afraid." And when she opened her eyes, Ingrid's sea-green eyes were traveling across her face. She flinched, as if she'd been touched.

Three months later, she was back in Hamburg, this time without Rahul, whose wife was expecting their first child within a few days. It was immediately apparent to Kavita that the other associates had assumed that Ingrid would collaborate with her on the housing colony project.

They were sitting side by side on the second day poring over blueprints in Ingrid's sun-lit office, when Ingrid ran her index finger lightly over Kavita's wrist. "Kavita," she said, the green eyes dark and searching, "shall we sleep with each other and get it over with? It's hard to concentrate on the job, otherwise."

Kavita felt a roaring in her ears. She swallowed hard, unable to look up from the drawings if her life depended on it. Her eyes focused on the red star in the middle of the blueprint until that was all she saw. The silence dragged on.

"I'm sorry," she heard Ingrid say, and for the first time since she'd met her, Ingrid sounded tentative and shaky. "Did I misread the situation?"

"I, I don't know what to say." Kavita forced herself to look up.

Ingrid exhaled sharply. "Boy. I sure made a fool of myself. Please. Forgive me." The briskness was back in her voice. "Can we just forget this happened?"

"Sure." She bit her lower lip.

Ingrid nodded. "Okay." She cleared her throat and then looked down at the prints again. "Now. What I suggest we do is submit the plans by—"

"I thought you were married." She had meant it as a question but it came out plaintive, more like an accusation.

Ingrid shrugged. "Hans and I—we have an arrangement. He accepts it."

The gurgle started somewhere deep within Kavita and suddenly, she was shaking with laughter. All these years. All this time that she'd lived like a nun, there had been people like Ingrid. She recalled the four years of college spent pining away for Armaiti and the wasted years since college when she'd not entertained any thoughts of romance, traumatized as she'd been by the memory of the humiliation at the police station when the constable had penetrated her through her clothes as a roomful of policemen had watched with leering eyes. Instead, for the past five years she had subjected herself every week to a furtive, shame-filled massage by a woman who had sensed, smelled, her loneliness and her hunger. The few times there had been the prospect of romance, she had not allowed herself to entertain the possibility. What a waste. What a waste of a life. She had been so worried about whether her brother would pull away from her if he knew she was gay, about the bewilderment and shame that would creep into Ma's eyes, about whether Rahul would continue to respect her, that she had walled off a whole section of her life. And during that whole time, in a different spot on the globe, there lived people like Ingrid and Hans.

"It's that funny, what I said?" There was annoyance and affront in Ingrid's voice but something else, something that tore at Kavita's heart—hurt.

She stopped mid-laugh and shook her head. "No. You don't

understand. I was laughing—at myself. Not at you." She looked deeply into Ingrid's face and a warm, tender feeling came over her. "Never at you."

She watched in fascination as the indignation on Ingrid's face softened and dissolved, like a lump of sugar in a cup of hot tea. "Have dinner with me tonight," Ingrid said. A vein pulsed at the side of her neck. "Please."

The feeling of tenderness lingered. "Okay. But we should get some work done, no?"

They went over the plans for another fifteen minutes and then Ingrid banged her hand on the table. "Ah, shit," she said. "Let's forget this. It's a beautiful day. Let me show you a bit of Hamburg. And then we'll get a bite to eat."

In the car, she was excruciatingly aware of Ingrid's hand resting on the stick shift. She noticed the fine hair on her bare arms, the manicured fingernails, the copper bracelet on the thin wrist. A shiver ran through her as she imagined those hands on her body. She turned her head slightly to look out the window. She startled as she felt Ingrid's hand on her thigh, as if she had willed it there. She continued looking out of the window until she heard Ingrid say, "Do you mind?" and again heard that tentative quality in Ingrid's voice.

She shook her head. "It's okay."

Ingrid laughed. "It's okay?" She moved her hand in slow, small circles across Kavita's thigh. "I usually get a stronger response than that."

Her throat was so dry that she didn't know if she could talk. Besides, as long as she looked out the window, she was not responsible for what was happening.

She caught herself. Dissociating. That's what she was doing. It was an old habit, born the night of her molestation at the police station. She had done the same thing during her first visit to the massage parlor in Cuffe Parade, when the masseuse had kneaded her breasts and then massaged the inside of her thighs. She had left the parlor feeling uneasy and confused, vowing not to return. But the next week, convinced that she'd misread the situation, she went back. This time, the woman's hands strayed to the inside of her thighs again. Only this time they did not stop there. This time, while Kavita bit down on her lip, the woman put one oil-slick finger inside her, and then another, and then another. Kavita lay immobile, fighting the desire of her body to move in time with the woman's increasingly aggressive movements. And after it was over, the woman went back to her regular massage, while Kavita lay there, scarlet-faced and rigid with self-loathing. But within that rigidity, there was a looseness, a lightness. It was that lightness, a sensation that was purely physical, an assertion by her body that seemed immune to the invective she hurled at herself, that took her back to the parlor the following Saturday. Each week she had acted as if it was her first time there, and each time she ignored the growing look of enjoyment in the woman's eyes as she relished the command she had over her silent client.

Now, fighting to ignore the fact that Ingrid's fingers were leaving a burning trail over her thigh, she caught her mind disengaging from what her body was feeling. Was she so far gone that she could not distinguish between the groping of a police constable intent on humiliating and frightening her and the honesty of Ingrid's desire for her? Between the masseuse who had serviced her for whatever reason—most likely for nothing more profound than the hope for a bigger tip—and the guileless way in which Ingrid had propositioned her? And was seducing her now?

"You know what?" she said, making no effort to keep the rawness out of her voice. "Do you mind if we go to my hotel?"

She felt Ingrid tense beside her. "You sure?"

She nodded and forced herself to face the woman beside her. "I'm sure."

Two hours later, Kavita lay in bed, stunned at what had passed between the two of them. Ingrid, however, claimed to be not in the least bit surprised. "Rubbish. I knew the moment I laid eyes on you. Honest."

"Knew what?"

"Knew . . . you. I knew you. Also, that the fit would be good."

Kavita giggled. "The fit? That sounds so . . . clinical. So mechanical. "

Ingrid had given one of her voluble shrugs. "What do you expect? I'm German."

Kavita was still smiling at the memory of that afternoon fifteen years ago when Ingrid emerged from the shower, a towel wrapped around her, her red hair wet and dark. "What are you smiling about, my lovely?"

"Just remembering the first time we . . . you know."

"The first time we made love?" Ingrid sat on the bed next to Kavita. "Still can't say it? All these years with me and you're still shy?"

She took Ingrid's hand in hers and placed it on her stomach. "I'm not shy." She looked deeply into Ingrid's eyes. "In fact, I'm pretty bold."

"How bold?" The green eyes sparkled like the beads of water on Ingrid's neck.

"This bold," she said as she undid Ingrid's towel.

The ring of her cell phone woke Kavita up an hour later. Beside her, Ingrid groaned and threw a pillow across her head, muttering darkly in German.

"Shush," Kavita said playfully as she flipped open her phone. "Hello?" She hunted for her watch on the bedside table.

"Hey. It's me. How are you?"

Shit. She'd forgotten to cancel the dinner plans she'd made with Laleh weeks ago. "I'm fine," she said.

"So where are you? Home?"

"No, at the Taj. My friend—my business associate—Ingrid is in town."

"Oh. You sound like you were asleep."

There was a sudden strained silence, as though Laleh had just realized the significance of what she'd said. Kavita's mind searched for a way out of the situation when a thought struck her: Ingrid loved her. She had flown into Bombay on an impulse after a long, weepy conversation in which Kavita had confessed her grief over Armaiti's illness and the squelched reconnection with Nishta. Suddenly she wanted to be free of all secrecy and lies. Laleh and Ingrid would like each other, she realized. All these years and she had never introduced them.

"I was," she heard herself say. "We were. Taking a nap."

Another silence, short and loaded this time, and then Laleh said, matter-of-factly, "Good. So, where are we going for dinner?"

She almost laughed out loud. Ever since they'd decided that they would visit Armaiti, she had agonized about whether she would acknowledge to Armaiti the torch that she'd carried for her, had spent hours calculating whether it was better to acknowledge the past or ignore it. And now Laleh had parted her apprehension and shame like a bead curtain.

She forced herself to focus on the conversation. "I don't know," she said. "You guys want to meet us at the Taj?"

"I'm thinking." The blast of a car horn chewed up a few of Laleh's words and then Kavita heard her say, "Tell you what. Why don't you and—your friend—come over here for dinner? I'll get something delivered from Khazana."

"Adish won't mind?"

"God, no. The poor chap is working so hard these days, he'll be happy to stay home."

"Okay. See you when? Sevenish?"

"Yup."

She hung up and rolled over to where Ingrid was snoring softly next to her. As usual, she ran her index finger over the crease on Ingrid's forehead and then stroked her cheek. Ingrid smiled in her sleep. "Hmmm," she mumbled. The smile grew deeper. "That feels nice."

Kavita leaned over and kissed the damp red hair. "Wake up, darling," she said. "I just made plans for us for this evening. Hope you don't mind."

"Where're we going? Can't we just get room service?"

"Well, actually, my friend Laleh invited us over. And I said yes."

Ingrid was wide awake now. The green eyes circled Kavita's face. "You're introducing me to your best friend?"

Hearing hope battling with disbelief in Ingrid's voice, Kavita felt a wave of remorse for not having done this sooner. "I am." She searched for Ingrid's hand under the sheet and held it. "I love you very much. I don't care who knows it."

"What on earth has brought this on?" Ingrid said wryly. Her eyes twinkled. "Or are you just in a postcoital rapture?"

Kavita laughed out loud and then immediately grew serious. "I've spent my life hiding from the very people who love me,

Ing. I'm not doing this anymore. I mean, until—until the news
of Armaiti, I used to think—I don't know—like I had plenty of
time or something. But now . . ." She shook her head. "Forget it.
I know I'm not making sense."

Ingrid lifted Kavita's hand and held it to her lips. "Yes, you
are. And I can't wait to meet the mysterious Laleh."

14

Iqbal could still feel on his forehead the imprint of the cool tile of the masjid floor where he had prostrated himself a moment ago. The cool was a welcome comfort from the hot, busy thoughts that raced like red ants through his mind. So was the peace that he'd felt during the evening namaaz, as the sonorous, musical chanting and the repetition of prayer—*Holy is my Lord, the Most High*—fell like raindrops over his fevered brain. His lips quivered as he stood up, his heart brimming with piety and compassion. It was better than any drug, this prayer. More powerful, more addictive, more necessary. It made him feel humble and powerful at the same time, gave him a way to see the world from afar, so that he could see how small the problems that occupied his days, really were. It taught him that the things from the material world that encroached upon him were unimportant, as inconsequential as fruit flies. *Shield us from the torment of fire*, he had just prayed, and already it was working, already serenity spread like an unclenched fist throughout his body.

"As salaam alaikum," Hassad said to him as Iqbal slipped into his shoes, and he smiled in response. "Wa-alaikum salaam," he replied. *Peace be with you.*

But as he descended down the stone steps of the mosque,

peace was already proving to be elusive. He remembered that he and Zoha were going to Mumtaz's house for a party tonight and his stomach muscles tightened at the thought. As much as he loved his nephew and niece, he hated visiting his sister. For one thing, his brother-in-law, Hussein, drank alcohol, drank openly and freely, as if he were a Hindu or a Christian. And Mumtaz acted so stiffly around him. After all these years, she still blamed him for her marriage, he suspected, and thinking about this, he felt a spurt of anger. What did they all expect from him? He was just a solitary being in a confusing world. He had done his best for her, in a time of burning, when everything— homes, neighborhoods, cars, hopes, innocence, ideals—was going up in smoke. Mumtaz had always been a romantic, that was her problem, her head turned by those Bollywood melo- dramas she used to watch incessantly as a young girl. She had wanted love, courtship, passion, really, she had wanted all the things that he'd had once with Zoha, he now acknowledged, and his heart twisted in bitterness. Look where their promising start, their shiny love had led them. Mumtaz was clinging to something as ephemeral as a child's balloon lost at sea. Over a girlhood fantasy, she had destroyed her relationship with him, the brother who had taken on a second job to pay for her dowry. Mumtaz, Zoha, all the women in his life were looking at him as if he was their bad mistake. When all he was, was a tired soul in a bewildering world.

He stepped onto the busy, noisy street full of hawkers and beggars and automobiles and felt the piety of just a few moments ago begin to drain out of him. In its place grew the familiar burdens of worry and resentment. He had a name for this syn- drome: Allah Left and Iqbal Returned. No matter how hard he tried, no matter how much he prayed, it was always like this. In the old days, the feeling of contentment used to linger longer, sometimes he was able to hold on to it all the way home, and then, wanting to continue that delicious, precious feeling, he would stop by the sweetmeat shop and buy some halwa for Zoha. And when she would protest about weight gain, he would tell her that as far as he was concerned she was still the most beautiful woman in the world, and he would mean it. But such moments of sweetness seldom arose between them anymore.

Iqbal looked at the night sky and swallowed the sob that was forming in his throat. Did Zoha think he was enjoying this, monitoring her every move? Did she not realize that when he had struck her for the first time in their married life, it was himself that he had really hurt? What had she called him last night? Her jailer. Him, Iqbal, who had battled the world for her sake. Zoha had been his first religion. From the day he had met her in college, he had lived to make her happy. Did she forget this? Or had she never known? He had fought with his own parents when they had balked at the news that their son wanted to marry a Hindu. He had even been willing to convert to Hinduism—Iqbal pinched himself now as punishment for that early blasphemy— for her sake. Apart from his college friends, everyone he knew had tormented him for marrying a Hindu girl. That much he had to give Adish and the rest—they had been open and total in their support. But they were mere children then. What did any of them know about the ways of the world? Leaving college and getting a job at the bank had been like waking up from a dream: the jokes on Eid about whether he had slaughtered a goat before coming to work that morning; the automatic assumption that he supported the Pakistani team during the India-Pakistan cricket matches; the hostile looks directed his way every time there was a terrorist attack anywhere in India.

The day he left the bank had been the happiest day of his life. Even though his colleagues had slighted him, taking him to a

Udipi restaurant for a farewell lunch, instead of the expensive Chinese restaurant they usually went to for dinner when someone left. Even though Zoha had looked at him in disbelief for the whole two weeks that he worked there after handing in his resignation letter. And, yes, even though—Ya Allah—she had suffered a miscarriage two months later. Because he had never believed, as she had, that it was her worry and stress over money that had caused her to miscarry.

A beggar woman trailed after Iqbal and he dug into the pocket of his pajama and flung a coin into her open palm. "God bless you, sir," she said before moving on, but he didn't hear her, thinking as he was about his scrotum.

He had had the vasectomy after Zoha miscarried the third time. The doctor kept saying he saw no rhyme or reason for the miscarriages. Be patient, he counseled. You are both still young and healthy.

But he could not deal with the stricken expression on Zoha's face after each mishap. Or the snide comments made by his mother about the barren womb of his "foreign" wife. And once they moved into the new neighborhood, he didn't *want* children with Hindu blood. Although Zoha had converted by then, it was too difficult, too risky, too confusing. He imagined seeing in his children's faces their Hindu grandfather's visage—the same man who had refused to look at Iqbal when he'd gone over to ask for Zoha's hand in marriage, a man who had never set eyes on his daughter since she'd married Iqbal, as if a dead daughter were preferable to a Muslim son-in-law. The Hand of God, he had thought after the third miscarriage. Allah the All-Knowing is behind the miscarriages, to spare us future grief. He did not consult Zoha about the vasectomy. But, still, he had not expected her outraged reaction. Some part of him had thought of the vasectomy as an act of love, of heroic self-sacrifice, a way of protecting his wife from the barbed comments of those around them. From now on, he could be the reason for the unnaturalness of being a young, healthy couple without children.

But she didn't see it that way, did she? Iqbal now said to himself. Of course she didn't. Why should she, when all she's been doing is looking for reasons to leave you?

His attention snagged by this last thought, Iqbal abruptly stopped walking, causing a bicyclist to almost run into him. He ignored the man's muttered curse. Of course. *Of course.* That explained the disquiet, the upheaval he had felt ever since she'd told him about Laleh's visit. Because even without knowing it, he had sensed this agitation, this restlessness in Zoha for—how long now? And the intelligent part of him, the Allah-blessed part, had figured it out before the rest of him had, the threat posed by Laleh's return into their lives.

But why now? Iqbal railed as he resumed walking. Now, when everything was already so hard? Even in his all-Muslim neighborhood it was impossible to escape the madness of a world thirsty for Muslim blood. How wrong their analysis in college had been. Back then they had seen the fight as between rich and poor, a global class struggle. Maybe the world had changed since then, or maybe Allah had seen fit to drop the scales from his eyes, but everywhere he looked these days, someone was out for Muslim blood. Iraq. Afghanistan. Chechnya. Kashmir. Sudan. Gujarat. Even on the streets of this cursed city. Hadn't he seen it firsthand?

But the affairs of the world were not his concern. He had humility now, unlike during his arrogant student activist days, when he had believed he could change the world. Now he knew that only Allah can change the destiny of an ant or an emperor. Now he had more pressing concerns, like the conversation with Murad earlier this week, when the latter had told him that business was bad and so he would have to take a pay cut. At first he had assumed that Murad was bluffing, getting even for his calling in sick the afternoon of Adish's visit. But when he realized Murad was not joking, Iqbal had been unable to look his uncle in the face, afraid that his eyes would show his contempt for Murad's obvious lie. Business was good, and for two months now Iqbal had been trying to muster up the courage to ask for a pay raise. It didn't come easy to him, this asking, this talking about matters of commerce. But Murad must've sensed something and had thought to preempt him with his outrageous untruth. And because Murad had no shame, the burden of shame had fallen on him, on Iqbal. He had been the one to look away, afraid of calling the thief a thief.

As he walked, Iqbal renewed his vow to hide the news of the pay cut from Zoha for as long as he could. He didn't want to revive the old discussion about allowing her to find a job. He was the man, the head of the household. It was his duty to support his wife.

At least there have been no new calls on Zoha's cell phone since the day Adish stopped by to see me, he thought. Seems like they have finally gotten the message. A car horn sounded, setting off a long string of horns, like the firecrackers that the Hindus set off at Diwali. Iqbal blocked his ears as he walked, frowning slightly. In retrospect, he was glad he had agreed to chat with Adish. He had almost refused, so upset had he been by Adish's showing up at his workplace. But he had noticed the unexpected wetness in Adish's eyes at his rudeness and something in him had weakened. Some hand of friendship had reached out from the past and tugged at him and he had agreed to lunch.

Iqbal sighed heavily. Could things have gone differently? he asked himself. Or was it inevitable that those college friendships had to end? Zoha had always blamed him for pulling away from the group. But this was not his recollection. What he re-membered was that they had begun to go their own ways even before graduation. Iqbal squinted hard, trying to part the veil of the past, and what emerged was a memory of him carrying a small vase of roses to the hospital for Armaiti the morning after the march. He remembered the large bruise on Armaiti's forehead and how she had drifted in and out of sleep, while her mother spoke in whispers and rearranged the pillows on Ar-maiti's bed. Where were the others that day? And then Iqbal remembered: he had left the hospital and gone directly to the courthouse, where Adish was waiting for him, Laleh's father at his side. Rumi uncle, who had agreed to represent the arrested students in court, had lectured both of them about their na-iveté, about the perils of political activism, but Iqbal had barely listened, anxious as he was to see Zoha, who had been arrested along with twelve of their comrades the previous day.

Even now, after all these years, in the middle of a crowded street, the hair on Iqbal's neck stood up as he remembered the shock of seeing Zoha and Kavita as they made their disheveled court appearance. It is as if they've been in jail for a year instead of a day, Iqbal had marveled to himself then. Kavita especially had looked half-crazed, but when he'd asked her if she was okay, she had looked straight through him.

It all began to come apart after that, Iqbal now thought. Laleh seemed to continually apologize to us for having missed the march. Kavita developed those strange eye tics and nervous habits, spinning around to look behind her even if we were just walking down a street. And if we asked her what was wrong, she just shook her head.

No, Zoha was wrong. He remembered that a few months before graduation Armaiti had won a writing contest cospon-sored by the Indian and Czech governments which took her to

Czechoslovakia for eight days. Upon her return, she had described to them in hushed tones how dark and drab Prague was, the soldiers with machine guns on the streets, the old ladies in black coats standing in food lines, the ever-present surveillance cameras in the hotel elevators. There had been a stunned silence, none of them knowing what to say or believe. "You're making it sound like something out of a CIA propaganda film, yaar," Laleh had finally said, and they had all looked at Armaiti, wanting her to deny it. Armaiti had kept quiet.

He and Zoha had gotten close in the months that followed. He knew it without her having to say it—for the first time, Zoha was letting herself imagine a future that featured him in a starring role, rather than her three friends. She was seeking him out now. Laleh was spending more and more time with Adish; Kavita had grown secretive and distant; Armaiti seemed disenchanted by the movement. Now, finally, there was a place for him.

Well, he would not let that place be usurped by the others. Not now, not after all these years, not after everything he'd sacrificed. Did Laleh and Kavita really think that they could swoop down into their lives after years of zero contact and scoop up his wife? Zoha was so impressionable. Always had been. And so influenced by Laleh, especially. And Armaiti. Iqbal increased his pace as his building came into view. He was very sorry for Armaiti's suffering. But what did she expect? That she could pick up Zoha as easily as he could buy a tomato at the vegetable market near his house? How blithely these Americans—yes, he considered Armaiti an American now—thought they could buy and sell people. Out of the whole lot of them, Adish was the only one he truly trusted. It was a good thing Adish had visited him, Iqbal decided as he walked past the vegetable market. He trusted Adish to keep his word. Let the others go to see their sick friend. Let them spend their money to visit a country that they had once condemned. None of this had anything to do with him. All he asked was to be left alone.

But there was still the matter of Zoha's cell phone. When to return it to her? When was it safe? Did he have the right to confiscate it? Was Zoha right? Was he holding his wife a prisoner? He had tried to ask such a question of the imam at his mosque earlier today, but the old man had looked at him with puzzled eyes. "What's the question, son?" he'd asked. "Cell phone belong to you. Wife belong to you. What is the problem?"

He had not dared tell the imam about slapping Zoha. To this question, he knew the answer. He was wrong. It was an unforgivable thing he had done, a gesture born out of a desire to protect his family from the intrusions of the outside world. But never again, he promised himself. I swear to you, Allah. May you chop off my hands if I ever strike a woman again.

He had almost reached his building when he remembered. The bruise. An ugly purple bruise and swelling had risen on Zoha's face where he had struck her. Mumtaz would notice immediately. Would Zoha cover for him? He could not be sure. Iqbal suddenly felt tired to his very bones. He glanced at his watch. Zoha would be dressed, waiting for him so that they could leave for Mumtaz's house. But the thought of facing his sister's hostility made him sick. Not tonight. He just didn't have it in him to put up with Mumtaz's attacks tonight. He took out his cell phone and dialed his sister's number as he climbed heavily up the rickety wooden stairs of his apartment building.

"Yes?"

"Hey, Choti," he said, lapsing into his nickname for her. "It's me. Listen, sorry about the last-minute cancellation, but we can't make it tonight."

"What's wrong?"

"Nahi, I'm not feeling well, yaar. Tell Husseinbhai I'm sorry. I just need to go to bed early."

"Is Zoha coming?"

He stopped climbing, stunned by the question. "No, of course not."

"Why can't she come alone?"

He could tell where this was headed. "She doesn't want to come without me, Mumtaz," he lied. "I asked her."

"Let me speak to her."

He gnashed his teeth. Mumtaz had always been like this, even as a toddler. Relentless. "I'm not home," he said shortly. "I was at the mosque."

"If you're well enough to go to the—"

"Mumtaz," he snapped. "Wish Husseinbhai happy birthday from us, okay? Khuda Hafiz."

"Wait," she began, but he hung up.

Iqbal shook his head in exasperation. He was so tired of Mumtaz and her seething resentments and misguided feminism. One of these days he would not keep his mouth shut. One of these days he would tell her to grow up, point out to her that she wasn't the only one who wore disappointment like an iron choker around her neck.

15

It was a feeling she had forgotten, this lightness of being, this feeling of wholeness. For years, everything had been a performance, a churning stew of anxiousness and achievement, of striving, of moving ahead. For years, she'd felt like a figure in one of Picasso's paintings, disjointed, cut up, her knees where her nose should be. Not a person so much as a patched-up doll. Hoping that the golden luster of professional success could hide the tarnish of her failed personal life. And help slow down the whirling, like a mad fan, that she always felt within her.

With the other three she had had that. A feeling of contentment, like ice on skin on a hot summer's day, like running your fingers lightly over a patch of grass. No need to perform, to even speak, because weren't there always three other voices speaking for you, vocalizing your thoughts and dreams, cracking your jokes, singing your heart's music?

And tonight. Nishta and Armaiti, still as distant as stars, flung into unreachable space. But Laleh with her, sitting across the room from her, warm and familiar as the sun. The red wine turning her lips purple. And Brahms—it was Armaiti, Kavita remembered, who had first introduced her to Brahms—-on the stereo. Nishta and Armaiti were not here, but Ingrid was, sweet Ingrid sitting on the couch next to her, her bare arm occasionally grazing hers. And dear old Adish, as painstaking and elegant a host as ever, rushing to fill their glasses, to replenish their plates, making sure they never excluded Ingrid from the conversation by dwelling on people she didn't know. A new foursome, and although they were a lifetime removed from those eccentric madcaps who had once been her best friends, tonight it felt enough—better than enough, it felt rich and precious and tender.

"She's drunk," she heard Ingrid say, and despite her immediate indignation, something in her thrilled to hear the quiet possessiveness in Ingrid's flat assertion.

"No I'm not," she exclaimed, but the last word somehow came out in a childlike squeak, so that she had no choice but to join the others in their laughter.

"This whole evening makes me wish I had a cigarette," Laleh said lazily.

"You smoke?" Ingrid said.

Laleh smiled. "Used to. Before the children were born." She pointed to Kavita with her chin. "This one, too. We all did. In college."

Ingrid turned slightly toward Kavita. "You never told me you smoked."

"There's a lot I haven't told you about me," she said saucily, aware that she was flirting with Ingrid, aware of Laleh's watchful, slightly incredulous gaze, but unable to help herself.

She felt rather than saw Ingrid and Laleh exchange conspiratorial smiles. "She's in a good mood today," Laleh said. "Generally she walks around all stooped and sulky, like she's responsible for every ill in the universe. You're good for her," she added.

"Thank you," Ingrid said lightly. "And I've heard so much about you for years now."

"Well," Laleh said. "I just wish that we'd met sooner."

Kavita heard the faint rebuke in Lal's voice but there was something else, too—regret? Self-chastisement? She looked up to see Laleh looking directly at her, her long, beautiful face serious, even sad. And then Laleh smiled slowly, and the warmth and love Kavita saw in her face took her breath away. She stared at Laleh wordlessly, unable to look away. She knew now without a shadow of a doubt that Laleh knew her secret, probably had always known. And that it didn't matter and probably never had.

Even as she looked away, Kavita had the weirdest feeling that Laleh and Ingrid were communicating silently with each other, that Laleh was handing her over to Ingrid, and that Ingrid was making some silent promise to Laleh. As discreetly as she could, Kavita pinched her right cheek. The numbness confirmed her suspicion—yes, she was drunk. You must be imagining things, she said to herself.

Adish, too, seemed to have picked up on some change in the atmosphere, because his voice was a tad too hearty as he said, "More drinks? Ingrid? Little more wine?"

"Don't mind if I do."

Kavita put a cautionary hand on Ingrid's knee. "We should be going, no?" she said.

"Bullshit, yaar," Adish said as he topped off Ingrid's glass. "Let the poor woman enjoy her drink."

"It will be hard to get a cab this late—" she began before he cut her off.

"Who said anything about a cab? You think I'm going to let you get in a taxi smelling like a bloody bevadi?"

"I'm not drunk," she said indignantly, punching him on the arm, but he just laughed as he fended her off. "Right, sure," he said. He turned to face Ingrid. "She was always a lightweight. Even in college."

"What was she like? In college?"

"I'd appreciate it if you people didn't talk about me as if I'm not here," Kavita said.

"Listen to her," Adish said with a grin. "Just like in the old days. She's trying her best not to slur her words."

"I certainly am not," she said, trying not to slur her words.

Adish got up from the couch. "I think I have a few photos," he said. "You want to see?"

"Adish, don't you dare——" Kavita said, but he winked at her and headed toward the wooden trunk in the corner of the living room.

The first photograph was of the three of them standing around Armaiti as she played the piano in her mother's living room. Armaiti's head was flung back, her mouth slightly open as she sang. Kavita stared at her own youthful face, noticed the intense way in which she was gazing at Armaiti. Would it be obvious to a stranger that the slim girl standing with one hand resting on the piano was in love with the piano player? Ingrid seemed to know, because she said, "So this is Armaiti?"

Their eyes met across the photograph. "Yes," she said.

Laleh had come across to where they were sitting and reached out to take the photograph. She stood studying it for a moment. "I know exactly what song she was singing that day," she said suddenly. " 'Bridge over Troubled Water.' Isn't that funny? I remember the day perfectly."

And just like that, Kavita heard it, heard Armaiti's voice, light as gossamer, soaring on the high notes like a bright yellow kite. *If you need a friend, / I'm sailing right behind. / Like a bridge over troubled water, / I will ease your mind.* What kind of a trick was youth that they had believed the words of a pop song as fervently as others believed in God?

She knew that Laleh was waiting for her to respond but found that she couldn't. All she could hear now was Armaiti's voice melding with hers on a hundred songs—*What do you see, my blue-eyed son? . . . Bluebird flying high, telling me what you see . . . A working class hero is something to be . . .*

"This one here played a mean guitar, let me tell you," Lal was saying to Ingrid. "She and that guitar were inseparable."

Ingrid turned to her, her eyes curious. "You play guitar? How come you never played for me?"

"I don't, anymore."

"Why'd you quit?"

There was no easy answer to that question. Kavita shrugged. "Because."

Laleh turned to look at her. "What was that song you wrote that we used to sing?"

Kavita blushed and shook her head. "I don't know. I forget."

But Adish and Laleh were smiling at each other, their eyes narrowing with the strain of remembering:

"*The years, like waves, drew us apart, / Out of mind, but not out of heart*," Laleh sang.

"Something, something, something," Adish hummed vaguely.

And then together they sang the chorus:

But we are all here.
We are all here.

Ingrid clapped while Kavita looked mortified. "This is so unfair," she said. "Bringing up youthful indiscretions."

"I think it's sweet," Ingrid said, patting Kavita's knee. She turned toward Laleh. "You know, I've never so much as written a poem in my life. But then, I have the perfect excuse—I'm German."

Kavita heard Laleh's delighted laughter.

They were still laughing when they heard a key turn in the

front door. "What the hell?" Adish said, staring. "It can't be the kids. It's much too early . . . ?"

The door opened and Ferzin let herself in. The girl walked through the hallway that led to the large living room with her head down so that she startled when she looked up and noticed the adults staring at her. "Shit," she said under her breath. And then, noticing Kavita, "Excuse me. Hi, Kavita auntie." She turned toward her mother, not bothering to keep the accusation out of her eyes. "I thought you all were going out tonight."

"We changed our mind," Adish said casually. "How come you're home so early?"

Ferzin took another step toward the group and Kavita noticed that the girl had been crying. Her stomach dropped. Laleh had mentioned earlier that Ferzin was out with her friends. Something must've gone wrong. "We really should be going," she said, throwing in a yawn for good measure. She nudged Ingrid as she got to her feet.

"Oh, no, don't leave because of me. I'm just going to my room."

"It's okay. We were leaving anyway."

"What's wrong, beta?" Laleh asked.

Ferzin stared at the ground. "I'm just tired," she said. "I'm going to bed."

"At least say hello to Kavita's friend," Laleh said. "This is Ingrid."

"Nice to meet you."

"Likewise."

There was an awkward silence and then Adish said, "Righto. Well, let me get my car keys. Be right back."

"Excuse me," Ferzin said, managing a smile. "Good night, everybody."

Laleh pulled on her lower lip as Ferzin walked toward her

room. Ingrid came up to where she stood. "Is she okay?" she asked.

"I have no idea." Laleh sounded puzzled. "Usually, coming home this early on a Friday night is a death sentence for her."

Ingrid laughed. "I thought only German kids couldn't stand to be around their parents."

"Don't you believe it." Laleh smiled at Ingrid. "This was such a pleasure. Hope to see you again."

"Oh, the pleasure was mine."

"Okay, let's go," Adish said, jiggling his keys.

"Bye." Ingrid gave Laleh a brief hug and then followed Adish out of the apartment.

"This was wonderful," Kavita said. " I'm so glad we did this."

"Ingrid's great, Ka. I'm happy for you."

"Thanks, Laleh," Kavita said softly. "You have no idea how much your accepting Ingrid means to me."

Laleh cocked her head. "What the hell does that mean? You don't just accept Adish, do you? You like him, right? I like Ingrid. It's as simple as that."

Kavita could hear the elevator doors open as she and Laleh walked toward the front door. "Love you, Lal."

"Love you, too, my darling. Call me tomorrow. We need to start planning for our trip."

Laleh knocked on Ferzin's door and when there was no answer let herself in. As she had expected, she found her daughter fully clothed and in bed, the tip of her nose a telltale red.

"What happened?" she asked as she sat on the edge of Ferzin's bed. "What's wrong?"

A storm of sobs was the answer she received, as Ferzin half

rose and threw herself into Laleh's arms. Laleh felt a pinch in her heart. Did children have any idea how much their tears hurt their parents? she wondered. She had heard her daughter cry a thousand times—over bad grades, parental injustices, unreliable boyfriends—and still it tore her into pieces, made her think that if she was granted one wish, it would be for Ferzin and Farhad to never be sad again. "Beta, what is it?"

"Tanaz won't speak to me."

Tanaz and Ferzin had been friends since they were seven. "Of course she will. You two fight and make up all the time."

"No, Mummy, this is serious. Honest."

"What happened?"

"Well, Zarir asked me to go on a date with him last week. And I knew that Tanaz likes him, also. So I didn't tell her. But she found out anyway. And now she's accusing me of betraying her."

Despite herself, a string of impatience cut through Laleh's earlier sympathy. Why did Ferzin's crises always involve boyfriends and sulking friends and juvenile misunderstandings? She remembered what she'd said to Kavita recently—that she was sometimes ashamed of her children. Loved them to pieces but was embarrassed by the lightness of their lives.

She waited until the judgment left her voice before saying, "And what do you think, darling? Do you feel like you did something wrong?"

"That's just it," Ferzin wailed. "I don't know. I mean, I don't think Tanaz has the right to tell me who I should go out with. And I had to lie to her because I knew she'd—"

"Wait a minute. You lied to her?"

Ferzin bit down on her lip. "Well, yeah. She asked what I was doing the evening I was meeting Zarir, and I just made up some story. I had no other choice."

And just like that, Laleh was back in a bright, sunny morning in August almost thirty years ago. The day of the march. Her mind played out the scene as if it were just happening: the vast crowd of protesters, and then, piercing the crowd like an arrow, a sweaty Adish running up to her. She had opened her mouth to thank him for picking up her migraine pills when he'd said, "You have to come home. Your mother's ill."

Beside her, Armaiti had gasped. "Oh, no. What's wrong?"

But Laleh had been suspicious, made uneasy by Adish's awkwardness, his strange demeanor. Why wasn't he looking her in the eye? Why was he shifting from foot to foot? "Adish," she said, "tell me the truth. Is Mummy *really* sick?"

Armaiti made an exasperated sound. "For God's sake, Laleh. Does it matter how sick your mummy is? The main thing is, she's asking for you. So go. We will manage without you."

And that's how quickly it had happened, the betrayal. Even today, she wasn't sure what she'd known, how much she'd understood, to what degree she was complicit. The only thing she knew for certain was that once she'd gotten over the shock and outrage of knowing that Adish had lied to her, that he had cracked like a stone pot under her father's pressure, and that once she'd been prohibited by her father to leave the house and follow Adish back to the march, a feeling of relief had seeped through her body like water through dry earth. Her worst fears would not be realized. Instead of spending the night in a filthy jail, she would sleep in her own bed.

"Mommy? Do you think I was wrong?"

Laleh blinked, brought back to the present by the plaintiveness she heard in her daughter's voice. Ferzin was hurting. She had to help. This is what she was put on earth to do—to comfort her children, to salve their wounds. But also to teach them something about living the kind of life that wouldn't require thirty years of soul-searching.

"Listen," she said. "I want to tell you something. About myself." She made a wry face. "Think you can listen? Or will it be too boring?"

She saw a look of surprise cross Ferzin's face. "No, Mommy. What?"

"Well, once when I was about your age, I did something that I'm ashamed of. To my friend Armaiti. Well, not exactly to her." She shook her head abruptly. "Forget it. It's too hard to explain." She smiled at Ferzin's serious face and stroked her cheek. "What I'm saying, darling, is this. Two things make us do bad things in life—fear and pride. I did my bad thing because of fear. I'm not sure what made you lie to your best friend, but here's a good bet—it's pride that's keeping you from apologizing to her. So don't sit on your pride. A good friend is worth more than that."

"But *I'm* not the one who said she never wanted to speak to me again . . ." Ferzin stopped and then frowned as a thought struck her. "Did you and Armaiti auntie ever fight?"

Had they? She couldn't remember. If they did, it certainly wasn't over some skinny young boy. "I don't think so. Anyway, it was different between us," she muttered.

"So how come you lost touch after she moved to America?"

A cold wind blew across Laleh's heart. She stared at her daughter wordlessly. Do you talk to your liver every day? she wanted to ask. Send love letters to your feet? Write an ode to your femur? Send a birthday card to your Eustachian tubes? That's how it is with Armaiti and me. She lives on my skin. She is part of my heart. So why did I need to acknowledge her presence every day? She opened her mouth to tell Ferzin this, to argue her case, and just then a voice in her head which sounded suspiciously like Adish's spoke an emphatic *Bullshit!* She had let Armaiti drift out of her life out of sheer laziness. What happens to a letter not mailed? To a phone call not made, an e-mail composed in the head but never written? What happens to a friendship that is not nourished?

But was that all it was? Laziness? Procrastination? The simple passage of time? The slow drift?

How nice to believe this. The tragic but inevitable unraveling of a friendship. How comforting, how blameless such a scenario would be. And untrue. No, the truth was harder than that. Going home from the march was the first secret she'd ever kept from Armaiti. The sad part was, Armaiti would've forgiven her immediately, would've even defended her stoutly and loudly, if she'd simply confessed to her moment of weakness. But the secret festered. It bound her to Adish and pulled her away from Armaiti. It made possible her future with Adish by severing her ties with Armaiti. And it proved to her that her dedication to the movement was not limitless after all, that she was a creature of creature comforts, that she was, ultimately, as her father always said, a middle-class girl playing at being a revolutionary. And the same turned out to be true for Armaiti: first, the disillusionment after she returned from that trip to Czechoslovakia, and later, the ultimate rejection—the move to America, the despised country of naked militarism and capitalism. If only we could've admitted our limitations, our humanness to each other, Laleh now thought. As it was, they couldn't. And it was embarrassment—embarrassment at their inability to live up to their own dream of themselves—that had made them drift apart.

"Mama, I'm not trying to be mean. I know you love Armaiti auntie very much."

Laleh smiled at the self-recrimination she heard in her daughter's voice. "I didn't think you were." She squeezed Ferzin's arm. "Call Tanaz and apologize. It never hurts to take the high road, beta."

"It's too late to phone . . ."

Laleh suddenly felt exhausted. She rose from the bed. "Okay. Your decision. But remember . . ."

"I'll just text her instead," Ferzin continued. "Okay?"

"Okay." Laleh went to the door and then looked back and grinned. "And make sure you grovel a bit. A little groveling never hurt a friendship."

16

Eleven o'clock and still she couldn't get out of bed. Nishta was awake now but too listless to start the day. At least she didn't have to cook lunch for Ammi today. Before he had left for work, she had requested Iqbal to drop off last night's leftovers for his mother. I'll make her a nice dinner, she'd promised. He had nodded and asked her to take care of the cold she'd told him she was nursing. Before leaving, he had come over and stood at the edge of the bed, a watchful expression on his face. Ever since he had slapped her, she felt his eyes on her at all times, the guilty eyes of a dog who had stolen his master's dinner and expected to be caught at any moment. And indeed, Nishta now thought, Iqbal *had* stolen something from her—stolen her last illusion, the story that she had told herself that had made these last few years bearable. For the past decade she had lived within the folds of self-delusion, continually making excuses for Iqbal: Yes, he had turned his back on the social movements that had once buoyed them, but in his telling, Islam supported the same goals of justice and equality that the movement once had; yes, he had forced her to wear the burkha, but he claimed it was for her own protection; yes, he had grown increasingly distant over the years, but at least he had never hit her.

The last thought made Nishta leap out of bed. Had never

hit her? Had her expectations of her husband really become so insultingly small? Had she broken her parents' hearts only to settle for these morsels? The estrangement from her family had carved a hole in her life so big that she had to will herself not to fall through it. And Iqbal's parents had never stepped in to fill the void. She knew that they had only accepted her because to do otherwise would have meant losing their son. It wasn't their fault, really. The divide between them and her was simply too great to bridge. The early years, in particular, had been very difficult. Coming from an affluent, high-caste Hindu family, she had always taken certain privileges for granted. But Iqbal's family was poor, and there were constant reminders of this: in the way her mother-in-law doled out her money, carefully, painfully, as if a rupee note were a nugget of gold; in the fact that Iqbal's family ate the government-sold rice and not the expensive basmati rice that Nishta had grown up eating; in the fact that her in-laws never "squandered" money on taking a cab or eating out. The cultural divides were even less bridgeable: Iqbal's parents could never watch television or follow the evening news without instinctively looking for the slights and slurs that they believed were leveled every day against Muslims. Watching a cricket match, which had always been a source of innocent fun, now assumed a new weight if the Indian team was playing the Pakistanis. Nishta could see their divided loyalties playing out in their conflicted faces.

No use thinking about the past, Nishta scolded herself, as she splashed cold water over her face. But she was in a bitter mood today, and long-buried resentments kept bubbling up. How dare Iqbal make it sound like quitting the bank was her fault. She remembered how abruptly he'd broken the news to her at the time. They had just left a housewarming party for Laleh and Adish, and Iqbal had acted so strange and formal that evening, she had been relieved when he suggested they leave. She was two months pregnant at the time.

"Did you see how they live?" he had hissed as they walked toward the train station. "These people who called themselves Socialists just a few years ago? Like bleddy colonialists or something."

"They've always lived like this. Laleh comes from money, and Adish, too. You know that. This is bullshit, Iqbal. And since when do we hate our friends because they're rich?"

"I don't hate them. I just . . ." He looked away. "I resigned at the bank," he said abruptly.

"Very funny."

"Nishta. I'm not joking."

Her stomach lurched. "What?"

He turned to face her. "I gave in my resignation. I'm leaving in two weeks. I'm going to help Murad run his shop. More money there."

She stared at him aghast. "Iqbal, are you mad? Murad's shop is so tiny he can barely support his own family. There's no place for you there. And now with the baby coming . . . My God, you could be branch manager in a few years. You know you're smarter than anyone else at that bank."

"It's already decided. I handed in my letter today."

It was a turning point in our lives, Nishta thought as she patted her face dry. Deeply religious, with a fourth-grade education, Murad was tickled pink at the thought of having his educated nephew working for him. He delighted in mocking Iqbal for his "English" manners, and told all their relatives that he had saved his nephew from destitution. A few times Nishta had tried to argue back, to deflate Murad's growing sense of largess, but Iqbal silenced her. He needed the job, he said. So she bit her tongue and put up with Murad's puffery. She also knew that

Murad was constantly haranguing his nephew for being a non-believer and for not attending mosque, and that Iqbal sometimes accompanied the older man just to appease him. But she was not worried. If anything, the trips to the mosque only served to re-mind Iqbal of how different he and Nishta were from the people around them. What she didn't foresee was that in time the trips would serve to remind him of how different he was from her.

Nishta sighed. Here it was almost noon and all she'd done was nudge the past into existence again. In a few hours it would be time to walk Zenobia home from her class, and she still had to cook tonight's dinner. Pulling her hair up in a bun, she glanced at herself in the bathroom mirror—and stopped. Her left cheek was still swollen from where Iqbal had struck it, and the area near her cheekbone was purple and sore to touch. Nishta shuddered. She saw her eyes, tired, unhappy, made dull with boredom and drudgery, and suddenly she wanted to leave this stifling house and run, kick open the door and run into the open streets, rip off her burkha, this costume of misery that Iqbal had inflicted upon her, and run. Run away from this life, to a place where he'd never find her. Her pulse began to race and her heart pounded, as if in imagining her escape she had actually begun implementing it. She walked out of the tiny bathroom into the living room, forcing herself to take deep breaths, to calm down. She went to the kitchen to get a glass of water, and when the doorbell rang she ignored it.

But it rang again, and then a third time, and, emitting a soft, frustrated *ooof*, she crossed the room and opened the door.

"Zoha jaan," a woman's voice squealed. "What is this behavior? You're a no-show to my party, and then I call and call but your phone is off. You were beginning to worry me, yaar."

"Mumtaz?" Her voice was tentative as her eyes adjusted to the dimly lit hallway.

"It's okay I stopped by, na?" Mumtaz pushed the door open further and breezed past Nishta and into the living room. "I wish you two hadn't gotten rid of your landline, yaar. I left two messages for my stupid brother but of course he didn't call me back." She spun around to face Nishta. "Kya khabar, bhabi? What news?"

Nishta ran her fingers across her hair. "Fine," she said weakly. "And you? How are the children? And Husseinbhai?" She stopped abruptly, watching Mumtaz blanch. "What?"

"Your face," Mumtaz said. "All banged up. What happened?"

"Oh, this." She forced her mind to arrange a plausible lie. "It's just . . . I walked into a door. The bedroom door was shut. I thought it was open." But she had never been a good liar and her voice trailed off and to her disgust she felt her eyes fill with tears.

"Bhabi, what's wrong? Is your face paining?"

She blinked back her tears. "No. I'm fine."

Mumtaz stared at her for a second and then she shook her head violently, as if she didn't want to host the thought that had flown into it.

"No," she said, as if losing an argument with herself. "Iqbal would never . . . for all his faults, he's no . . . Did he do this, Zoha? Hit you?"

"He didn't hit me. Just a slap. Nothing, really. Happened so fast it scared him more than me. And you know how my skin is. Everything shows. It doesn't hurt at all." Her voice sounded tinny and ridiculous to her own ears.

Mumtaz took her by the hand. "Zoha jaan. Come sit down. I'll make some tea. No, come sit."

She allowed herself to be led to the old sofa, but after a few minutes she rose and followed Mumtaz into the kitchen. From the doorway, she heard herself ask, "Has Hussein ever hit you?"

Mumtaz spun around, shaking her head vigorously. "No, bhabi. Never. He's far from perfect, believe me. You know the problems in my marriage. I've kept no secrets from you. But at least he never forced me to wear purdha, like you. And never this." Her eyes flashed. "I'll kill Iqbal. I swear, I'll . . ."

"Mumtaz," Nishta said gently. "He's your brother. Remember how much he loves you."

Mumtaz shrugged and looked away. "That relationship ended a long time ago," she said.

"I'll never understand why."

Mumtaz poured out two cups of tea. "Someday I'll explain. But today we are talking about you." She frowned. "I'm no longer a child, bhabi. Besides, you've done more to help me than my own brother has. What you said to me on my wedding day, I'll never forget. About coming to you night or day if I needed help in my marriage. Not even my own mother said that. They were all so happy to get me off their hands. The fact that Hussein is fifteen years older meant nothing to them."

Nishta heard the bitterness in her sister-in-law's voice. "I never understood why you married him in the first place," she said. "You were so young."

"I was a child," Mumtaz said. "Had dreams of being a commercial artist. Marriage was the last thing on my mind."

"Then, why?" Nishta asked, remembering how emphatically she had argued with Iqbal at the time, and how secretive but adamant he had been.

Mumtaz shrugged. "None of this matters now. Ancient history." She sat down on the sofa, balancing the teacup on her lap. Reaching over, she pulled Nishta beside her on the sofa. "So tell me. Why did he strike you?"

Nishta started at the beginning. Told Mumtaz about her excitement about Kavita and Laleh's amazing, unexpected visit.

Her shock and sadness at the news about Armaiti. Iqbal's paranoid, unsympathetic reaction. How he forbade her from contacting the other two again, and, when she argued, his confiscation of her cell phone. Adish's attempt to plead his wife's case. Iqbal's reaction to this. The exchange of heated words over dinner. His hand flying to her face, severing in an instant the connection that they had shared for decades.

"Ya Allah," Mumtaz breathed when she was done. "He took your cell phone? What kind of a man does this? Who has Iqbal become?"

"I ask myself this question daily," Nishta whispered.

The women stared at each other for a moment, their chins trembling. Then Mumtaz took her index finger and lightly rubbed the bruise on Nishta's face. "He never was the same since after the riots," she murmured. There was something in her voice that Nishta couldn't identify.

"Well, the riots were terrible." Nishta shuddered. "We all saw things no human being ever should. And we were lucky. At least we were spared."

Mumtaz gave a short, bitter laugh. "Yah. We were the lucky ones."

Again, something in her voice that Nishta couldn't quite place. "Are you and Hussein . . ." she started again but Mumtaz cut her off.

"Forget Hussein and me," she said. "I want to do something for you. I want to help you."

"Thank you, sweetie. But there's nothing anyone can—"

"Yes, I can. Don't say that. Don't say there's nothing I can do." Mumtaz stared into the distance for a second and when she spoke, her voice was wistful. "I was really little when all of you used to come to our house. But I still remember your friends. My God, it was like having movie stars descend upon us."

Nishta sighed. "Those days are long gone."

Mumtaz opened her purse and pulled out her cell phone. "Here, bhabi. Use this. Call your friends."

Nishta shook her head. "No thanks. I don't want to get you in trouble."

Mumtaz snorted. "I'm not afraid of anybody," she said. "Perfectly legal, talking to a friend on the phone." She put her cell phone on the coffee table in front of them.

"Mumtaz, what's the point?" Nishta said. "I have nothing in common with them anymore. And for all I know they're already in America."

"Sheesh." Mumtaz rolled her eyes. "Just listen to yourself, Zoha. All I'm asking you to do is return a friend's call and you have a list of excuses longer than the Great Wall of China." She gave Nishta a little push. "Go get their phone number. Just go, na."

Kavita was in a foul mood. It was Ingrid's last day in town and already she was missing her. The three days had gone by so quickly and Laleh and Adish's easy acceptance of Ingrid had made her feel even more warmly toward her girlfriend. Who was about to get on a plane in another seven hours.

So what the hell were they doing at work? Why the hell was she letting that ass Rahul monopolize Ingrid's time? "You guys going out of town?" Rahul had asked when she'd told him she was taking a few days off because Ingrid was coming to Bombay. And, stupidly, dumbly, she had answered, "No." Which Rahul took as an invitation to leave multiple messages on her phone, asking her to drop by the office with Ingrid so he could say hello. Finally, she'd suggested to Ingrid that they swing by for fifteen minutes this morning. The fifteen minutes had turned into two hours and Rahul seemed in no hurry to stop picking Ingrid's brain about their newest collaboration.

Kavita was headed toward Rahul's office when she saw Mohan, her assistant, come toward her. "Phone call for you, madam," he said.

"Take a message. I'm still on vacation, remember?"

"I tried, madam. Says it's urgent."

She gritted her teeth. Clients could be so pushy. "Nothing that can't wait until tomorrow." Hand on Rahul's doorknob, she turned her head. "Who is it?"

"Says her name is Nishta, madam. Says she is—"

She was flying down the hallway before he could finish the rest of his sentence.

Mumtaz looked at Nishta and shook her head. "Look at you," she said softly. "Ten minutes on the phone with Kavita auntie and your whole face looks different. Color in your cheeks. Even your eyes are shining."

Nishta smiled self-consciously. "Kavita is so warm. She's always been so . . ."

"You should go," Mumtaz said abruptly. "With them. Since they haven't left yet. I can help you. I have money—I'm a rich man's wife, remember?"

"Mumtaz, it's okay. This is not your problem. You heard me tell Kavita I couldn't go. Please don't involve yourself in this. I don't want to open a rift in the family."

Mumtaz got a stubborn look on her face that Nishta recognized from her years of living with Iqbal. "Bhabi," she said. "I can't help you if you don't want to help yourself. But I think you should go. A dying woman has asked for your help. I think you should honor her wishes."

Nishta rose tiredly from the couch. "I swear, you and your brother could convince a starving man to not eat." She attempted a laugh but it fell flat.

Mumtaz stood to face Nishta. There was a slight wetness in her eyes. "You know, Iqbal's been running other people's lives for too many years. I think it's time for him to stop."

The room fell silent. Nishta looked away first. Mumtaz was saying something else but Nishta didn't hear her. Her mind was replaying the innocent question that Kavita had posed to her just before they'd hung up: Why hadn't she called them from a pay phone if Iqbal had hidden her mobile? The answer made her lips twist with bitterness: because of some misguided sense of loyalty to Iqbal. Because she had claimed Iqbal's shame as her own, pulled it tight over herself, like a second skin. The realization embarrassed Nishta, made her realize how fuzzy and distorted her thinking had become. Between Mumtaz's outrage and Kavita's question, she could see her own complicity in her captivity.

"So what are you suggesting?" she whispered. "That I leave without Iqbal's permission?"

Mumtaz pulled on her lower lip. "I don't know," she said. "Maybe Hussein can knock some sense into my brother's thick skull." She looked away for a second and then focused on Nishta. "Let me talk to Kavita auntie again. I don't know anything about going abroad." She made a face. "At least you've been to Dubai. I've never even left India."

Nishta put her hand on the younger woman's shoulder. "Mumtaz. I know you want to help. But please don't call Kavita again. I don't want to get their hopes up. I . . . I . . . God, I don't want to get *my* hopes up. Iqbal will never let me go."

But Mumtaz was already redialing Kavita's number. Nishta stood around purposelessly for a second, biting her nails and then began pacing around the small room, listening to Mumtaz's end of the conversation. When Mumtaz signaled for a pen and writing paper she hurried into the kitchen. Hunting through the kitchen drawer, she saw, in a sudden flash, the rest of her life with Iqbal, the slow descent from middle age to old age. The future looked unimaginably dull and blank, a slow, funereal procession of days and years that led to nowhere beautiful.

Mumtaz looked up as Nishta walked back into the living room; she grabbed the pen from her to jot down whatever Kavita was saying. "Yes, yes, of course," Mumtaz said. "Definitely. No problem, auntie. Thank you so much. I'll be in touch. Okay, bye."

"I don't know why you're doing all this," Nishta said as soon as Mumtaz hung up. "I can't go anywhere."

Mumtaz held her finger to her lips. "Shh. I need your passport."

"What?"

"Your passport. I need it."

Nishta blinked. "What for?"

Mumtaz smiled impatiently. "Kavita auntie said we have to make a visa application online. So we need your passport, ration card, financial papers. Then they call you for your interview. Your friends already have their visas. But she said they'll postpone their trip until you get your interview."

"Wait. Wait," Nishta said, rubbing her forehead. "Mumtaz, I don't even have enough money to go from here to Pune, let alone to America."

Mumtaz looked insulted. "Nobody asked you for money," she muttered.

A few days ago she had prayed to an unknown god for help. And here, sitting next to her, was an answered prayer, in the unexpected form of Iqbal's own sister. Mumtaz, who was planning her trip to America as blithely as if she were planning a picnic at Hanging Gardens. Was this yet another mindless detour, another joke that life was playing on her? Could she trust this?

"I can't," she said. "I can't. And I don't want to involve you in this."

Mumtaz sighed heavily and stared at Nishta. "Let me ask a simple question," she said finally. "If you didn't have to worry about what Iqbal thought or what Ammi will say or where the money will come from, what would you do? Would you go? Yes or no?"

"I don't know——"

"Yes or no?"

"Well, yes. Of course. Armaiti was one of my best friends."

Mumtaz nodded. Then she said, "I'm younger than you, bhabi. But let me say something. In this life, most of the time we live and sacrifice for others. For husbands, for children, for aging parents. And that's good. It's the natural order of things. But once in a while, we must do something for ourselves. The secret is knowing when it is your turn." Mumtaz's eyes blazed like sparklers as they rested on Nishta's face. "This is your turn, Zoha. *Take it*."

Nishta blinked back the tears that formed unexpectedly. She reached out and caressed Mumtaz's left cheek. "You are so sweet to me," she said. "But I can't."

Mumtaz's voice was a whisper. "Let me do this. For me. Not for you. For me." A film of sweat shone on her upper lip.

A dim, blue flame of suspicion ignited in Nishta's mind. *For me?* Why was Mumtaz so anxious to help? Was she using her as a pawn in some age-old rebellion against her brother? But the suspicion was doused by the slow excitement that built in her body. Was this really possible? That Mumtaz would help get her out? Luck had not been her friend in so long. Could she trust it now? Could she trust it?

"Mumtaz, are you sure? This is not a game, you know. Iqbal is going to be very angry."

Mumtaz clucked her tongue dismissively. "Don't worry so much, na. I know how to handle my brother." She paused, and then grinned. "Let's just do this one step at a time. No law that says you have to go just because you have a visa, correct? But definitely a law that says you can't go if you don't have a visa." She snapped her fingers. "So let's get your visa. Simple."

"Okay," Nishta said. "Okay." She went to the Steelcase cupboard and opened the inner safe where she and Iqbal kept all their valuables. She found his passport right away. But not hers. It took her a few seconds to realize that Iqbal had removed it. She didn't bother hiding her shock when she returned to the living room. "It's gone," she said woodenly. "Iqbal must have taken it."

The two women sat in embarrassed silence on the sofa, not looking at each other. Then Mumtaz said, "I'm sure I know where he put it. After all, he's not taking your passport to work with him everyday." She turned toward Nishta. "You know that safe that Ammi has? I'll bet you anything he's hidden it there."

Nishta shook her head no. She was in shock over Iqbal's treachery. How far will he go? she wondered. Where will it end? Who is this man I've spent all these years with?

"Yes, you do," Mumtaz insisted. "It's the small brown one where Ammi keeps her wedding jewelry. We took her jewelry out of it and gave it to Sharma uncle to hold for us during the riots, remember? Ma told him she trusted him like her own brother." There was a vibration, a tremor in Mumtaz's voice. But it barely registered, like the roar of the traffic under her window.

"I think so," Nishta said vaguely.

"You stay here. I know the code. I'll go visit with Ammi for a few minutes and then tell her I need to borrow her jewelry for a party. I'll be back soon."

Mumtaz returned twenty minutes later and triumphantly pulled the blue book out of her handbag. "I knew it. I'm telling you, I can read my brother's mind better than anybody."

"Did Ammi see?"

"She was in the other room. Don't fret so much." She tossed the passport on the coffee table and turned toward Nishta. "There's something I should say," she began. "On behalf of my whole family, I apologize to you."

"Don't be silly," Nishta said. "You had nothing to—"

"No. I mean it. I had—I feel responsible for who my brother has become. Stealing his wife's cell phone, hiding her passport. It's shameful, but I understand why he has become this way." Mumtaz swallowed hard and then shook her head abruptly, as if to dismiss any softening toward Iqbal. "But I don't excuse it. In fact, I reject it." She paused for a second. "One thing I promise you, bhabi. I will help you. Even if it means bearing Iqbal's wrath. And in any case, I know Iqbal. He can't stay angry for long. Once you return from America, he will forgive me."

Nishta forced a blankness to fall across her face. Because she had almost said it out loud: If I go, I'm not coming back. If I can escape the prison my life has become, I am flying away forever.

17

Laleh had the driver drop her off at the entrance of the club that she and Adish belonged to. She usually avoided visiting the club in the evening. The diamond-encrusted women in their silks and chiffons, their bossy, preening husbands who asserted their power by barking orders at the waiters, their whiny children who harassed their tired-looking ayahs while their parents played cards or stuffed themselves with oily, heavy food—Laleh reacted to all of them as if they were personally insulting her. If she went to the club at all, she usually went in the afternoon, to swim for an hour. Or she might occasionally treat a friend to lunch there, on the verandah overlooking the sea, before the evening crowds descended.

But Adish came here after work three nights a week to play tennis, and this was one of those nights. Laleh had made her peace with the fact that he would be home late tonight, but as the evening wore on she found the waiting to be unbearable. Not when she had such wonderful news to give to him.

"Just stop here," she told the driver. "I'll call when I'm ready."

As she approached the tennis court, she spotted Adish immediately. He was ready to serve, reaching up on his toes to smack the ball, when he caught sight of her. He stopped, called out something to his partner and hurried toward her. "What's wrong?" he said immediately.

"Nothing. Nothing's wrong," she said. "Can't I just come to watch you . . ."

"Bollocks." Adish pulled a white towel off the chair on the side of the court and mopped the sweat off his face. "What is it? The children?"

"Go finish your game," she said, suddenly annoyed at herself for not having waited until he got home. Poor Adish. Tennis was his one relaxation. She smiled to reassure him. "Everything's okay. I just have some news to give you. But it can wait."

Instead, he trotted over to where his tennis partner was waiting impatiently. "Sorry, yaar. Family situation. Do you mind if we stop?"

"Just when I was about to beat the pants off of you." The other man grinned. "Well, I'll see you day after tomorrow."

They found a quiet spot near the swimming pool and Adish ordered a scotch for himself and a cocktail for Laleh. "So?"

"We—Kavita heard from Nishta." She waited for him to react, but he stared at her impassively. "Nishta contacted us. Turns out Iqbal had confiscated her cell phone. Can you imagine?" She waited for her own revulsion and outrage to be reflected on Adish's face but it had turned to stone.

"Say something," she finally urged.

"What do you want me to say?"

She ignored his last remark. "She wants to come. To America, to see Armaiti. So we have to figure out how to help."

"Why are you telling me this?" There was a flash in Adish's eyes that she knew meant trouble, but she wasn't about to acknowledge it.

The waiter set their drinks before them along with a bowl of beer nuts. Adish popped a fistful into his mouth, chewing hard, his eyes never leaving Laleh's face. "You know I gave my word to Iqbal," he said. "You know I would never——"

"Adish," she said urgently. "This is our friend. She is in a bad marriage. We can help her. What is there to discuss?"

Adish closed his eyes. "Iqbal was our friend, too. My mother always told me one never knows what goes on between a man and a woman. And Iqbal has suffered so much. I wish I could tell you some of the things he told me."

He was getting that stubborn look on his face, the lower lip jutting out, that Laleh had come to know only too well over the years. She knew she only had a few minutes to get it right. "It was Mumtaz who phoned Kavita," she said quietly. "Iqbal's sister. Why? Because even she knows injustice when she sees it." She saw Adish raise an eyebrow at the mention of Mumtaz, and she pressed her advantage. "He makes her wear a burkha, janu. A *burkha*. He's broken her spirit. You remember what Nishta used to be like, so carefree and easygoing. She's a nervous wreck these days. Why should she continue living like this? Tell me. Just so that you can say you kept your word?"

"A promise is a promise."

"Damn your promise." She had spoken louder than she intended, and he put a warning hand over her wrist. She shook it away. "A promise is only meaningful if it is just."

"I know a lot of lawyers who would disagree with that interpretation, sweetie."

She stared at him in anger. "What do you think this is, Adish, some bloody game? I'm not discussing some esoteric principle here. I'm asking . . ." Angry tears filled her eyes. "I came here to ask you to help." She rose from her chair. "Forget it. I'll take care of this myself."

"Laleh." Adish's voice was low but urgent. "You're making a scene. Now sit down and let's talk like adults."

She looked down at him, focusing on the tiny bald spot that had started on the top of his head. "No. You talk. You spend your life discussing things, clinging to your ridiculous promises." She moved away from the table and then stomped back. "You know what you promised Iqbal, don't you? You promised to keep your mouth shut and look the other way. That's all you promised him, darling." She shook her head. "Forget it. I'm going home."

"Wait," he called, but she ignored him.

Adish didn't get home until ten that night. Laleh had calmed down enough to regret her outburst at the club. She waited for him to enter their bedroom but when he didn't after fifteen minutes of being home, she went into the kitchen where he was sitting with the children.

She noticed immediately that he wasn't making eye contact with her. And, apparently, so did their son. "So what did you guys fight about?" Farhad asked after a few minutes and they both jumped guiltily. "Nothing," she said. "No fight," Adish stammered.

Farhad looked at them languidly and grinned. "Then how come Papa didn't kiss you when he came home?" he said.

Adish smacked his son on the arm. "Mind your own business," he said. "You're turning into a bloody nosey parker."

Farhad grinned more broadly. "It *is* my business, that you two get along," he said as he opened the fridge and took out a can of Coke. He paced the floor in a manner that reminded Laleh of her father. "Imagine if you two kept fighting," he said. "Soon you'd get divorced. That means Papa has to give Mommy half his money. Then let's say both of you remarry. Your new spouses may have their own children. That means"—Farhad threw his hands open for dramatic effect—"my inheritance is cut in half. Possibly more."

"You keep this up and you'll be lucky to have any inheritance at all," Adish said.

"Speaking of inheritance, can I have some money now?" Ferzin chimed in. "I'm going to a night-show with my friends," she added.

Adish turned to Laleh. "What do these kids think we are? Do they just see us as walking, talking moneybags?"

She shrugged, but a smile played on her lips. Adish seemed to have softened toward her. Thank God for the kids, she thought. They had a way of diffusing the tensest of situations. "It's not their fault they have the world's most generous father."

"Not to mention the world's prettiest mother," Farhad said immediately. As she looked at her gangly son—the unruly eyebrows, the crooked smile—Farhad, ugly in that beautiful way teenage boys were, Laleh felt love stir in her heart. Why didn't Nishta have children, she wondered? That would have helped her so much.

Adish's eyes twinkled. "Arre, saala, stop flirting with my wife."

Laleh sat there a little longer and then returned to the bedroom. Adish followed ten minutes later, unbuttoning his shirt as he entered. "We'll need Nishta's passport information," he said casually, as if resuming a conversation. "I'll contact Joseph and have him make a visa appointment for her. It's lucky we didn't pay for your tickets yet. Now we can get all three."

She flew across the room and flung her arms around him. "Thank you. Oh, I just . . . thank you. And I'm so sorry about the horrible things I said."

"No. My fault. I let my pity for Iqbal blind me to the real victim here. And that's Nishta."

"We already have her passport number, by the way. Mumtaz gave it to Kavita."

"Good work." He picked up the phone and then looked at the wall clock across the room. "I'll call Joseph first thing in the morning," he said.

Laleh tugged at Adish to sit on the bed next to her. "So what happened? Between the time I left the club and you came home? To change your mind, I mean?"

"Nothing." He stared at his feet and then turned toward her. "I just decided a few minutes ago, while talking to the children. While looking at Ferzin." He paused and when he spoke, there was a tremor in his voice. "If some bugger told my daughter that she had to wear a chador each time she left the house, I would choke him. I wouldn't care if he was a boyfriend, husband, nothing." Even as he spoke, a muscle on his forearm twitched, as if he were performing the action. "And you said—didn't you say Mumtaz called? Iqbal's sister?" Laleh nodded. "Well. So obviously even his own sister disagrees with what he's done," he said, as if to himself.

Laleh put Adish's hand in her lap and stroked the twitching muscle. "You're a good man, Charlie Brown," she murmured. "I don't know how you do it, but you come through time after time."

Adish grinned. "They don't call me Mr. Fixit for nothing."

Laleh smiled. "This is the best present we could've given Armaiti," she said.

"You want to phone her?"

Laleh considered. "She's on vacation. With Richard and Diane. I don't want to disturb her. I'll send an e-mail to Diane."

She bit her lower lip. "I guess her coordination is bad enough now that she can't type anymore. Diane does her e-mails for her."

Adish kissed her cheek. "I'm sorry." He rose to his feet. "I'll go brush my teeth. And then let's go to bed, okay? It's getting late."

18

Nishta clutched the thin plastic bag that contained the potatoes and spinach she would cook later today. Muddy, dirty water ran into the streets, and she lifted the hem of her burkha as she gingerly made her way. The bazaar was teeming with people, and although it was still morning the heat was unbearable.

The first time she had ever worn a burkha was fifteen years ago, but she still wasn't used to the claustrophobic, buried-alive feeling. Iqbal had accompanied her that first time, and for a few moments a childish delight, a mild form of hysteria had enveloped her. As a little girl she had been enthralled by the idea of invisibility, of using pens with invisible ink, of donning a cloak that would allow her to move around undetected and unseen. Every Sunday she would stop whatever she was doing to watch the old American series *Invisible Man* on television. Now it seemed as if that old childhood wish had come true; if not for the fact that Iqbal was by her side, she could wear this cloak and disappear within it, be reduced to nothing more than a pair of eyes looking out onto the world, spying on it while it couldn't spy back. Like a uniform, the burkha conferred instant anonymity—it obliterated her features, swallowed up her identity, made indistinct her facial features, and even her shape. She could be a potato in a sack, for all the difference it made. The anonymity made her feel powerful—she could stick her tongue out at the world and it would never notice.

But the next second, the panic hit. She felt as if she were in an underwater cave, drowning, crying for help but unable to make her voice heard. Her face broke out in sweat brought on by the unimaginable heat under the hood and a heart-pounding fear that was existential. It felt like death—a slipping away, a disappearance, an obliteration—except that instead of being in bed surrounded by weeping relatives, she was standing in the street under a noonday sun surrounded by thousands of strangers. She felt a screaming begin in her ears, a deafening screech, as if there were an airplane stuck inside the burkha with her.

"I can't," she said to Iqbal, "I'm sorry, I can't." But he was looking straight ahead, a peculiar smile on his face, and she realized that she had to speak louder to be heard from under this polyester coffin that she was wearing. The fact of being unheard simply added to the feeling of death, of not existing, and her panic must've registered in the force with which she squeezed his hand because he turned to her and said, "What?"

"Home," she gasped, and when she saw him cock his head in incomprehension she said, more loudly, "I want to go home. I'm sick."

They turned around immediately and ten minutes later she was lying on their bed, the ceiling fan turned on high, a glass of water by her side. She had torn off the hood as soon as they'd entered the house and Iqbal had helped her remove the rest of the garment. When she could finally speak, she turned to him and said, "That was horrible. I felt like I was drowning." He nodded gravely, not responding.

Three days later he came home from work and suggested they go to the seaside. She readily agreed, but when she came into the living room wearing her regular pants and blouse, he raised an eyebrow. "Where's your niqab?"

She stared at him, and as he met her gaze a lump formed in her throat. "After what happened to me, you still want me to . . . ?" Her voice trailed off, disappointment and disbelief mixing together.

He smiled his new smile—the patient, serene, paternal smile that he often cast her way these days. "That was your first time, Zoha. Of course it was hard. Remember the first time you wore a sari? You must've tripped a few times, na? So we just have to practice."

"We? We have to practice?" She rushed into the bedroom, bundled up the dreaded object, came back to where he was sitting on the sofa and threw it at him. "Here. You wear it. You practice."

He shook his head sadly. "You are so childish." He rose from the sofa. "Fine. If I can't get my wife to go to the seaside with me I'll go alone." He got to the front door and then turned around. "Have you seen how the brothers in this neighborhood look at you, with lust in their eyes? Don't you care about—"

"Then they're the ones who should wear the burkha," she interrupted fiercely. "On their dicks."

His face flushed with anger. "I will not have you talk like this in my house. You have a filthy mouth, Zoha." She watched as his Adam's apple bobbed a few times as he struggled to control his temper, and then he spun around and pushed open the front door.

That was fifteen years ago, Nishta now thought with wonder as she deftly wound her way around the marketplace. She stopped for a moment to set down the plastic bag and pushed up the sleeve to read her watch: 9:58 a.m. She had two minutes to reach Yasmina, the young vegetable vendor who sold her wares on the east side of the market. Habit made her turn around and glance up at the fifth floor of her apartment building. Almost immediately her mother-in-law, sitting on the balcony as she did every day of her life, waved to her. Nishta marveled at the fact that even at this distance, Ammi could spot her among all the other clad women. The old woman knew the comings and go-ings of everyone below her and Nishta felt her hawk eyes on her as she picked up the bag again and moved farther away. Another few steps and she would be out of Ammi's range. She made a sharp turn onto the main road, dodging the crowds and huffing a bit as she hurried. She listened with distaste to her breathing, amplified under the dark shroud she was wearing. You need to lose at least ten kilos, she chided herself. She knew she was eat-ing too much, eating carelessly, out of boredom. And who could exercise while wearing a sack?

Maybe in America she could . . . But she couldn't complete the thought because she had found Yasmina's stall. The vendor was bickering with an old man over the price of two cabbages, and Nishta waited impatiently for them to get done. She resisted the temptation to offer the few coins that were standing be-tween the customer and his purchase. She must do nothing that would draw attention to herself. For years she had railed against the anonymity that the burkha imposed on her. Now she would make it work in her favor.

She checked her watch again, saw that it was ten o'clock, and just then Yasmina's mobile phone rang. Yasmina picked it up and answered, looking up at Nishta and smiling with her eyes. And then, as arranged by Mumtaz two days ago, she handed the phone to Nishta.

It took her a moment to maneuver the phone under the hood of the hijab. In that moment, Nishta died a million deaths. Please don't let them hang up, she prayed. "Hello?" she said finally.

"Nishta?" It was Kavita's voice, crisp and clear. "How are you, darling?"

"I'm fine. Fine." She struggled to control the shaking of her hands. "But I shouldn't talk for long."

"Understood. Okay, listen. The appointment is for eleven on Friday. We don't really have a choice on dates. So, I hope it will work for you?"

She had no idea if it would. Or how she would get out of the house. But she nodded. "Yes. It's okay."

"Great. Let's meet at ten-thirty. You know where to come? Tirupathi Apartments. Can you remember that? It's across from Mahalaxmi temple. You have to check in there, and then they'll take you by bus to the embassy."

"Yes. Okay." The shaking had spread through her whole body. Was she sick, she wondered? She forced herself to concentrate on the conversation. "Kavita. One other thing. Can you phone Mumtaz? Tell her the date and time and ask if she can pick me up. I'll tell—I'll say we're going shopping."

"I can do that." Kavita's voice sounded so calm and competent, so close, Nishta thought she would cry. "How will she confirm with you, though?"

She thought quickly. "Call her now. And call me back at this number. Can you?"

"Five minutes," Kavita said and then there was silence.

"Thank you," Nishta said after she handed the phone back to Yasmina a second time. She dug into her purse and took out a five-rupee note.

"No need, miss," Yasmina said. "The other lady already paid."

Nishta smiled. Mumtaz must've paid Yasmina a handsome amount for the use of her phone for her to refuse a tip. "My phone is still in the repair shop," she said. "May need to trouble you again."

Yasmina appeared to reconsider. "Your wish," she said, accepting the note. "Just to make you happy."

Oh, you've made me happy all right, Nishta thought as she walked away. She marveled at how quickly things had changed because of Mumtaz's fortuitous visit. Thank God for Iqbal's slap, she thought. If Mumtaz had not noticed the swelling, they would have never discussed her marriage. And Mumtaz might not have been so willing to help. Even now, it made Nishta a little suspicious that her sister-in-law would so readily align herself with her, and against her own brother. It all seemed too easy—Mumtaz's sudden appearance, her willingness to believe her story, her insistence on her visiting Armaiti, her pledge to help even if it meant deceiving her brother. None of it made sense.

She shook her head. She had stayed up late last night watching *The Bourne Identity*, and that's why she was like this today, suspicious of everything, even of Mumtaz, who had been a little sister to her ever since they first met. And she, who had always believed in women helping each other, who had read *Sisterhood Is Powerful* when she was sixteen, who, in Kavita, Armaiti, and Laleh had known the true bonds of sisterhood, she should know better than to doubt Mumtaz's sincerity.

As she walked, Nishta heard an unfamiliar sound, and for a second she thought it was an insect trapped under the hood of her burkha. And then she recognized it. She was humming.

19

Florida in July was not Armaiti's idea of a good time, but Richard had asked her to go with him, and, except for that one time when he'd begged her not to divorce him, she had never been able to refuse him anything. So here they were, the three of them, at the vacation home of one of Richard's clients, a seven-bedroom villa on the beach in Ponte Vedra. And although it had been a short flight and they had flown in on the client's private plane, Armaiti was stunned by how exhausted and drained she felt.

They had just finished a tour of the house, Armaiti doing her best to hide her shudders at the gaudy furnishings, when Richard turned a critical eye upon her. "You look awful," he said. "Why don't we order in tonight? And maybe you can take a short nap until the food arrives?"

A wave of irritation rose in her, unbeckoned. "Thanks," she said. "You have such a wonderful way with words."

To her chagrin, Richard laughed. And slapped her playfully on her rump. "Go take a nap," he said. "You'll feel better."

She was about to argue when she saw that Diane was nodding her head in agreement, and all the fight went out of her. Besides, the thought of shutting her eyes for a few minutes suddenly felt welcome.

But once she slipped under the top sheet and stretched out on the soft bed, she became even more aware of how deeply, inconceivably tired she truly was. The realization made her heart pound. It was a new kind of fatigue, this. Not the wet-noodle fatigue she would feel after swimming nine laps in the pool. Not the tiredness she used to feel in grad school after pulling an all-nighter, or the limp, hungover feeling after returning home from a party at four in the morning. Not even the exhaustion she'd felt when Diane was young and she would collapse in bed at the end of the day and fall asleep before Richard could turn off his night light. There had been something life-affirming and joyous about that kind of tiredness. What she felt now was different—a darkness shading the edges of her fatigue, a feeling that was almost pain, not the muscle-burning fatigue of yore but something that seeped from her very bones. Despite the air conditioning in the room, a film of perspiration formed on Armaiti's face. She knew that the two people she loved most in the world were in the next room, only a yell away, that they would burst in at the slightest cry for help. But still, she felt irreducibly alone. For the first time since the diagnosis, she had an intimation of what death would be like. She would die alone. And not in twenty or thirty years, either. She would die alone, and soon. Even if Richard and Diane were by her bedside, as they undoubtedly would be, she would die alone. She felt dizzy with panic at the thought and kicked off the top sheet, not wanting to be by herself for another second. But it required energy to leap out of bed, to drive her toes into her slippers, and hurry out of the room and rejoin the living. And Armaiti found that she didn't have it in her. A sob expanded like a balloon in the back of her throat.

Maybe it wasn't too late to start the radiation. Richard and Diane had been right all along—she had been a stupid, stubborn fool for refusing treatment. No wonder her daughter sometimes looked at her like she was some kind of a monster. Because only monsters chose death. Giving in to death without a fight was unnatural, irresponsible, an abdication of sorts. The desire to live was cross-stitched into every living thing. Why had she thought she was any different? Every organism on earth, every bug and plant, scuttled, strained, grew, or flew toward life. Maybe that was what the soul that dear Mamma used to talk about really was—that hollow cup of fire, that straining toward the sun, that instinct that was buried deep inside every breathing thing. How clear this seemed to her right now, in this silent room.

Inviting Laleh and the others to join her had been another mistake, Armaiti thought. What the hell were they coming all this distance for? To see her corpse? Because that's what her body felt like, heavy, weighed down with sandbags. Planning for their visit had been a great diversion, but it had also prevented her from taking her daughter's entreaties seriously. How easily she had pivoted from the graveness of her diagnosis to the excitement about their coming. As if she were planning a regular college reunion, for God's sake. When the truth was, she could barely lift her head from the pillow.

"I can't. I can't lift my head from the pillow," she heard herself say groggily when Richard shook her awake a half hour later.

"Sorry. You can sleep again after you eat."

"I'm not hungry."

"You haven't eaten all day. Come on, now."

"First you force me to sleep. Then you force me to wake up," she grumbled, even as she rolled out of bed.

"Sorry," he said again.

She smiled thinly. "I'll be there in a sec. Let me tidy up a bit."

In the bathroom, she studied herself in a mirror whose edges were studded with seashells. How thrilled Richard and Diane would be if she announced that she would start the radiation as soon as they returned, that she had come to her senses, that they had been right all along. But could she give them this? "Mummy," Armaiti whispered. "Help me. What should I do?" As if in response, she saw her mother's gaunt, haggard face as she lay dying. Her mother, Jerbanu, a timid, diffident woman, had always done the right thing, had always played by the rules, had treated her doctors as if they were gods and their advice as if it were gospel, and still she had died a slow, miserable death. This is what you didn't factor in earlier, Armaiti told herself, when you were thinking of immortal souls and unnatural behavior. The fact that the math doesn't add up, that the odds are awful, regardless. If only it were a choice between living and dying. If only. But it isn't. It's between dying on your own terms and dying on someone else's.

She stared at her reflection for another second, then turned away, eager to rejoin her family. Her mind was made up. She would exit on her own terms.

As always, Richard had ordered too much food. Armaiti's stomach turned as she saw the row of take-out containers on the kitchen counter. "We're having a party?" she muttered and missed the flame that leapt into Richard's eye.

"We're hungry, even if you're not," he snapped abruptly.

Armaiti startled at his tone and glanced over to where Diane sat hunched over her plate at the kitchen table. Richard always got pissy when he was hungry, she reminded herself. "Go ahead and eat, then," she said, but Richard shook his head and handed her an empty plate. She eyed the contents of the containers, her stomach heaving as she saw the various meats swimming in a sea of brown sauce. She took two tablespoons of fried rice, a pinch of noodles, and spooned some kung pao chicken onto her rice.

"That's all you're gonna eat?" Diane demanded as she took

her place at the table and Armaiti chafed against her proprietary tone. "For now," she said mildly. She would be lucky if she could get two teaspoons of this meal down. How could she have ever loved Chinese food? How could Diane and Richard sit beside her and wolf down this gruel? Didn't they know how sick the smells were making her?

As she ate, she tried to ignore the anxious looks Richard was casting her way, the way his eyes followed the movement of her fork from the plate to her mouth. She knew her hand was trembling, and hated that he had noticed. Those sky-blue eyes that she had always loved now seemed like the eyes of some bird of prey, watchful, attentive, shiny, not missing a thing. A dull feeling slowly built inside Armaiti's chest, and it took her a few minutes to realize that it was anger.

Richard finished the last of his meal and rose to get seconds. "I'll get you some more while I'm up," he said, reaching for Armaiti's plate.

She put her hand across her plate to prevent him from picking it up. It was a white plate with a navy-blue border and a blue star in the center. "I'm not done with this," she said.

Richard sighed. "You need to keep your strength up, Armaiti," he said patiently. "You know what the doctor said about . . ."

Armaiti loosened her grip on the plate for a second and then knocked it off the table with the back of her hand. Richard jerked back as the plate shattered by his feet on the tile floor. "What the—?"

She was half-aware that Diane was watching them with her mouth open, looking from one to the other. But the feeling in her chest was sharper now, and the plate had smashed with such a satisfying sound that her hand moved involuntarily toward Richard's empty plate, and before he could stop her it joined

its companion on the floor. He leapt back. "Armaiti!" he thundered. "Are you nuts? What do you think you're doing?"

"Mom—"

The fatigue that had almost turned her bones to ash earlier
now made her eyes burn with anger. "What I'm doing is, I'm
asking you to leave me alone. To stop watching me. Stop monitoring everything I eat or do or say. The two of you will put
me in my grave sooner than necessary if you keep this up." She
heard her voice, thick with anger, unrecognizable, and she knew
she was frightening them, but she didn't care. The anger was
bringing her back to life, pulling her away from that dark, tomb-
like room where an hour ago she had first seen the cold, clammy
outline of death.

"I'd stop watching you if you'd take care of yourself," Richard snapped.

She shook her head. "You're not getting it, Richard. I have a
friggin' brain tumor. You think fried rice is gonna cure that?"

Richard blinked rapidly. "That's low, Armaiti. Really low."
He turned away from her, his Adam's apple moving compulsively.

"No. What's low is you patronizing me. Treating me like an
imbecile. Telling me when to sleep and what—"

"Mom, please." Diane's voice was appeasing. "We're only
trying to help."

"Don't. Don't help me. You *can't* help me. Don't you see?"
And now the tears came, pouring down her cheeks. "I'm dying,"
she whispered. "And you can't help me."

"Mom. Don't."

"And I don't want to. I don't want to die." There. She was
saying the words. But why did the fact that she was saying them
surprise her so? Why hadn't she said them earlier? Had she been
so deluded, had she really tried to be so brave for Diane's sake

that she had actually convinced herself that dying wasn't a big deal? Who had she fooled? No one except perhaps herself.

But apparently she wasn't done. Because she heard herself say, "I want to live. To see my only child marry. To hold my grandchildren." She turned toward Richard, whose blue eyes were bloodshot. "To live to a ripe old age. A ripe, old age."

The fatigue was blinding her now, and she rested her head on the cherry table, feeling the cool of it against her flushed cheek. Diane got up and stood over her and stroked her hair. "Mom. C'mon, now. It's okay. Everything's okay."

But Richard, she noticed, didn't console her. Instead, while she sobbed quietly into the wood of the table, he found the broom and swept up the pieces of broken china. "I'm sorry," she began, but he shook his head dismissively.

"Don't worry about it." And then, as if he couldn't help himself, "Maybe you should go back to bed."

She sighed and rose slowly to her feet. She stood on her toes to give him a kiss on the cheek but his eyes were opaque. She had hurt Richard. But even more than that, she had scared him, Armaiti realized, by revealing the full extent of her anguish. She would not even allow herself to think of what her little scene had cost her daughter. But the look on Diane's pale face as she walked her to the bedroom was her answer.

"Stay up with your dad for a bit," she whispered to Diane just before closing her eyes.

She fell into a deep sleep until two a.m. and then was wide awake, her mind replaying what had transpired in the kitchen. Not a good way to start your vacation, she scolded herself. As for smashing those expensive plates in a house that they were guests in, her mother would have been appalled. But, God, Richard had pissed her off.

But the next minute, her lifelong loyalty to Richard rose to the surface and made her defend his actions. He meant well, Richard. He had always protected her, and the fact that she now had cancer was no reason for him to stop, or for her to get sensitive about it, was it?

She tossed back her covers and got out of bed. She waited until her eyes adjusted to the dark and then made her way out of her room and across the hallway to where Richard slept. She stood in the doorway of his room for a second and then moved to the edge of his bed. "You asleep?" she asked in a low voice.

"I'm awake," he answered immediately, although she could hear the grogginess in his voice. "Are you all right?"

"Fine," she whispered. "Is it okay if I spend the night with you?"

There was the slightest of pauses before Richard shifted in bed to make room for her and said, "Sure." His voice was neutral, but she knew he had heard and accepted her apology.

They had never slept in the same bed since the divorce. No matter where they traveled, Armaiti had insisted on having her own bedroom. Her insistence had hurt Richard deeply, she knew, and now she had no more desire to hurt him. *Now I lay down my sword and shield.* She got under the covers and rolled onto her left side, resting her body against his. He spooned her, and she took his hand and held it against her chest. She felt his breath in her ear, and it sounded exactly like the breathing of the ocean outside their window. She had not slept in the same bed as Richard for five years and yet it felt like it had been only yesterday, like sleeping under an old quilt. "This is nice," she murmured and felt him nodding behind her. "It is," he replied.

Richard left early the next morning for a meeting, promising to call her when they broke for lunch. Armaiti stayed in bed for another half hour and then rose and wandered into the kitchen. Richard had already started the coffee and she poured herself a cup. She stared out of the glass doors to the ocean. The fatigue from last evening had thankfully left her and she felt a whimpering gratitude. She felt like she was once again occupying her own body, that the woman who had had a meltdown in this kitchen yesterday was a stranger she was happy not to get to know.

Armaiti poured herself another cup of coffee as she pondered whether to wake Diane up or go for a walk alone. This house was giving her the heebie-jeebies. Too rich for my blood, she thought. The cost of the chandelier that hung in the foyer alone could have kept a family of eight in India alive for years. Not that she, too, had not gotten used to the finer things in life. Richard, after all, came from money, the only son of a prosperous Boston businessman who had made his fortune in real estate. And Richard had not done too poorly in his own export business. The cottage in Nantucket, which now belonged to him and his sister, was worth several million dollars. But this house felt different. The Nantucket house was a scruffy, comfortable place, where sand and dog hair and wet swim trunks and yellowing paperbacks and brutally competitive Scrabble games all merged into one happy, messy stew. The tea kettle that had a permanent place on the old kitchen stove was dented and looked as if it hadn't been cleaned properly since Richard's parents had bought the house in 1954. The beautiful hardwood floors were polished but scratched, and nobody would ever dream of shooing Daisy, Jordon's beloved basset hound, off the old leather couch. By contrast, the Ponte Vedra house was a monument, something that one felt like buying admission tickets to before entering.

She was just slipping on her sandals when Diane entered the kitchen, her curly hair a crazy mess on her head. Armaiti grimaced as she caught the wary, guarded look her daughter flashed her way. Poor Diane. What a fright she'd given her last night.

"Good morning, sweetheart," she said in her most energetic voice.

Diane immediately looked relieved. "Good morning," she said. "What's with all the noise?"

"Oh, sorry. I thought I was being quiet."

Diane smiled. "It's okay. I couldn't sleep, anyway. For once." She noticed the sandals. "You going for a walk? Dad's left?"

"Yes and yes. Want to come?"

"If you give me a couple of minutes to change."

"Don't change too much." It was an old joke between them and Diane rolled her eyes before she left the room.

The sun was a red bindi dot on the forehead of the sky as they started their walk. The sea was calm this morning and the powdered-sugar sand stretched for miles in either direction. Ahead of them, a little girl in a red swimsuit turned cartwheels on the sand as her grandparents walked a few paces behind her. An old Asian woman stopped every few seconds to pick up seashells, which she placed inside a cloth bag. Armaiti swerved as a large black dog chasing a Frisbee almost knocked her over. She brushed away the apologetic "Sorry" that the young man throwing the Frisbee mouthed toward her.

"So. I need to apologize for last night," Armaiti began, but Diane shook her head.

"Mom. It's okay. You were just having a bad night, is all. It's okay. Honest. Dad's fine, too."

Armaiti smiled. I wish Mamma was alive to see Diane, she thought. She would've been so proud of her granddaughter.

They walked along the edge of the ocean in peaceful silence, Armaiti struggling occasionally to keep up with her daughter's stride, but determined not to slow her down. But after a few minutes a thin film of sweat covered her body, and despite the warm breeze, she shivered. Her breathing must've grown more jagged, too, because Diane stopped suddenly and pointed to the hard, tamped sand. "Let's sit for a few minutes," she said, and Armaiti nodded gratefully.

Growing up in Bombay, she had always felt the sea to be as familiar as the sidewalk outside her home. But today it felt strange and foreboding to her, an undiscovered, undulating continent, mysterious and unchartered, harboring secrets and hidden things, home to creatures and life forms she knew nothing about. All her life she had believed she knew the ocean, but now she realized that its workings had been kept from her as surely as if it were from a different planet—the ridges and valleys of the ocean floor, the continual bloodbath where bigger creatures preyed on smaller ones, the millions of human and animal bones and the debris from shipwrecks and plane crashes that lay at its bottom.

The clarifying principle. The phrase came into her head so clearly and fully formed, she thought for a moment that someone had said it out loud. But it was just Diane and herself, sitting on the warm sand, and her daughter was staring straight ahead. Besides, the phrase wasn't new. She had heard it before—but where? And then she remembered. Of course. During her student activist days it was a phrase they bandied about all the time. Every time they planned a strike or each time they planned a protest outside a college or a factory gate, someone would ask, "Okay, so why are we doing this? What's the clarifying principle here? What's our rationale for this?"

Death was the ultimate clarifying principle. Sitting at the water's edge, watching the foamy white curl of the waves, Armaiti saw the curvature of the earth, saw everything around her with a new attentiveness. She felt as if she had accidentally wandered backstage and was witnessing the stagecraft that went into making the planet—gravity, magnetic fields, the earth's burning core. She was seeing the mechanisms of the universe, the hidden things that controlled this big, blue clockwork of a planet. Armaiti felt her eyes widen, as if to better see it all, to take in, to absorb, to reach that point where she felt her bones melt into this warm sand, where the hot blood in her body became the salt water of the sea, where her breathing and the breathing of the ocean became one. This was probably the last time in her life she would visit the ocean; from now on she would simply have to listen to the rumbling of her blood to know that she carried it within her.

The clarifying principle: she was not the only one who was dying. She looked around the beach and saw how it would appear a hundred years from now. That little girl in the red swimsuit doing cartwheels on this beach would be a pile of bones in a cemetery somewhere. The descendants of the seagulls whose cries sounded alternatively like shrieks of laughter and cries of complaint would all be dead, even the progeny of the little chicks who were bobbing up and down on one foot in front of her. All that would be left of the hunched Asian woman they had seen earlier would be a brownish-yellow photograph that a grandchild might someday find in an old trunk. Every fish that currently swam in the water would be dead and the seashells that she was crunching under her feet like crisp autumn leaves would have become sand that another child would use to build a new castle. Only the ocean, the ocean would still roar, magnificent and proud, and that, too, only if this dreadful species that she belonged to didn't figure out a way to screw it up completely.

Her thoughts did not depress her. Rather, all seemed startlingly clear: it was a finite planet, with finite resources. Someone—she—had to go to make room for new life. Death was simply a way to sweep the planet clean.

She couldn't decide if she was being silly or wise, sentimental or profound. But for the first time since she'd received the news of her dying, she felt at peace.

She wanted to share this insight with her daughter, give Diane something she could remember and hold on to during the hard, cold months that were inevitably to come. Something pure and beautiful to make up for last night. She looked at Diane's clear, sharp profile, and as if on cue Diane said, "What?"

But what came out was simply, "It's peaceful here. I feel—peaceful."

"Good." Diane squeezed her hand. "I'm so glad."

And Armaiti had a great feeling of letdown, as if she had failed in some important parental duty.

"Shall we walk some more?" Diane murmured, her hand still resting on top of her mother's.

"In a moment. You want to walk ahead, baby?"

Diane leapt to her feet. "Just for a few minutes," she said. "I'll look for you on the way back, okay?"

She nodded and followed her daughter's jaunty, self-assured walk down the beach. After all this time, it still took her breath away, that this beautiful, confident girl was hers. Armaiti smiled to herself. Last night was the closest she'd come to giving in to Diane, questioning her right to live on her own terms. But she had no such doubts now. The clarifying principle made clear the impermanence of things. It was an illusion, all of it—this life that they clung to, this earth that they battled over—a collective exercise in self-deception. The world was perishable. She wasn't the only one who was dying. Even love, that great, cherished human commodity, even love was not forever or immortal. It was stupid and dishonest to pretend that it was. In order to live, love needed to be remembered. In seventy years or so, there would be no one left on earth who would remember her.

Diane had disappeared into the haze of the morning's sunlight and Armaiti looked away to face the ocean again, and as she did, she felt something come loose inside her head. That's how she remembered the feeling later, as if a mechanical part, a knob, say, had come loose inside her head and had caused instant dizziness and blurriness of vision. The world around her, so sharp just a second ago, disappeared and became a fuzzy image cast by an old, creaking projector. Her own feet as she sat on the sand, were out of focus. The ocean lost its distinctive shape and form, gave up the individuality of each wave to become a diffused, amorphous, gray-blue mass.

The inclination was to panic, of course. Every cell, every electrical impulse in her body was ready for battle, to go into overdrive. And Armaiti gave in to her fear, caught in its undertow. She blinked furiously and shut her eyes but each time she opened them the world remained unclear. She looked around to see if Diane was heading back, but the beach looked deserted and the few figures on it seemed unrecognizable. Even in her panic, the irony registered—a few minutes ago she had followed her daughter's walk with her eyes. Now, she wouldn't be able to distinguish Diane's figure from those of strangers. As the moments ticked by, she fought to control her fear. She would not cry for help, she wouldn't. It would frighten Diane to see a crowd of people gathered around her. Besides, Diane would be back this way in a little while. Maybe her vision would right itself by then. Even if it didn't, even if it took a little longer, it didn't matter. Diane would help her up, and the two of them would make their way back to the house. It was not as if she were blind or anything. She could see. This was not much different than the blurriness that occurred after the doctor dilated her pupils during an eye exam. Maybe it was a side effect of the steroids. Or even the changes in pressure from flying. It had been a choppy flight—maybe her ears were still clogged.

But even as she came up with comforting scenarios, another thought swept through her mind like backwash, the dark knowledge gleaned from late-night readings about her condition on the Internet. This is it, she thought. The slow, relentless beginning of the end.

20

Nishta had flung the hood of her hijab to uncover her head as soon as they'd left her neighborhood. After she and Mumtaz got out of the cab in front of the Mahalaxmi temple, she willed herself to not lower the veil again, despite the strangeness of bright sunshine prickling her face.

Disoriented, shaky, unused to the sun in her eyes, she held Mumtaz's hand as they crossed the busy street and headed toward Tirupathi Apartments, where she knew Adish and Laleh would be waiting. Despite the crowd, she spotted Laleh immediately and waved to her. "Hey, girl," Laleh beamed as they approached her.

"Hi," Nishta said. She felt breathless, her head reeling from the novelty of being in an unfamiliar neighborhood, of standing on the sidewalk chatting to Laleh as if it were the most natural thing in the world. She looked around. "Did Adish not come?"

"He's here somewhere. You know how he is—can't stand still for even a second." Laleh extended her hand. "Hi, Mumtaz. I'm Laleh. I can't believe how long it's been. You were a kid when we last saw you."

A man was hurrying over to them and Nishta saw that it was Adish—sweet, gentle Adish, looking the same as ever, just a little grayer and more plump, but with the same smiling eyes and the fleshy lips that gave him a slightly open-mouthed look. She started to say hello and promptly burst into tears.

Adish looked shocked. "Arre, Nishta. Don't cry, yaar. What's the matter?"

Laleh threw an understanding look her way. "He always has this effect on women," she said drolly to Mumtaz, who chuckled dutifully.

Adish moved to put a comforting arm around Nishta and then hesitated, as if her cream-colored burkha made this simple, informal gesture difficult. "It's okay, Nishta," he murmured. "You are safe here."

"I'm all right." She smiled, wiping her tears with the back of her hand. "Really. I just . . . it's so good to see you, Adish."

He grinned, the dimples making deep grooves into his pudgy cheeks. "My pleasure, yaar."

Beside her, Mumtaz shifted. "What time is the appointment? We can't be late."

"We're in good shape," he replied. "But I want to go over a few things, achha? Some questions they will ask." He pivoted toward Nishta. "Basically, they want to make sure you're not going to overstay your visa, okay? So anything you can say to convince them you're coming back is good. What papers did you bring? Bank statements? Tax returns?"

"I brought this." Thrusting her hand into the pocket of her robe, Nishta fished out a business card for Ahmed Electronics. "This is all I could come up with—on short notice." She did not mention that their bank balance was small enough to be inconsequential in establishing her motives for returning to India.

Adish blanched. He glanced quickly at Laleh and then recovered. "Okay," he said. "Well, we have the e-mail from Armaiti and the letter from her doctor. That should help."

Nishta smiled. "Don't worry," she said. "It will be enough." She glanced at the entrance. "Should I make my way in?"

"Yeah. They'll take you by bus to the embassy. Once you're there, things should move pretty fast. We'll be here when you return, okay?"

Laleh stepped up and squeezed Nishta's shoulder. "Stay calm," she said. "Good luck."

Twenty minutes later, the shuttle dropped her off at the embassy. She sat on a wooden bench until it was her turn. Nishta's heart was pounding as she was directed toward an elderly immigration officer. This is it, she said to herself. It's all up to you. Everything ends here if you don't get the visa.

"Good morning," she said brightly, into the glass partition that divided them.

The man looked up at her briefly. "Morning," he mumbled. "May I ask the reason for your visit to the United States?"

"I have a friend who is very sick." She slid the note from Armaiti's doctor under the glass and stood silently as he reviewed it. When he looked up, his face was impassive. "How long will you be away?"

"Maybe three weeks or so." Her voice shook and she hoped he hadn't caught it.

The American nodded, gazing at her appraisingly as he did so. Nishta forced herself to look him in the eye. "You travelin' alone?" he asked.

"With two of my friends. We were all in college together." She casually mentioned the name of the prestigious South Bombay college she'd attended and the fact that she'd majored in French. She saw the man's eyes widen slightly at the last detail. "So, you parlez-vous français?" he said.

She smiled. "Oui, je sais parler français."

"Indeed." The officer leafed through some other documents and then looked up. "Here's the bottom line," he said. "I don't see any evidence of your finances here. I need some sort of guarantee that you'll return to India after your stay."

There it was. Her chance to get it right. Nishta drew herself up to her full height and cocked an eyebrow. "Well, my husband and I are not rich, if that's what you mean. My friends are buying my plane ticket. But my husband is here. We were college sweethearts. And he's here in India. That's your guarantee."

She saw the man's face break into a startled smile, as if he had just tasted something sweet. And then he blushed. In that moment, she knew that she had won. She had just written her ticket out of India.

Her performance, her conjuring and channeling of her former self, surprised even herself. And it made her hopeful as she exited the embassy. She had believed that the old Nishta was dead, smothered under the weight of the Zoha she'd become. But Nishta had come roaring back and had not been satisfied until she'd earned—yes, earned—her U.S. visa. Had not relaxed until the officer had stamped her passport and said, "Good luck with your visit, my dear."

Three pairs of eyes turned to look at her when she emerged from the compound and onto the street; three faces gazed at her in anticipation, eager to be elated, prepared for disappointment, ready to take their cues from her. She savored her moment of power. Then she smiled and said, "Got it," and Adish hooted and Lal hugged her and Mumtaz stood proudly, tears glittering in her eyes. "Congratuations, bhabi," she said.

Nishta touched her right hand to her forehead in a gesture of thanks. "Without you . . ." she began, but Mumtaz brushed her thanks away.

"Anything for you, Zoha jaan," she said.

"Kavita called while you were in," Lal broke in. "She wants to know if we can all meet for lunch."

Nishta shook her head in regret. "We can't," she said. "I have to pick up my niece in a few hours. And traffic is so bad . . ."

Adish checked his watch. "I'll get you home with time to spare," he said. "I promise. Come on. It's Kavita's birthday the day after. You will be my present to her."

Half an hour later, they were sitting at the Hotel Marine Plaza, overlooking the sea. Nishta stared at the water greedily. She and Iqbal hardly ever went to the seaside anymore. She leaned out of the large window, taking deep breaths, inhaling the moist, salty air.

"Remember how we used to go to the seaside for hours?" Kavita said to her before turning to Mumtaz. "We used to bunk classes and come here instead," she explained.

"And yet all of you were good students," Mumtaz said. There was a breathless quality to her voice that Nishta recognized as the eternal tone of the little sister looking up to her big brother's friends. How unimaginable, how foreign we must've all seemed to Iqbal's family the few times we visited him, she thought. How brave Iqbal had been in taking his bohemian, unconventional college friends to meet his conservative parents. She felt her heart spasm at the memory of those days.

Adish had excused himself soon after they were seated and now he walked back to their table, talking into his iPhone. "It's Joseph," he whispered to Laleh as she looked at him inquiringly. "I called him. I just want to know what dates are available." He sat at the table and wrote on the paper napkin as he spoke into the phone. "Okay, bossie, keep looking. I want a few more options, okay? Phone me later tonight. Ciao."

He turned to face Mumtaz and Nishta. "That was my travel agent. He gave me a few possible flights." He looked at the napkin, scratched something out and looked up again. "How are we going to get you out of the house, Nishta? Is there any way to get through to Iqbal? To appeal to him? I hate doing this surreptitiously, yaar."

A furious Laleh kicked him under the table but he ignored her. He stared at Nishta, who looked down at the plate in front of her. "I cannot talk to Iqbal," she said finally. "If I could think of another way to do this, I would."

"She's right," Mumtaz said. "I know my brother—once he makes up his mind, Allah Himself cannot make him change. Believe me, I know," she added, and there was something so bitter in her voice, it made them all look up.

Adish opened his mouth to say something but Lal spoke first. "I think it's time to stop thinking about Iqbal and start thinking about Nishta. She's made clear that she wants to go to see Armaiti. That's good enough for me."

She looked directly at Adish, who held her gaze for a second before lowering his eyes. "Okay. Guess I know when I'm outnumbered," he said, but when he looked up none of the four women looking back at him was smiling. "Okay," he repeated. "How soon can everyone leave?"

"Maybe in three weeks or so?" Nishta started to say when Kavita interrupted.

"That's too long. We don't have that long."

"Meaning?"

"Meaning Diane called this morning. With bad news, I'm afraid. Armaiti's had a setback."

"What?" Laleh said.

"Ya Allah," Mumtaz breathed.

"It happened a few days ago, while they were in Florida. It seems her vision is pretty bad. And her balance. Her right leg has suddenly gotten very weak." Kavita's voice trembled. "Anyway, what I'm thinking is, we should go now. I mean, soon. As soon as we can."

There was a second's silence as nobody dared make eye contact with another. Mumtaz spoke first. "I will help," she said to Nishta. "I will get you out. Don't delay, bhabi. Otherwise, your trip will be futile."

And Nishta buried the immediate, treacherous thought: But that's not the whole reason for my leaving. She had said as much to Laleh on the way to Adish's car, as she and Laleh fell behind Mumtaz and Adish, told her that her intention was to not return to Iqbal at the end of three weeks. "Does Mumtaz know about this?" Laleh had whispered and she had shaken her head no, guilt making her cheeks burn.

Now Nishta said, "Iqbal comes home late on Thursdays. He has a trustees' meeting at his mosque on that day. Can we leave on a Thursday?"

"I'll work on it," Adish said promptly. "Actually, a weekday is probably better, anyway. Flights are hard right now—peak summer vacation time and all. But I'm sure Joseph can pull a few strings."

"Mr. Fixit," Kavita and Laleh said in unison and their chuckle cast away the somberness that had descended on them. "That was his name in college," Nishta explained to Mumtaz. "Any problem you had, you went to Adish."

Laleh stroked her husband's arm affectionately. The waiter came with their drinks and they ordered their meal. When he left, Mumtaz said, "A plan is emerging in my head. I think I know how to get you out of the house on that day."

"You're good at this subterfuge game, Mumtaz," Laleh said. "We could've used you during our student days."

Mumtaz flashed a broad smile. "I grew up on Enid Blyton," she said. "*Secret Seven, Five Find-Outers*. All those adventure books. And later, Nancy Drew. Now my children read them. So it's all here." She tapped her head with her index finger. She turned toward Nishta. "Don't worry, bhabi. You're going to America. It's as good as done. In fact, you're already there. Just visualize it."

She turned to face Laleh and Kavita, who were exchanging bemused smiles. "My other favorite author is Norman Vincent Peale," she declared. "I believe in the power of positive thinking."

BOOK
TWO

BOOK
TWO

21

One o'clock in the morning and sleep had disappeared, much as she hoped to disappear from home three days from now. Nishta lay on her back, staring at the ceiling, listening to the sounds of the city at night—the firecracker-like *phat-phat* sound of motorbike engines, the occasional howling of a nearby dog, answered by another stray down the street, the drift of voices as small groups of young men walked down the street, making no allowances for the sleeping world, the dry heaves of the old trucks grinding their way down the road. She remembered with a sharp longing her bedroom in her parents' large, beautiful flat. How muffled the sounds of the night had seemed in that bedroom. But then she recalled how she had tossed and turned in her single bed, her body aching for the man who now slept beside her, and she smiled mirthlessly at the irony. What was that wonderful quote by Truman Capote? More tears have been shed over answered prayers than unanswered ones.

Iqbal mumbled something in his sleep and she turned her head slightly to look at him. He was lying on his side, and the light from the fluorescent streetlamp allowed her to study his features. As she had a million times, she took in the beautiful, delicate face—the long eyelashes, the thin, curved lips above the bearded chin. As Nishta watched, Iqbal's hand twitched, and she fought the urge to cover it with hers. He was frowning now and she strained to hear what he was muttering. Pity swept over Nishta. The agitation that filled Iqbal's days also dominated his nights. Iqbal deserved better, she suddenly thought. Maybe her foreignness, her Hinduness, had prevented her from recognizing or taking seriously the grievances that stuck to him like postage stamps. Maybe, as he had recently admitted, he had died a million deaths trying to shelter her against the everyday bigotries and discrimination that he had faced because of their marriage. Maybe when they counted the casualties and death toll from the 1993 riots, they should've counted men like Iqbal also, good, open-hearted men who died a spiritual death in those riots, men whose lives were spared but whose spirits burned along with those who were set on fire in their homes or out on the streets, whom the mad mobs consecrated with gasoline and then set aflame. Men who learned the wrong lessons from those riots, who came to believe that all that stood between them and the fire next time was the strength that came from numbers, who moved into dense, overcrowded bastis to live among their own kind, who subjected themselves to living with people with whom they shared a religion and not much else.

Nishta's throat ached with sorrow. Despite all that had happened between them, she loved the man sleeping next to her. Felt protective of him. Because despite the sober attire and attitude, his humorless demeanor, the bearded visage, the religious garb, the twinkle-eyed college boy he had once been occasionally shone through. She saw it in his wide smile sometimes when he wasn't being guarded, or when his eyes grew misty when an old song from a 1950s Hindi film came on the radio, or when he came home drenched from a downpour and grinning like a schoolboy.

She realized with a pang of regret that she had conveyed a one-dimensional portrayal of Iqbal to Laleh and Kavita. She had fed them an easy caricature—young Socialist grows up to become a conservative Muslim—and although shocked and disappointed, they had accepted her version. But she remembered now how beside himself Iqbal had been when he'd heard about the Taliban's destruction of the Buddhist statues. "Savages," he'd sworn, his eyes blazing. "Barbarians. No right they are having. Those statues belong to the world." She remembered how upset he'd been after the planes had brought down the towers, how he'd looked at her with tears in his eyes and said, "Today is the worst day of my life. These people make me ashamed of my faith."

"Iqbal," she heard herself say. "Are you sleeping?"

He opened one eye and said, "Not anymore." But there was a smile in his voice and she was encouraged.

"Sorry. I can't sleep."

He leaned on his elbow and raised his head, stifling a yawn. "You're sick?"

"No, not sick. Just sad."

He was immediately alert. "Why, my bibi? Why sad?"

"I keep thinking about Armaiti." Even as she said these words, she came to a conclusion: Iqbal's reaction would determine whether she would leave or stay. Yes, three days before she was to leave for the airport, she was still ready to shut that door, to live out the rest of her days in this bed, with this man. But she had to believe that there was a reason to stay.

She waited. For him to respond. For the course of her destiny to be decided by what he said.

"No use thinking about sad things, Zoha," he finally said and she felt disappointment fall and settle like soot on her skin.

"How come you never slip and call me Nishta?" she said

inanely, to prevent him from hearing what her body was screaming—*You failed. I gave you a chance and you failed.*

"We're going to talk about your name in the middle of the night?" he asked mildly, and when she didn't respond, he added, "I have to work tomorrow. Try to sleep."

Her mouth puckered, as if she'd tasted something sour. She blinked back her tears as she realized that Iqbal was settling back into sleep, unaware of the agitation she was feeling. She waited long enough to steady her voice, and then she said, "Don't you care about Armaiti at all? Do you never think about the old days?"

He let out an exasperated hiss. "Woman. You don't have to get up each morning and take two trains just to reach work. So you can lie in bed and indulge in nostalgia. But some of us have mouths to feed. Now, what is it you want me to say?"

Was that suspicion she heard in his voice? Had she given something away? "Nothing," she said hastily. "Nothing I want you to say. It's just that—"

"You want me to say that I'm sorry about Armaiti? Someone I haven't talked to in donkey's years? Someone who moved to America and married a rich, fat American? Who has had a nice, cushy life and has never had to get up early and catch two trains to get to work? Let me tell you something, Zoha. If I'm to shed a tear, it won't be for people like Armaiti. If I'm going to cry, I'll cry for Umar. You remember Umar? Attends our mosque, works at the post office. Lung cancer at thirty-four. And still he delivers the post, walking around the streets of this filthy, polluted city. Why? Because his salary supports seven people. I'll cry for him before I'll cry for Armaiti."

Nishta trembled from the bitterness she heard in Iqbal's voice. "But she's our friend," she cried. "You yourself used to say that Armaiti was the sweetest person in college. Remember how she used to—?"

"This world is full of kind people, Zoha," Iqbal said. "But kind people didn't stop me from losing my job at the bank. Kind people didn't stop the genocide in Gujarat. And they won't keep Umar alive. And I must say, I'm surprised at your definition of friend. Someone who didn't care to contact you for over twenty-five years, who suddenly decides she must see you again before she passes away—that's a friend?"

"That's unfair." Nishta dug her fingernails into her hand to focus her anger. "We are the ones who pulled away from them. You began to act so peculiarly around our friends that it was easier for me to stay away rather than to make excuses for you all the time."

Iqbal was silent for so long that she wondered if she'd gone too far, but when he spoke his voice was distant and mild. "You've let one visit from the past turn your head, Zoha. You're still a child, beguiled by candy at the fair. These rich people, they're like cotton candy—sweet, but spun out of air." He yawned and turned on his side. "Your place is here, Zoha—with your husband and your in-laws. Now go to bed and let me sleep for a few hours in peace. Please."

He rolled on his side, his back to her and she listened in astonishment as Iqbal fell into his regular breathing in just a few moments. His house is on fire, his wife is burning next to him and he sleeps, she thought with wonder. Because his pitiless words had singed her, had made the last of her illusions go up in smoke. She wondered now why she had felt so tenderly toward him just a few moments ago, what had made her give him another chance. This emotional seesawing is the reason why you've spent all these years in hell, she scolded herself. You're like a dog that whimpers when kicked and then wags his tail each time his master pets him absentmindedly.

She turned her face on the pillow to look at Iqbal's bare

back. She had an urge to run her fingernails down that smooth back, to draw blood, to shock him out of the mask of complacency that he wore. And then she thought: He's no longer my responsibility, my work-in-progress. For the first time, she saw Iqbal as separate from her, unlinked, unrelated, an individual whose smiles, frowns, moodiness, laughter, sexual urges, illnesses, religious beliefs, were none of her business. She blinked her eyes in surprise at the revelation, and as she did, she felt Iqbal receding from her, saw the distance between their two bodies grow.

She had never understood the custom of a Muslim man being able to divorce his wife by merely repeating the word "talaq" three times:Talaq, talaq, talaq. I divorce you, I divorce you, I divorce you. It had always appeared too simple, too easy, like a child's recitation of a magical incantation. Now she understood something: that the words were merely an outward expression, a delayed airing of an emotional process that had already taken place. That indifference was the true divorce. After that, it was just words. After that, it was merely action.

So she didn't bother saying those severing words to her husband's sleeping back. Mumtaz was right. The departure for America had already happened. Now, Inshallah, there only remained the task of getting her corporeal body there.

Two o'clock and here he was, at the window seat in their living room, staring out at the dark waters of the sea and the blinking neon lights in the distance. He'd gotten out of bed a half hour ago, afraid of waking Laleh up because of his restless tossing and turning. The house was peaceful at this hour, the children safe in their bedrooms, his wife sleeping silently in theirs. Everything I love in this world is here, within my reach, Adish thought, and a soft joy came over him. But the next second, the dread that had woken him out of a deep sleep punctured his contentment.

He had woken up a half hour ago thinking about the hours and days after Nishta would leave on a plane with his wife and Kavita. Was there a way to keep Iqbal from ever finding out their involvement in getting Nishta out of the house? Probably not. So he had to figure out what Iqbal's reaction would be when he found out that he had betrayed him. Broken a promise he had made, after having looked him straight in the eye when he made it. What would Iqbal do? How far would he go to restore his sense of honor, to avenge the betrayal? That was the question he needed to answer: How far would Iqbal go? Adish thought over the possibilities. A cursory Internet search by Iqbal would reveal the name and location of Adish's business. A look in the phone book would yield his home address. What if Iqbal showed up here? On an evening when he was not home? When perhaps the children were home alone? What would he do? What if, dear God, what if Ferzin was alone at home?

Adish felt his heart pounding and forced himself to take some deep breaths. He tried to remember all the details of his lunch with Iqbal, sifted through the memory of his talk with Iqbal for any clues that could predict his future behavior. He recalled that Iqbal had done nothing to the pervert who had mo- lested Mumtaz. In the face of that grave an injury, he had kept quiet, been passive, had instead scuttled out of the neighbor- hood like a bloody mouse. Iqbal had always been a milquetoast, Adish thought, and the white beard couldn't cover the fact that he had a wobbly, weak chin.

Adish laughed as he realized what he was doing: reducing the threat of Iqbal by emasculating him. Who the hell was brave in the days following the 1993 riots? he asked himself. When all it took was one wrong move, a wrong look or word—hell, if you cleared your throat wrong you could end up dead. And suddenly Adish's cheeks burned with embarrassment at the rise of a long-buried memory.

South Bombay, where he lived, worked, and played had been mostly immune to the savage hatreds that had gripped much of the city, but upon Lal's insistence, he had stayed home from work for a few days. But on the fourth day, restless and bored, he had announced that he was going for a short walk. He had left his compound and headed toward the sea, which meant walking past the small slum on the way to the water. As he approached the slum he heard yelling and came upon a group of six men who were beating and kicking a young man who lay writhing in the dirt. He stopped, stunned. The first thing he realized was that the crowd of onlookers who usually congregated during any street fight was missing. In fact, the street was preternaturally calm and empty. Adish recognized a couple of the men, ne'er-do-wells who hung around the neighborhood and ran the occasional errand for him. "Ae!" he shouted out, all the authority of his class in his voice. "Stop. What the hell are you doing?"

They turned at the sound of his voice but their feet kept up their deadly dance. The man on the ground screamed in pain. Adish saw something gleam in the hands of one of the men. It was a knife. Adish saw something glint in all their eyes. It was malice and a kind of insolence he had never seen before. He shivered.

One of the men reluctantly tore himself out of the group and walked up to Adish. "What are you doing here, seth?" he asked dully. "No place for you to be."

Despite his fear, Adish felt his temper spike. "I'm going to the sea," he said gesturing. "Is that illegal? Or do you thugs now own the streets, also?"

The man smiled humorlessly. "We own nothing, seth. We

poor people. It's these Muslim dogs who own everything." He spat on the ground.

Out of the corner of his eye, Adish noticed that the others had stopped beating the man on the ground as they listened to what was transpiring between him and the man who stood in front of him. His hand curled inside his pants pocket to grip his cell phone. Have to phone the police, he thought.

He could tell from the man's eyes that he had followed the movement of his hand. "Listen," he began, but the man shook his head.

"No, Parsi seth," he said. "You listen. This is not your fight. We have nothing against you and your people. You turn around now and go home. Like a good Parsi schoolboy, you go home."

At this, the rest of the mob began to laugh and jeer. "Go home," they repeated. "Parsi bawaji," they teased.

Adish felt his face break out in sweat. Still, he stood his ground, trying to decide what to do next. "Let that man go," he said feebly, "and I will leave."

At this his confronter emitted a cry and raised his right hand in a threatening, chopping gesture. "Jao. Get lost. Last chance I'm giving you. Otherwise you will take that insect's place."

He had fled. The memory of his retreat made his cheeks burn with shame all these years later. He had not stopped walking until he had reached the safety of his building and then stood leaning against a wall in the lobby until he regained some control over his body. Laleh had looked up with a "Back so soon?" but he had merely shaken his head and muttered an evasive, "Nothing's stirring, not even a sparrow," before going into the living room and turning on the television set.

No wonder Iqbal had not confronted Mumtaz's molester, Adish now thought. That alone predicted nothing. Well, they would just have to be careful for a few days after Nishta left.

He'd talk to all the security guards in the building, warn them to screen any man who fit Iqbal's description. And then, after a few days, he'd pay Iqbal a visit. See if he could reason with him. When Laleh returned without Nishta, they would pretend to be shocked by her perfidy. Later, he could even offer Iqbal a job in one of his many companies, take him into the folds of his business empire. Double his salary. He could help Iqbal, he really could.

As for Nishta, God knows what was going to happen to her. This was something he'd tried to say to Laleh—that just because Nishta had decided not to return to India with the other two, didn't mean that she could stay. Richard had apparently told Armaiti that he would make sure that Nishta was safe, but what the hell did that mean? Armaiti, he had no doubt, would've moved heaven and earth to help Nishta. But Armaiti was fighting a monster illness. She would be in no position to help. Which meant they had to believe Richard, and how well did any of them know him?

Adish rubbed his forehead. He tried to calm the machine-gun thoughts firing in his head. He opened the sliding glass window a little bit more and breathed in the warm night air. As he shifted on the marble seat he felt a movement behind him. It was a rumpled-looking Ferzin. "Hi, Dad," she said. "I got up to get a glass of water. Why are you sitting here in the middle of the night?"

"Couldn't sleep, beta. Just thinking."

Ferzin sat down next to him, and he was suddenly very glad for the company. "What about?" she said.

He hesitated, unsure of how much to share with her. The children had been involved in their feverish plans to get Nishta out of the house and to the airport, had overheard many of their phone conversations with Mumtaz. "You know, just about the upcoming trip," he said vaguely.

Ferzin frowned. "You mean about Nishta auntie?"

"Yes. Among other things."

"How will Iqbal uncle react when he finds her gone?"

Adish looked at his daughter with relief. At least one other member of his family had the smarts to worry about this. Laleh, he knew, was treating this as some kind of game. No, that wasn't it exactly; it was that she had been more energized by plotting Nishta's escape than she had been by anything since their college days. The Laleh of the last two weeks had reminded him of the old Laleh—tireless, indefatigable, driven. Except that instead of planning a student demonstration she was planning the rest of Nishta's life. And she did not seem to realize how immeasurably higher the stakes were. If she had fretted for a second about Iqbal's reaction, she had never mentioned it.

"I don't know, deekra," he confessed. "That's what has me worried." He looked at his daughter, wondering how much to draw her into his circle of fear. Then he said, "But we'll have to be careful for a few days after they leave. You understand? If you're home alone, I don't want you to open the door unless you know who it is."

"I told you we should get a dog," Ferzin said promptly, and he laughed.

"God, you're your mother's daughter for sure. You two never miss an opportunity to press home your point."

She spread her arms apart in an elaborate gesture and then gave him a quick hug. "Don't worry so much, Dad. I'm sure it will be okay."

"Hope so."

She got up from the seat, yawned, and held out her hand. "Come on. Go to bed. You need to sleep."

He took her hand, bemused by the role reversal. Wasn't it just a blink of an eye ago when he was the one calming her nighttime fears, putting her to bed? "Thanks, sweetheart," he said. "It was nice talking to you at this hour."

"Just don't make it a habit," she said as she disappeared into the kitchen.

———

She must've fallen asleep at the drafting table, because she was woken by her mother shaking her by the shoulders. "Oi, Kavita beti," the older woman said. "What kind of a life is this, working so hard? Get up now and sleep properly, in your bed."

She woke up with a groan and stared bleary-eyed at her mother. "What is it?" she asked.

"I got up to use the bathroom and saw your light was still on," Ma said. "Do you know what time it is?"

"I'm leaving in three days, Ma. I have to finish this project before I can go."

"Project-froject be hanged. Who will look after you in 'Merica if you get sick?" the old woman cried. "Even as a child, you got sick if you didn't get enough rest."

Kavita grinned. "I'll sleep on the plane." But she leaned forward on her stool and rested her head on her mother's belly.

"It's my job to worry," Ma said, stroking her hair. "After I'm dead and gone, no one will worry about you."

Kavita peered up at her mother. "Will you be all right, with me away?" she said seriously. "Rohit has promised he will stop by often." She had badgered her irresponsible brother into that promise.

"Pscht." Ma made a dismissive sound. "Tell him not to bother," she said. "All he cares about is his maharani wife and his spoiled-rotten son. I'll be fine with my Rekha looking after me." Rekha was the twenty-two-year-old servant who had started working for them when she was fifteen.

"That's the only reason I'm going—because Rekha is staying here at night," Kavita murmured. "But you phone me night or day if anything is wrong, okay?"

Ma got the woe-is-me look on her face that she usually did when Kavita went away. "I'll be fine," she said. "God takes care of the sick and feeble."

Kavita turned away to hide her smile. Ma could be so dramatic.

The old woman began to roll the blueprint on Kavita's desk. "Now come on. Go to bed. Very late it's getting."

Kavita placed her hand on the drawing. "A few more minutes, Ma. You go on now. I'll be done soon, I promise. I have to fax this to Germany first thing in the morning."

Ma snorted but backed away. "You youngsters work much too hard," she muttered as she left the room.

Kavita smiled. Ma had no idea how much money it cost to run this household. Her father had left them a good inheritance, but without Kavita's well-paying job, the money would've run out long ago. And speaking of money, she needed to buy a few more gifts before they left for America. She looked at the clock. If she could get this project completed tonight, maybe she could go to Cottage Industries and buy some gifts before going into work tomorrow.

She and Laleh had gone shopping last weekend. They had bought a few outfits and shoes for Nishta to wear in America, knowing that she would have to sneak out of the house with the clothes on her back. Kavita had wanted to buy some kurtas and a few pairs of shalwar khameez for Armaiti but Lal had stopped her. "Ae," she'd said in the middle of FabIndia. "Maybe we shouldn't buy her so much? For one thing, we don't know Armaiti's size anymore, yaar. And also, you know, who knows how much longer . . ." Her voice had trailed away and they had not dared look at each other for a few moments. In the end, they had gone in together on a very nice silver-and-turquoise bracelet for Armaiti, but both women had lost their appetite for shopping and they soon gave up.

But she needed to buy more presents for Diane, Kavita thought. Diane would be their link to Armaiti in the coming months and she was determined to play a role in the girl's life. She resolved to go shopping the next morning.

She worked for another forty-five minutes, then collapsed on her bed with the night light still on—and immediately realized that her exhaustion was so deep as to make sleep impossible. After a few futile moments, she flung back the sheet and leapt out of bed. Ingrid would be on her way to work, and if she was lucky she'd catch her on her mobile.

"Hi," she said when Ingrid answered with a short "Da?"

She heard Ingrid's gasp of pleasure. "Kavita? What a nice surprise." There was a shuffling sound and then Ingrid said, "But it's the middle of the night there, no?"

She laughed. "Almost morning." She paused. "I was up working. And then I couldn't sleep."

"Well, your loss is my gain," Ingrid said warmly, and Kavita could've hugged her. "So? You all set? Ready to leave?"

"Not really. There's a million things to do. But I'll send the drawings of the Burnside project to you later today."

"I wasn't worried about that. But I'm worried about you. You going to be okay in America?"

"I think so. I mean, I know it will be hard. I don't really know what to expect from Armaiti, you know? I'm just hoping she doesn't look too sick. And there's the whole deal with Nishta. Just hope we get off smoothly."

"That's quite a plan you have there. To get Nishta out of the house."

Kavita chuckled. "That's Laleh and Mumtaz in action."

There was a short silence, and then Ingrid said, "You're gonna say something to Armaiti? About the past and all that?"

"I don't know." Kavita plucked at a small pimple on her cheek.

"I'll just have to wait and see. She may be too sick." She sighed heavily. "I wish you were coming with me."

"Me, too. But this is better. The four of you need this time with no interruptions." There was a suggestive pause. "And if I were there, there would be interruptions, if you know what I mean."

Kavita smiled.

"Besides, I'd be so jealous."

Kavita was stunned. Ingrid had practically built her own religion out of espousing the evils of jealousy. "Of what?"

"Of you and Armaiti. The fact that you loved her for so many years."

She was more moved than she could've anticipated. "You have nothing to be jealous of. That was—I was a girl then. A kid. What I have with you is . . ." She choked on her words, not wanting to betray the purity of her love for Armaiti while also trying to let Ingrid know how much she had come to value her.

"Hush, baby. Are you crying? That wasn't my intention. I'm sorry."

And then she was indeed crying. "I'm just tired," she said. "Sorry. I . . . I'll be glad when we get on that plane and when I see Armaiti. It's just not knowing what we'll find—" She shut up abruptly.

They chatted for a few more moments and then hung up. Kavita fell into a deep sleep minutes later.

The lovely things:

The reflection of the traffic lights on the slick asphalt streets of Bombay after a rain shower. The Atlantic Ocean during a thunderstorm, its waters turning silver and green and majestic.

A solitary squirrel racing on the smooth, white skin of a snowy lawn of a ski lodge in Colorado. The sand mandalas made by the Buddhist monks at the art museum.

She was in love. Hopelessly, helplessly, tenderly, in love with the world. A sob formed in Armaiti's throat as she lay on her couch, the weak afternoon light pouring in through the large windows. What she had believed was indignation or rage or a deep intolerance for injustice came down to this: she was irreducibly in love with this bewitching planet, this thrilling life, this heartbreaking species she belonged to, with its capacity for stupefying destruction and breathtaking magnanimity. It all astonished her—the vivid greens, the searing blue of the sky, the splendor of the ocean, the pockmarked perfection of the moon, the stunning grandeur of her own backyard. Yellow, Armaiti thought. You could devote an entire lifetime to the study of yellow.

Color. She was obsessed with color. There was the red of the Shiraz that Richard had opened the night before. The burnt orange of the handcrafted cherry table in the hallway. The glitter of a computer chip, the history of human intelligence shrunk into a capsule. The muted gold of this leather couch she was napping on. It made you greedy, intoxicated, made you want to open your mouth and bite into the richness of the world. It made you want to never leave it, never miss out on a day of this party, this wild carnival ride.

A tear rolled down Armaiti's cheek. This was the hardest time of the day, afternoon, when Diane was out running errands, when the house was quiet and still and all she wanted to do was breathe alongside billions of others. The quiet hour when thoughts became prayers—*I want a few more years, please. I want to live. Pain-free, of course*—and prayers devolved into bargains.

She wiped the tear away and stared at the ceiling, her mind careening between past and present.

The lovely things:

Coming home from college to find her mother asleep and waking her up with a kiss on the forehead. The green misty hills of Mahabaleshwar the summer before Daddy died. Seeing a double rainbow the day Kavita and she had skipped class and gone to the beach. The dogwoods flowering in Harvard Yard as Richard kissed her deeply and tenderly, that first time. Richard's pale, strong hand on her darker body, his fingers spread out across her pregnant belly. Singing along to Joan Baez's "Honest Lullaby" as Diane played on the floor with her building blocks.

Potatoes boiling on the stove, the wintry afternoon light pouring into her kitchen as the cats dozed and purred on the kitchen table. Diane coming home from preschool, jabbering away about her day, her upturned face a flower in the sun. George Winston's "Pachelbel's Canon" playing on the stereo on Christmas morning. A Thanksgiving Day when Richard, Diane, and she had sat on the couch, eating Chinese takeout and watching Three Stooges videos.

Armaiti lay on the couch and thought about how much she would miss the lovely things.

22

dish yawned again and Laleh pivoted in the passenger seat to look at him with concern. She knew that after he dropped her off in Mahim at the women's shelter where she volunteered every Thursday, he had at least another half hour's drive ahead of him to the suburb where his meeting was. "Why are you so tired this morning?" she asked.

He rolled his eyes. "Bad night. Just couldn't fall asleep."

"I'm sorry. I heard you get up."

He sighed. "I kept thinking of what will happen after you leave."

Laleh smiled. "I know. I'll miss you, too."

Adish looked puzzled, then shook his head. "Thanks. But that's not what I meant."

"What, then?"

"I was awake half the night worrying about Iqbal when he finds out Nishta is gone. He'll come home and she won't be there. How soon before he notices her passport is missing? Iqbal's not an idiot. It's a matter of time before he puts two and two together."

Laleh shrugged. "I don't care about Iqbal. I just want to do this to help Nishta. And to repay my debt to Armaiti."

She regretted the words as soon as they'd left her mouth. But it was too late.

"Repay your debt?" Adish asked sharply. "Are you still obsessed with thinking you've caused Armaiti's tumor? Is that why we're going through all this, Laleh? To appease your conscience?"

"You're not getting what I meant," she said.

"So what did you mean?"

She shook her head impatiently. "Forget it."

"No. I'm not forgetting it. I want to know what you meant." Adish took his eyes off the road to look at her. "You better be sure you're thinking this through, Laleh. It'll be hard, but we can still back out. You better not be using Nishta as a pawn, just to satisfy Armaiti."

Laleh felt her face redden. "Take that back," she said. "You know me better than that."

"Okay," Adish said. "Okay. I'm sorry."

They made light, desultory conversation the rest of the way until Adish pulled into the dusty compound where the shelter was housed. "Thanks for the lift," Laleh said stiffly, not looking at him. She turned to get out of the car.

"One sec," Adish said, touching her wrist. He looked at her for a moment, his brown eyes searching her face. "Are you sure you're doing this for the right reasons, Laleh?" he said finally. "I mean, we're on the verge of breaking up someone's marriage. And the consequences could be severe."

Several hours later, Laleh watched as Farhad took his third helping of rice, cauliflower, and chicken. Beside him, Ferzin sat playing with her food. Farhad eyed his sister's plate. "You're not eating this?" he said, pointing with his fork to the cauliflower on her plate. Before she could respond, he scooped the vegetable onto his plate. He chewed for a few seconds and then looked at his mother. "Why aren't you having dinner?"

"I told you before. I'll eat when Daddy gets home," she said shortly.

"But he's playing tennis tonight. It'll be late when he returns."

Farhad, she could tell, was in one of his argumentative moods. And she was in no mood for a second argument today. She got up from the dining chair. "I know. It's okay." She went into the bedroom, picked up the car keys from the dresser, and came back. "I'm going out for an hour or so," she said.

The children looked startled. "Where're you going?" Ferzin asked.

"Out," she said, and before they could ask any more questions she walked out the front door.

As she entered the lobby, she spotted Murthi, one of the building's watchmen, and pulled out two twenty-rupee notes. "Can you run a quick errand?" she asked. "I need a small garland. See if the flower shop is still open, would you?"

"Any special kind, madam?"

She shook her head. "Just an ordinary garland—a couple of roses, some jasmine, bas. I'll wait for you in the car."

"Shall I call for your driver, madam?"

"No. I'm driving."

Ten minutes later, she was in the silver Maruti, headed toward Marine Drive. It had rained earlier in the day and the evening air felt heavy as a secret. She turned on the air conditioning. The string of flowers, rolled inside a newspaper bag, lay on the passenger seat, filling the small car with its sweetness.

She had been so busy all day that she had not had a chance to evaluate what Adish had said to her in the car this morning. But now she knew: as always, he had hit the nail on its head. As much as she'd wanted to rescue Nishta, some part of her had also wanted to present her—present the three of them—to Armaiti as a gift. And, yes, ever since she'd heard about Armaiti's condition, she had been indulging in magical thinking. As long as she was responsible for Armaiti's condition, she could also fix it. It had been the only way she could deal with the immensity of her grief.

But the truth was, she had lost Armaiti a little at a time over almost thirty years, starting when Armaiti had told her that she was applying to grad school in America. Laleh had been shocked but had done her best to hide the fact. "Why?" she had asked, flinging her arms open. "Everything you love is here."

Armaiti had hesitated, a pained expression on her face. "I'm not happy, Lal," she'd finally said.

"Why ever not?" she demanded. "And what about the movement?"

"The movement," Armaiti repeated, as if testing the words out. She paused for a long time. "I've spent four years in the movement, Lal," she said. "And I'm only twenty-one. I'm—I'm tired. Tired of being scared every time I see a policeman. Of feeling guity every time I buy a new pair of pants because someone else can't afford bread. Don't you ever get that way? And I've been thinking . . . what if we're wrong about some of this stuff, Lal? What then?"

Laleh looked straight ahead, unable to answer. A thousand thoughts skated though her head, but the most persistant one was: Without Armaiti, what will I do?

"Why would we be wrong?" she said finally, knowing that Armaiti was waiting for a response.

Armaiti swallowed. "Czechoslovakia was horrible, Lal," she said. "Gray. Gloomy. Depressing. Everyone looked old and tired. I tell you, the worst slums in Bombay look more cheerful than Prague did. And there were soldiers with machine guns everywhere in the city. Out in public, on the streets."

"I know. You told us already. But maybe there was a military exercise or something going on."

"No, Lal. It's like that all the time."

She was quiet then, not knowing what to do with this information—the thought that their dream might have a hollow core; the extent of Armaiti's disillusionment with the movement; Armaiti's abandonment of the poor, beleaguered country of their birth; the glass-coated string of loneliness that was cutting through her body at the realization that Armaiti was going to leave her, had in some ways already left her.

She did not trust herself to speak, fearing what sorrow or hurt or pleading might bubble up in her voice if she opened her mouth. They walked in silence for a few minutes. Then Armaiti asked, "Are you angry with me, Lal?"

"Don't be silly," she said gruffly, putting her arm across Armaiti's shoulder. They walked down the street this way, much as they had done since childhood. "I hope you go to America. And I hope you find whatever you are seeking over there."

The tears were rolling down Laleh's cheeks as she sat at a traffic light, and she was glad for the Maruti's tinted windows. She turned on the CD player and the second verse of "The Boxer" came on. As always, the forlorn lines made her imagine what Armaiti must have felt like when she'd first arrived in America. How friendless, how scared and lonely Armaiti must've been during those first months in America.

Lai la lai
Lai la lai la la la la lai
Lai la lai

Laleh was driving fast now, flying past the old Art Deco buildings and overtaking the other cars. The rolled-up windows and the soft whir of the air conditioner muted the honks of the vehicles that she passed. She turned the stereo up even louder, so that the music fell on her like a heavy rain. The day's last sun drew its streaks of scarlet across the sky. Laleh's heart felt like a building about to collapse under the weight of the emotions she felt.

> I am leaving,
> I am leaving,
> But the fighter still remains . . .

She and Armaiti used to sing the last verse at the top of their lungs. The lyrics to "The Boxer" were burnt into her soul, were part of her DNA, and after all these years they still got to her, a testimonial to a battered, bruised resilience that she was beginning to understand better and better the older she got. It was a wonder that they had loved this song so much in their teenage years—what part of it could have possibly spoken to them? How could two fifteen-, sixteen-, and then seventeen-year-old girls have understood the quiet resignation, the tentative pride, the longing for home, that lay at the heart of this song? After Armaiti had left for America, Laleh would think of her when she heard the lines about the bleeding New York City winters and the pocketful of mumbles, and worry about her friend. But today, in the car, she heard the song differently, and thought of Armaiti in a new way, as a survivor—*But the fighter still remains*—hanging on, waiting for them to reach her.

The song reached its soaring climax, the lyrics giving way to the *Lai La Lai*'s, a rising tidal wave of sound that gave the song its anthem-like power. Laleh imagined it—the two of them, Armaiti and her, and then a whole generation, soaring, transported, being lifted on the shoulders of those *Lai La Lai*'s, marching together, resisting, fighting back, defying death together. Her melancholy was so pure and acute it tipped over and became joy.

Her hand reached involuntarily for her cell phone, even as she eyed the clock on the dashboard. Eight-fifteen. Which meant it was ten forty-five in the morning where Armaiti was. Her right hand was dialing Armaiti's number even before she had completed the mental calculation.

"Hello?" Armaiti's voice was husky, as if she was still asleep.

"I'm so sorry," Laleh said, "Did I wake you?"

"For you, Lal, I'll wake up even from the dead."

There was a short, brittle silence as they both digested what Armaiti had said, and then, to Laleh's relief, she heard Armaiti's characteristic giggle. "Sorry. That was a bad joke."

Laleh smiled through the lump that was forming in her throat. "Only you, Armaiti."

"So. All packed? Where are you?"

Laleh groaned. "Not even close. I've left it until the morning. I'm at Marine Drive," she added as she spotted a red Honda City pulling out of a parking space and eased up behind it.

"Marine Drive." Even over the miles, she could hear the wistfulness in Armaiti's voice. "The Queen's Necklace. Is it as beautiful as I remember it?"

Laleh's eyes shone with tears. "Imagination is always better than reality, right?" she murmured.

"Is Adish with you?" Armaiti asked.

"No. I just came by myself." She hesitated, her reasons for this sudden pilgrimage to the sea a little unclear even to her. "I just needed . . . time to think. Alone."

"What's wrong?" Armaiti said immediately and Laleh smiled to herself. Has anyone ever known me as well as Armaiti? she wondered and then felt a twinge of guilt at what she imagined was a betrayal of Adish.

"Hey, talk to me. What's on your mind?" Armaiti's voice was urgent in her ear.

"Oh, we had an argument this morning," Laleh said. "Adish and I."

"About your coming?"

"No. Not at all." She hesitated again, questioning her own motives, wondering why she was telling Armaiti this. "He was upset because I—I feel responsible for your illness." Now that she'd said the words out loud, Laleh could hear how foolish they sounded.

Armaiti made a sound that could've been a chortle. "How? What do you mean?"

"Well, I thought—maybe the concussion you suffered from the laathi charge may have somehow caused the tumor?" Cringing as she said it.

Armaiti laughed. "Oh my God, I'd forgotten about that. Laleh, don't be stupid. That was decades ago. And my mother died of cancer, remember? If you want to blame anything, blame my lousy genes."

Laleh felt her body go limp with relief. Armaiti didn't even remember. "I know. I'm an idiot. Adish has been saying the same thing—that I was being absurd."

"Lal. Darling." Armaiti sighed so mightily it felt like a gust of wind in Laleh's ear. "Can I say something? One thing I've learned is, none of this matters. Honest."

Laleh switched hands. She had been pressing the phone so tightly to her right ear that it was throbbing with pain. "What do you mean?" she said.

"Lal, when I was in Florida, I felt like I finally understood something."

"So tell me."

"Well, it's very silly, really. The kind of hackneyed, dime-store wisdom that you're supposed to get when you're . . . dying."

"So tell me."

"I divorced Richard five years ago because he had an affair," Armaiti said. There was a flatness to her voice that Laleh had never heard before, as if she were reading lines from a book. "I never told you this, right? I was too embarrassed, as if his cheating on me was my fault. But guess what, Lal? Turns out Richard is the one who has done more for me these past months than anyone else—not counting Diane, of course. So all I'm saying is, everything that seems so important—our quarrels, or philosophical differences—in the end, it doesn't matter much. You know? In the end, what matters is what remains."

"I can't wait to meet Diane," Laleh said. "If she's anything like you, I will love her . . ." She corrected herself. "I will love her, anyway."

"She's so excited to meet you. She's even volunteered to help me cook a full Parsi dinner for all of you."

"Armaiti. Don't you go exerting yourself. The last thing you should do is cook for us. We will do all the cooking and cleaning after we land there."

Armaiti's voice was as innocent as a child on Christmas morning. "Well, I was thinking of making a few of my mother's recipes. Remember my mom's fried fish? And her sali murghi? You used to love it."

Laleh groaned. "You're a bitch."

"Listen, you idiot," Armaiti said. "If you think I'm not going to cook for my best friends who I haven't seen in donkey's years, you have another thing coming."

"Two more days," Laleh said with wonder, "and we'll all be together."

"Come to us safely."

Laleh sat in the Maruti for a few minutes after hanging up the phone, going over the conversation. What had Armaiti said? In the end, what matters is what remains. A picture of Adish's dimpled face rose before her eyes and she felt her chest tighten with love. How much good fortune had been strewn her way, starting with a man who still put up with her crankiness and ir-rationalities, who stayed loyal and devoted to her, as if she were the flag of his country. How absurd that she would bring even a dollop of grief into Adish's life. Really, she should be genuflect-ing with every step, giving thanks for all the riches in her life.

She gripped the bag holding the garland of flowers, opened the car door, and stepped onto the sidewalk. The sky was dark now and so was the sea as it crashed against the boulders. Laleh sat on the concrete ledge and swung her legs around so that she faced the water. She removed the garland from the newspaper bag and looked quickly to her left and right. Although flowers were biodegradable, she still felt a tremor of guilt at what she was about to do. Last year, while at the seaside with Adish, she had chased after a man she had caught tossing a plastic bag full of garbage into the water. The poor man, a servant in one of the nearby apartment buildings, had cowered as she'd lectured him about the ecology of the sea and then explained that he was merely obeying the orders of his mistress. Laleh had entertained the thought of marching up to the woman's apartment to deliver the same lecture when Adish had caught up with her and talked her out of it.

Now she cast a quick look around her, then whirled the garland over her head like a lasso before releasing it. It flew over the boulders, the white of the jasmine gleaming against the dark, and then landed in the water. "For you, Armaiti," Laleh said to herself. "A prayer for you. For a miracle to happen. For another ten, twenty years." This had been her original prayer, the purpose of her trip tonight, but now, fresh from her conversation with Armaiti, she added another: "If not health, if not long years, then peace. And here's a prayer for Diane. For our children. For all our children."

Her thoughts were hot and inchoate as she felt the pinpricks of withheld grief across her face. And finally, rising like a whale from the murky waters of her sorrow, another prayer. "Forgive me," she pleaded to Armaiti and then realized that since Armaiti had never blamed her for anything, there was nothing to forgive. The only person who had ever held a moment of youthful weakness against her, who had ever woven that moment into a lash with which she had bloodied herself, was herself. She narrowed her eyes to follow the movement of the garland as it floated on the water, and as she did so, the first of her tears fell onto her cheeks. "I forgive you," she whispered to that idealistic but frightened girl from so long ago. "I forgive you."

23

Flowers. She wanted to buy enough to fill each room of the house with dozens of bouquets. Armaiti knew it would come across as ostentatious, that her friends might be a little shocked by such extravagance, but she couldn't help herself. This was the last party she would probably ever throw, and she wanted it all—flowers and candles, good wine and food. Last night she had pulled out the old notebook in which her mother had painstakingly written down all her recipes in the months after she had left India for Harvard. She and Diane were going to revive several of those recipes for a feast the evening their guests arrived. Richard had suggested that they order in from Maharaja but she had refused. "I'm cooking," she'd said flatly. "No matter what."

It had given her something to look forward to these past few days, which had not been good ones. The blurry vision was now a fact of life. It was strange how quickly she was accepting each new insult that her body offered up. When she went out, she now used the motorized wheelchair that Richard had rented immediately upon their return from Florida. She was just so grateful to still be mobile, given how grim the doctor in the emergency room at the Mayo Clinic in Jacksonville had looked when Diane had taken her in after the episode at the beach. Since then, she had relinquished much of her care to Diane and Richard, and the strange part was, she didn't mind it so much. The physical fatigue that was always present had blurred into mental exhaustion—she was tired of fighting her family. Instead, a quiet resignation had taken over. She recognized that everything they suggested came from a desire to protect her, to prolong her life by keeping her safe and healthy. She had once been a young mother herself and understood a thing or two about wanting to protect those you loved—even if that love occasionally felt like handcuffs. So be it. Since Florida, she had said those three words to herself over and over again: So be it. Thy will be done. She was through with fighting Richard, hurting Diane, asserting her will against theirs. They loved her. That was the only truth that mattered.

Plus, there was now one major imperative—she had to be in respectable shape when the others arrived. Diane, Richard, and she had come to an unspoken truce—she would follow their commands about everything that pertained to her health. In exchange, she alone would make decisions about the upcoming visit. This was her last hurrah, and father and daughter seemed to understand this. "It's okay, Dad," Diane had interjected when Richard had insisted that Armaiti not exert herself by cooking. "I can help Mom with all the actual work. She'll just have to supervise."

But before they could start shopping for food, they had to buy flowers. She wanted her guests to walk into a house that looked and smelled like paradise. They would be exhausted after their twenty-hour flight and the flowers would revive them. Sunflowers, Armaiti thought, as she moved around in her wheelchair at Whole Foods. Lots of sunflowers. And roses, of course. The hydrangeas she would clip from her garden. Oh, if only the three of them had come in the spring. How to possibly convey to them the scent from the rows of lilacs that bloomed in her yard? Armaiti reached out unsteadily for yet another bouquet. "Take it easy, Mom," gasped Diane, who was pushing a cart that was already half full. "You know we've already ordered a dozen bouquets from Costco for tomorrow. We don't even have vases for all the new ones you're buying."

Armaiti frowned. "So? We'll just buy some cheap ones from the Dollar Store. I want at least five bouquets in each of their bedrooms."

"They won't even have room for their suitcases. Besides, somebody might be allergic, you know?"

Armaiti tossed back her head and laughed. "Allergic? Darling, no one in India is allergic to anything. Just breathing that foul Bombay air is like smoking a pack of cigarettes a day. You think a few flowers will bother them? I tell you, we Americans have become so soft and . . ."

"Yeah, yeah, yeah, and all Indians have cast-iron stomachs. And amazing immune systems. I know. Jeez."

She smacked her daughter's hand playfully. "Getting too big for your britches, Di," she said.

Ten minutes later, they left the flower section, ignoring the incredulous looks the other shoppers were casting at Diane's overflowing cart. "I want to pick up some cheese," Armaiti said.

"There's no room in the cart."

"Okay. Go get me a basket. I can balance it on my lap."

"I don't want you to exert yourself, Mom."

"Diane." Armaiti stopped her chair in the middle of an aisle. "I want you to listen to me now. The next few days, I'm going to forget that I'm sick. Okay? At least, as much as my body will allow me to. I . . . these might be . . . I just want to have fun with my friends, okay? And if the price for that is a little bit more fatigue or dizziness or whatever, well, that's a price I'm willing to pay." She could see she was upsetting Diane and so she softened her tone. "I know you mean well, darling. But, please—let go a bit? Please try?"

Diane gave her a rueful smile. "Okay. But I want you to be healthy for when they get here."

"Me, too, darling. There's nothing I want more. Now, come on, look at the list. What else do we need?"

Laleh had just finished zipping the red suitcase when Adish came into the bedroom. "All packed?" he asked Laleh. "Bags ready to be taken downstairs? I want to load the van early. That way, no last-minute tension."

"Yup. Have you called for the watchman to carry them down?"

"What do we need the guy for? Farhad can take one and I'll take the other. Plus your carry-on."

"You're forgetting the bag I'm carrying for Nishta. She won't have any clothes of her own."

"Shit. I did forget about her suitcase." Adish groaned. "Okay, Nishta's suitcase makes sense. But you're only going for three weeks. How much stuff do you need to carry?"

"Well, who forced me to carry a marble Taj Mahal replica for Richard? The bloody thing weighs at least fifteen kilos, I swear. What's Richard going to do with it?"

"He'll love it. You're going to be guests in their house, Lal. You have to take some gifts, no?"

Farhad ambled toward their room and stood leaning in the doorway. "Bags ready?" he asked.

"In a minute." Lal turned back to Adish. "Well, at least one of the bags is over the twenty-two-kilo limit, thanks to your bloody statue."

He shrugged. "Try and talk them into letting it go. Or pay the fine, what else?" He glanced at his watch. "We better leave a half hour earlier than planned. There might be traffic on the way to Nishta's." He unzipped her overnight bag. "How much room do you have in here?"

"Why? I still have to put some books in there."

"Forget it. I need the space. I ordered a bunch of mithai for Armaiti. Jalebis, suterfeni, halva. We have to stop on the way to pick it up. And all that has to go into your carry-on."

"Adish, are you mad? We don't even know if Armaiti still likes those sweets. Or whether she can eat them."

He smiled at her indulgently. "She will. Trust me." He shushed her by holding two fingers to her lips. "Lal. I haven't sent anything for Armaiti. Just indulge me."

"You have your passport?" Mumtaz asked for the third time and nodded when Nishta pointed silently to her handbag. "Good," she said nervously and then got up from the couch. "Oh. I almost forgot," she said and opened her own purse. She took out a bundle of notes that had been folded over and secured with a rubber band. "This is for you, bhabi," she said. "For spending in America."

Nishta gasped. "I can't. How . . . how did you get this? It's dollars, yes?"

"I have a friend whose husband travels a lot. Bought from him."

Nishta's eyes widened with fear. "Did you tell them about me?"

Mumtaz shook her head vehemently. "No, Zoha, of course not. I told them it was for a friend. And don't worry, they don't even know I have a brother." She held out the bundle again. "Take it. You will need some money there."

"There is no way I can repay you for all this."

Mumtaz smiled shyly. "Actually, there is." She took out a small piece of paper. "Here is my waist and hip size. If you can bring me a pair of 7 For All Mankind jeans, I'd be grateful. They're very hard to find here." She made a face. "Even though Hussein won't let me wear them outdoors, I can wear at home."

Nishta felt her face redden. It was one thing deceiving Iqbal. But Mumtaz? She wanted to caress the innocent face with the big, trusting eyes.

She looked away. "Okay," she said. "I will bring these."

"Shukriah, Zoha jaan." Mumtaz turned her head toward the kitchen. "Do you still have any more of those mutton cutlets you made for lunch?"

Nishta smiled, glad to be able to do something for her sister-in-law for a change. "Of course. Shall I heat some?"

"Oh, no. I'm full. But I'll take two for Hussein, if you don't mind. He loves your cooking."

They had had lunch upstairs with Mumtaz's mother earlier in the day. The old lady was thrilled that her daughter had stopped by unexpectedly. She was even happier to see that Mumtaz was wearing a pink burkha. "Allah be praised," she exclaimed. "What do we owe this miracle to?"

"Hussein wanted me to," Mumtaz said.

The old woman nodded understandingly. "One must always keep one's husband happy," she said.

Nishta had been stunned at how easily the lies slipped off Mumtaz's tongue. She's enjoying this, she thought with amazement. It's like she's getting back at all of them. But what for?

"Shall we warm the food?" the old lady had said and it didn't escape Nishta's notice that even though Mumtaz was sitting right there, her mother-in-law was looking pointedly at her. She doesn't get to see her daughter too often, she reasoned with herself, and then almost laughed out loud at her next thought: What do you care? You'll be out of here in a few hours. This is the last meal you will ever serve this cranky old woman. "Sure, Ammi," she said demurely, keeping her eyes to the ground.

They had returned to Nishta's flat after lunch, after Mumtaz promised her mother she'd come say goodbye before she left to go home that evening. Now, they sat on the couch making chit-chat. "Amazing how time doesn't budge when you're watching the clock," Mumtaz said, and Nishta heard the nervousness in her voice.

"Promise me you'll make sure that you'll leave before Iqbal comes home tonight?" she asked.

Mumtaz let out a groan. "God, Zoha. What a worrywart you've become. I've told you a hundred times. When Ammi goes indoors at eight to eat dinner—*foos!*—I'll dart out of here fast as a mouse."

Nishta sighed. "But what about later?" She gestured toward the note sitting propped up on the coffee table. "After he reads my letter? Your Ammi will mention you were here today. Surely he'll come knocking on your door to . . ."

"Bhabi. You're not thinking straight. You know the plan. I'll just pretend to be as shocked as everyone else."

"But he'll question you, Mumtaz. You know Iqbal. If he's suspicious at all . . ."

"Let him be as suspicious as he wants." Mumtaz's voice grew defiant.

" . . . and the first thing he'll do is check the safe for the passport," Nishta continued. "How long before he—"

"Hussein can deal with my brother," Mumtaz interrupted. "None of his violent behavior will work in my house."

"I didn't mean . . . Iqbal would never hurt you. I just meant . . ."

"Who knows? Would I have ever thought my brother would raise his hand to you?" Mumtaz shrugged. "It doesn't matter. He can't do anything worse to me than what he's already done."

Nishta reached out to take Mumtaz's hand in hers. "Sweetie," she said. "What did he do?" Had Iqbal sexually abused his sister when she was little? It seemed unfathomable, but she'd learned that it was a common enough story—cousins, brothers, fathers, touching little girls, fondling them, doing worse. "Did he hurt you?" she asked cautiously. "Touch you wrong?"

Mumtaz looked confused for a second, and then, as Nishta's meaning dawned on her, she gave a startled laugh. "Oh, God, no. Nothing like that. My God, Iqbal was so protective of me when we were young." She fell quiet, and when she looked up, her eyes were red. "I was molested, didi. But not by him."

Nishta let out a cry of outrage, and, at this, the younger woman roughly brushed away her tears and forced a gaiety into her voice. "Forget it. Ancient history. And today's a happy day. No need for all this sad talk."

"I need to know," Nishta said but Mumtaz stopped her. "Another time. After you come back I'll tell you the whole story." She leapt up off the couch. "Now come on. Let's go pick up Zenobia from her class."

Kavita eyed Ma dispassionately, trying to gauge whether the sudden illness was real or a manifestation of the old lady's usual hypochondria. She remembered that the last time she had gone out of town—not out of town, really; she'd just told Ma that, while she'd spent three days with Ingrid at the Taj—she had come down with the same nebulous symptoms.

"You go finish your packing, beti," Ma croaked. "I'll be okay."

"Can you describe what's wrong?" Kavita asked again.

Ma sighed. "Just shaky."

Shaky. Giddy. Jelly-like. Feeling upside down. Like my brain has turned to yogurt. This was the medical terminology Ma typically used to describe her ailments. It drove Kavita up the wall.

She got up from the chair next to Ma's bed and went into the kitchen, where Rekha was making chapatis. "Go sit with her for a few moments," she asked and then went into her bedroom. She dialed her brother Rohit's phone.

"What?" he said.

"It's Ma. I can't tell if she's really ill or what. And I leave for the airport in about an hour. Can you come over?"

"She's just upset you're leaving," Rohit said in the blithe tone that set her teeth on edge.

"Congratulations on your medical degree. Not to mention your psychic powers."

"Funny," he said, in that abrupt way of his.

"Well, can you come over?"

"Not now. I'm busy."

She forced herself to stay calm. "Rohit," she said, thinking for the umpteenth time how telling it was that her brother's name rhymed with "shit." "Ma could be sick. And I won't be here. She'll be alone with Rekha. Can you pretend to care?"

He made an exasperated sound. "Tell you what. I'm going to the club at eight. I'll stop by before that. Okay?"

It was the best deal she would get today. "Promise?" she said.

"Whatever."

His callousness stung more than it had any business doing. "Okay," she said, trying to control the dangerous tremor in her voice. "Thanks. I'll see you."

"Hey, Ka?" Rohit said. "You take care of yourself, understand?"

Her disproportionate gratefulness at his casual remark told

her how much stress she was under, how emotional she was about this trip. She eyed the clock. Did she have time to squeeze in a quick call to Ingrid? "Thanks," she said. "You, too. I'll see you soon."

Ma had gotten up from her bed and was lying on the couch in the living room. "She insisted," Rehka said. "Said she wanted more light."

Kavita nodded. "Feeling better, Ma?"

The old woman groaned in reply. "The time of my dying is fast approaching, beta. I'm just a burden to you."

Rekha and Kavita exchanged the briefest of smiles. They heard this line every time Ma was unwell. Kavita dug into her jeans pocket and fished out a few crumbled hundred-rupee notes. "Keep this," she said to the maid. "In case you have to call Dr. Shah or buy some medicine."

Ma shot upright on the sofa. "What are you doing, handing out money like sweets?" she cried. She leaned forward to pull the money out of Rekha's hands. "Giving the girl ideas," she muttered to herself. "Spoiling her. No sense." She fell back on the couch with dramatic flair, still clutching the money in her hand.

Kavita noticed that the little exercise had restored the color in Ma's cheeks. "Sorry," she mumbled to Rekha as the servant left the room. "Come see me before I leave." She stood at the doorway and looked back at the reclining woman. "Your first-born will drop by for a visit this evening," she said.

Ma raised her head slightly. "Will he be bringing that nasty wife of his?" she said.

"Not sure. But Prince Charming has consented to a visit. That's good news, isn't it?"

Ma glared at her. "It's not his fault. That wife of his has poisoned him . . ."

Kavita shook her head. "Oh, Ma, stop." She had heard this tirade a thousand times before.

She was still shaking her head as she went into her bedroom. She wondered whether to weigh her suitcases one more time, but she and Rekha had done that twice last night. She had been done with her packing by nine last night, the inside of her suitcases as precise and neat as an architectural drawing. Now there was nothing to do but wait for the phone call that would tell her that Laleh and Adish were downstairs, waiting to pick her up.

Armaiti noticed Devdas's eyes widen as she entered his grocery store in her wheelchair. She had not been in here since her diagnosis, she realized. Her heart sank at the thought of explaining her condition to the genial, talkative owner of India Food Emporium.

"Arre, Armaitiji, kya hua?" he asked, his middle-aged brow creasing with concern. "Accident or what?"

She flashed a warning look at Diane before she turned to him with a smile. "Just not feeling well," she said evasively.

"Arre, Ram," he breathed. "Nothing serious, I hope?"

She was about to open her mouth to reassure him when she heard Diane say, "Nothing serious. Just cancer."

She turned slowly to face her daughter—any sudden movement made her head spin—and saw that Diane was staring defiantly at her. Please don't make a scene, Armaiti pleaded silently with her eyes. Even though she had very few ties with India, some ancient sense of propriety made her close-mouthed around people from the home country. Especially Indians who looked at her with creased brows and inquisitive eyes, as Mr. Devdas was doing right now.

"Cancer?" Devdas flinched involuntarily. "No, no, no. Impossible. Not to someone as sweet and kind as you, madam."

Armaiti emitted a low growl of frustration that was audible only to Diane, who pulled the shopping list out of her mother's hand. "I'll pick up what you need, Mom," she said hastily and Armaiti saw that she was avoiding eye contact with her.

Armaiti spent an excruciating ten minutes listening to Devdas tell her story after story of people he'd known—well, actually, heard about, he allowed—who had beaten cancer. He also suggested a myriad of cures—urine therapy, a mixture made from goat's milk and six cloves of garlic, a paste made from turmeric, tamarind, and crushed red brick, a massage oil made from tiger's meat. Yes, tiger's meat, he repeated sagely, as if it were a common item he sold in his store. Or, if madam was interested, he would phone his uncle's cousin, who was a faith healer in Milwaukee. Very powerful, faith healing, hadn't she heard? Armaiti felt her life trickling away as she sat in her wheelchair, unable to get away from the man. A customer entered the store, picked out some Indian snacks, and waited to pay at the counter but Devdas ignored him. Armaiti pointed out the waiting customer but it was useless—Devdas gesticulated wildly, his manner got more and more agitated and persistent, his brow more furrowed. He railed against the dangers of chemotherapy—Armaiti didn't have the heart or the energy to tell him she wasn't using it—the perils of vaccines, antibiotics, and Western medicine in general; made wild and dubious claims about the low rates of cancer in countries like India; tried to extract a promise from her to immediately stop eating corn, sweet peas, and chicken, all of which apparently corrupted a person's aura and caused cancer. "If you eat meat, madam, eat goat. Very, very safe."

After ten minutes of this, Armaiti had had enough. Politeness be damned, she thought. Surely dying had a few advantages and the abandonment of good manners was one of them. She spun her wheelchair around in the middle of Devdas's sentence. "Excuse me," she said abruptly. "I must find my daughter."

She found Diane on her haunches, picking out the cans of sliced mangoes from the bottom shelf. "Sorry," the girl said preemptively.

Armaiti was not appeased. "We'll talk in the car," she said in the clipped manner she slipped into whenever she was angry. "I'll wait for you outside. Use the credit card to pay for everything."

Devdas insisted on helping Diane load the groceries in the car and then watched with much shaking of his head as Diane helped her mother in. Every few seconds he struck his forehead with his palm, as if swatting invisible flies. It was, Armaiti knew, both a gesture of disbelief and an expression of sympathy. It grated on her enough that she did not respond when Devdas yelled, "Good luck, madam!"

"What a stupid man," Diane said as soon as they'd pulled out of the parking space. "He kept trying to tell me what cures you should try while bagging my groceries."

"Yeah, I heard them all, thanks to you." Armaiti was furious and she saw no reason to disguise the fact. She turned to face Diane. "What made you do it, Di?" she asked. "Don't you think it's my business to tell whoever I want to?"

Diane swallowed hard. "It is. I'm so sorry. I don't even know why I blurted it out. It's just that . . ." She shook her head. "No. I won't make excuses. I don't know why I did it."

Armaiti felt the anger leaving her, like a bird flying off her windowsill. "Okay," she said. "Let it go." She put her hand on her daughter's knee. "Shall we stop at Aslaam's to pick up the lamb? It's on our way. That way, we can go home and I can rest for a bit before we start working."

Diane looked at her immediately. "You're tired, Mom?"

Would Diane ever speak to her again without that clutch of

anxiety in her voice? She supposed not. It was just one more thing she'd lost along the way—the simple casualness of her interactions with her daughter. What a difference it made to know—to really *know*—that life was finite. "Just a bit, honey. Nothing that a long nap won't fix."

"Shit. We're going to be late picking up Kavita," Adish said. "I hadn't counted on this bastard wedding procession holding up traffic."

"Mommy told you not to stop for the sweetmeats," Farhad said languidly.

Adish glanced back at him. "Chup re, chumcha. Remember, you're stuck with me at home for three weeks."

"As if I don't know," Farhad said, and Adish and Laleh both burst out laughing at his aggrieved tone.

"It's not a punishment living with your father, you know, sonny," Laleh said as the car inched forward.

Farhad stretched his long frame in the back of the SUV. "He's a bloody tyrant, yaar," he complained to his mother. "He gets grumpy when you're not home."

Laleh smiled to herself. There were worse things in life than her son being aware of how much his parents missed each other when they were apart. "I'll be back soon," she said.

"Okay, listen," Adish said to his son as he entered the lane where Kavita's apartment building was located. "You jump out when we get there and help Kavita auntie with her luggage, okay? Think you can manage all the suitcases?"

"Why can't you come with me?"

Adish pretended to be affronted. "What am I paying your gym fees for, you useless bugger?" He pulled inside the gate and eased into a parking space. "Now go."

"Janu, careful how you talk to him," Laleh said gently, after Farhad had exited the car. "Sometimes you are a little rough."

Adish looked at her with pity in his eyes. "Lal. Please. This is between us men. I know how to handle that boy. Give me some credit." He paused. "Besides, that little swine knows how much he means to me. He knows I would give my life for him."

Laleh felt an exquisite sweetness pierce her heart. They had built something together, she and Adish. Not a brave new world, perhaps, but—a world. A life. A family. "Thanks," she said.

"What for?"

"For everything. For putting up with me. For being in my life."

He put his arm around her, pulled her toward him, and squeezed her tight.

"You just come back to me, safe and sound," he said gruffly.

They had picked Zenobia up from her class and dropped her off at her grandmother's flat an hour ago. And now, Nishta waited in her apartment for Mumtaz to return from saying goodbye to Ammi.

There was one more thing she had to do before she left this place forever. Nishta picked up Mumtaz's cell phone and dialed the phone number that she had never forgotten, the number that, as far as she knew, had not changed since her childhood. Please let Mama answer, she prayed. Please let her pick up.

"Yes?" It was a male voice, old, tentative, but unmistakably her father's. Nishta's hand shook. Her mind went blank. She had not considered the possibility of her father answering the phone. Would he stay on the line long enough for her to tell him that she was leaving India? Would he convey the news to her mother? Or, praise God, would he relent and let her speak to her mother, one last time?

The voice, more impatient now, said, "Yes? Hello?"

"Daddy."

The silence on the other end was different now, heavier, more textured. And then, before her heart could either be despondent or rejoice at the fact that her father was holding on, she glanced at her phone and saw that the call had ended. He had hung up on her.

For a second her anger was so blinding, she couldn't see. Hideously proud, bigoted old man. Monster. Keeping her away from her own mother. And then the anger dulled into the usual acceptance, a grudging forgiveness. They had been right, in the end, hadn't they? Marrying Iqbal had been a bad idea.

She would write to her mother from America. Tell her everything. Ask for forgiveness—and also offer some. Most likely Mama would return it unread, as she often did. But maybe she'd open it, once she saw the foreign postmark.

In order to take her mind off what had just happened, she picked up the letter on the coffee table, twirling it in her hand. For a moment she was tempted to slit open the envelope and reread the note, which she had written hastily this morning. She had written it as a kindness to Iqbal, to spare him the terrible unknowing, the blind, aimless searching for his missing wife. But now she wondered if she had revealed too much, had tipped her hand too much. She shook her head. By the time Iqbal read the letter, she would be on a plane. Mumtaz was right—worrying had become a bad habit.

She rested the envelope against the brown bowl and bit her fingernails, glancing up at the clock. A moment later, she leapt up from the couch and dialed Adish's phone. He answered immediately. "We're about fifteen minutes away," he said. "That gives you enough time?"

"I'm ready," she said, willing Mumtaz to make her way down.

"No worries if you're a few minutes late," Adish said. "I'll just circle around. Chalo, we'll see you."

"See you," she repeated, and saying the simple words made her feel better, made what was about to happen seem real. She had expected to be assaulted by a battalion of emotions— sadness, guilt, regret—as she readied to leave, but all she felt was a jittery anticipation. All she wanted to do now was put the simple plan that Mumtaz had devised into action, to slip unseen into the backseat of a car being driven by Adish. She realized that she had exhausted all the other emotions she had expected to feel. The sorrow she had expected to feel at so momentous a step had been used up, had dissipated under the weight of Iqbal's numerous humiliations. Now there was just the lip-chewing anxiety about avoiding her mother-in-law's omniscient gaze, and making the drive to the airport unevent- fully, and the eagerness to find herself safely ensconced in a plane, strapped in her seat, her best friends on either side of her.

She heard the door open and Mumtaz walked in. "All done," she grinned. "Zenobia is doing her homework. Ma is enjoying her cup of tea on the balcony." She pulled off her pink burkha as she spoke. "Did they phone?"

"Yes. Five minutes ago. They will be there soon."

"Okay." She tossed the burkha over to Nishta. "Put it on."

As Nishta made her way into the bedroom, she heard Mum- taz say, "I had one more idea. We can't take any chances. You know how sharp Ma's eyes are when you don't want her to see something."

"What's the idea?"

"We'll exchange handbags. That way Ammi won't notice the difference."

Nishta swallowed the quick pang of regret she felt at losing the leather handbag she had owned for over twenty years. Iqbal had bought it for her, at a shop in Colaba. "Okay," she said. She eyed herself in the bedroom mirror for a quick second, and then, shaking her head at this ridiculous vanity, stepped into the pink burkha.

The contents of Mumtaz's purse were in a pile on the coffee table when she returned to the living room. "I'll arrange it later—after you're gone," Mumtaz said. "But just check you have everything. Passport? Money?"

"It's all here," she said dully. Now that the moment of departure had arrived, her movements were heavy and slow. She stood in front of Mumtaz, taking in the beloved face that so resembled Iqbal's, her brain struggling to comprehend how to say goodbye to the woman in front of her, who had risked so much, for reasons she still didn't quite understand. How to say goodbye to this cramped, gloomy apartment that she had despised since her first day here but which was still one of the few things in the world that belonged to her? How to take leave from her life with Iqbal? How to bid farewell to the memory of the young couple who had once believed that the forces that destroyed millions of others—religion, parental opposition, money issues—would not destroy them?

"Bhabi, you must go," Mumtaz said, giving her a gentle push. "They will be waiting."

"You will be safe, yes? Promise me you'll leave before Iqbal comes home?"

"For the millionth time, yes. I will." Mumtaz gave a sudden grin. "Who knows? Maybe after you return we can tell Iqbal the whole story. About how I helped you, and all."

"No." Her voice was sharp. "You must promise never to reveal your role to Iqbal. No matter what. If he asks about the passport, just say I told you I needed it to open an account or something. Make it sound like I tricked you, also. That I casually asked you to look for it in Ammi's safe when you went to borrow the jewelry."

"Okay, Zoha, just relax. . . . "

"Mumtaz, this is not a joke. Promise me."

"God. You are so intense. Okay, I promise. Happy?" Mumtaz took a step toward Nishta and caressed her cheek. "You enjoy your time with your friends, okay? And return home safe and sound."

It was a good thing she'd sealed the note before placing it on the table this morning, Nishta thought. She took Mumtaz's hand in both of hers and kissed it before holding it up to her eyes. "Khuda Hafiz," she said.

"Khuda Hafiz, bhabi. God be with you. Bon voyage. And remember my jeans."

Nishta collected Mumtaz's handbag and lowered the hood of her burkha. She stepped into the darkened hallway and then deftly made her way down the familiar stairs, stepping carefully over the broken one at the bottom. She exited the building and stepped into the street. The evening market rush had begun as housewives and office workers vied to buy the day's last produce for their dinner. She didn't turn to wave to Ammi as she usually did. She remembered to pull herself up from the waist and tried to imitate Mumtaz's jaunty walk. She swung her handbag loosely from her wrist as Mumtaz had done earlier today and resisted the urge to look back to see whether her mother-in-law was watching her from the balcony. Please don't let Ammi recognize me, she prayed.

She got to the end of the street and just before turning onto the main road, swung around to wave goodbye to her old life. It was safe at this distance, she knew—even her mother-in-law's vision was too weak to spot the difference between her daughter and daughter-in-law.

Nishta turned the corner and then she was free.

They drove for about two kilometers in silence, Nishta sand-wiched between Farhad and Kavita, and then Farhad said, "I've never sat next to a lady in a burkha before." Adish guffawed and the others joined in, until Farhad finally grew uncomfortable and said, "What? It wasn't *that* funny."

Nishta tossed the hood of the burkha over her head and turned toward Farhad so that he could see her for the first time. "It's not you, sweetie," she said. "We're not laughing at you." She reached over and took his hand. "I'm just so pleased to meet you finally. Laleh's son."

Adish cleared his throat. "Ah, excuse me. I had a little some-thing to do with the creation of the boy wonder also."

"He's right," Laleh said promptly. "He had a *little* something."

And just like that, the years fell away and they were back to the old days of joking, teasing each other, talking over each other, their voices loud and clear, their laughter strong and un-complicated.

Farhad looked from one to the other, his eyes wide. "You guys are crazy, yaar," he finally said, shaking his head. "I'm glad I didn't know all of you when you were in college. You all must've been wild."

24

Wait here," Iqbal told the taxi driver as he pulled up in front of his building. "I will be back in less than five minutes. Just have to change out of these." He pointed to his white pants, which were torn and muddy near the knee.

His right knee was beginning to ache by the time he climbed the four flights of stairs. If only he'd had time to chase after the bastard college boys who had pushed him onto the railway platform as the train was coming to a halt. He had intervened on behalf of the young Catholic woman they had been harassing during the ride, and this was their childish revenge—giving him a shove as he leaned out of the open doorway, ready to disembark as the train pulled into the station. He had broken his fall with his open palms but had landed on his right knee, hearing the thin cotton pants rip as he hit the concrete. He rose almost immediately, saw the grinning face of the ringleader as he melted into the crowd, and was about to give chase when he remembered. Today's was not just a regular weekly meeting. The imam from the main mosque was gracing them with their presence, Allah bless his soul. He couldn't afford to be late tonight.

Usually he walked the half-mile from the station to the

mosque. But eyeing his torn pants, Iqbal had made a quick calculation—if he jumped into a taxi, there would be enough time to go home and change and still get to the mosque on time.

Iqbal tried to look at his watch in the dimly lit hallway. Maybe he could take a few minutes to have Zoha put some iodine on his knee before he left again. As he removed the keys from his pocket, he grinned at little Murzi, who was tearing down the hallway in his tricycle. "Salaam, Iqbal uncle," the boy yelled, and before Iqbal could respond, he was gone, his fat little legs pedaling away. Grinning to himself, Iqbal inserted the key in the latch, turned it, and let himself into his flat.

The first thing he noticed was the darkness in the living room. He frowned, puzzled. Was Zoha out? Upstairs at Ammi's place? But then he saw the light in the kitchen and made his way toward it. He was about to part the curtain that led from the living room to the kitchen when it was pulled back from the other side and he almost collided with someone hurrying out. "Zoha," he gasped, afraid that he had scared her with his early homecoming and then gasped again as he recognized Mumtaz.

"Sister?" he said. "What's wrong? Where's Zoha?"

He watched in puzzlement as Mumtaz's face convulsed. An icy feeling filled his body. "Is Zoha not well?" he said. What else could explain Mumtaz being here at this hour?

Mumtaz looked at him blankly, as if he were speaking to her in a foreign language. As his fear grew, he resisted the urge to shake her. "Choti," he said. "What's wrong? Why are you here?"

And now his mind registered what had been there all along—Mumtaz was dressed in a burkha. In Zoha's blue burkha, as a matter of fact. A raindrop of suspicion fell onto Iqbal's mind. His hand involuntarily searched for the switch on the living room wall and he flipped it on. In the light, he saw that what he'd mistaken for blankness on his sister's face was something else—Mumtaz looked scared, and trapped, and—guilty. Her dark eyes searched the room, and she was making small, almost imperceptible movements away from him.

The fear in his chest was so sudden and viselike, it felt as if a large animal had placed its front paws on his chest, choking him, making it hard to breathe. His eyes swept around the small living room for more proof of Zoha's absence, but what he saw was the blindingly white envelope that sat upright against the brown bowl on the coffee table. He looked from Mumtaz to the envelope and saw that she had seen him notice it. He opened his mouth but no sound emerged, and yet she flinched, as if he had spoken. His fear grew even larger, curling like hot smoke from his chest to his stomach. Extending his hand as if to hold Mumtaz in place, his open palm facing her, he backed away, his eyes still on his sister, until his calf bumped into the coffee table and then he turned a bit and reached for the envelope.

He had almost torn it open with his index finger when he heard Mumtaz say in a flat voice that made his hair stand, "She's gone. Nothing you can do to stop her."

"Gone where?" he asked but then he was reading the short note Zoha had left for him, explaining her need to see Armaiti once again, accusing him of destroying something that had once been precious and alive, telling him she would always love him but didn't know when she would see him again.

He looked up from the note, his eyes bloodshot, feeling orphaned, widowed, and childless all at once. A tiny muscle twitched painfully in his left cheek. He had never felt this lonely or naked or bereft. Despite the ugliness that had flared between him and Zoha on occasion, he had never doubted that they loved each other, that they would remain woven into each other's lives like old trees that grew around and through each other. How many times had he thought that the words of that old song—

Zindagi kuch bhi nahi, teri meri kahani hai—were about him and his Zoha. Life is nothing but the story of your life with mine. And now he was holding a note that told him that he would have to live out the rest of his story alone. He would not know where her story had taken her, which new characters would enter it, how long each chapter would be, and whether he would be reduced from hero to villain. Because Zoha had left him. Zoha, whom he had loved from the first day they'd met, who had made it impossible for him to ever seriously look at another woman, for whom he had snapped his mother's heart into two like a cheap pencil, for whom he had borne a thousand insults that cut like barbed wire—*that* Zoha had left him.

And Mumtaz had helped her. That much was certain. Mumtaz, his blood, the colicky baby sister he used to sing to on hot nights when she couldn't fall asleep, the toddler for whom he had purchased her first set of crayons, the adolescent whom he used to painstakingly tutor in geometry and science, the ruined young woman whose life and reputation he had saved by marrying her off to a wealthy and powerful man, this Mumtaz, this poisoned blood, this snake, had driven Zoha away from him. The two women he had loved above all else, yes, even more, Allah forgive him, than Ammi herself, had conspired to destroy his home, his izzat, his family name, had smeared shame upon his face like feces.

He heard a strange sound in the room and looked up startled. Then he saw his sister's eyes widen with fear and realized that the sound was coming from him, that he was growling, baring his teeth, like a mad dog. He saw that he was frightening Mumtaz, but the growling just grew louder and he felt his feet whisk him across the room, and then he saw two heavy hands land on Mumtaz's shoulders and recognized that they were his. Then he was shaking her and he tensed as he waited for her to scream and after a moment, he knew that she would not. Instead, a curl of spit trickled down the side of her mouth and she said, "Go ahead. Hit me. You didn't spare your biwi. Why would you spare me?"

Inexplicably, his eyes filled with tears and as he blinked, he felt the rush of madness leave his body and felt himself become human again. He yanked his hands away from Mumtaz's shoulders as if they were hot burners. "How dare you. I love Zoha. What do you . . ." He was close to crying, humiliated by Mumtaz's words, the way in which she had expected him to strike her.

There was iron in Mumtaz's eyes now. "You have a funny way of showing your love to women, bhaijan. Slapping your wife, marrying off your sister against her will. Where does it stop?"

He felt the blood rush to his face. "That's what this is about? Revenge from so many years back?"

She opened her mouth to reply but he shook his head, noticing the clock behind her. Time. Maybe there was still time. He had a taxi waiting downstairs—if the bastard cab driver had not left by now. "When did she leave?" he asked. "How long ago?"

Mumtaz looked him in the eye. "It's too late, Iqbal. They've probably reached the airport by now. Let her go. Her friend is dying. It's only for three weeks, for God's sake. You'll manage. I'll bring you home-cooked food every day."

He stared at her, wanting to believe her, but then he looked at the note in his hand. "Then why does she say she doesn't know when she'll be back?"

He watched as the color drained from Mumtaz's face. "What?"

"This line," he yelled, jabbing the letter with his finger. " 'I'll always love you but don't know when I'll see you again.' "

Mumtaz's eyes went hazy with confusion. "I . . . don't . . . she said she would be back. I gave her . . ."

Her confusion scared him more than her bravado of a few seconds ago. Zoha was leaving India. Maybe forever. He felt a shaking start in his legs and climb through his body. He willed his mind to focus, to think, to calculate the time it would take to reach the airport at this hour. His mind steered off course, drove him into a future unimaginably barren and bleak, careened into a past that seemed filled with failure and missed opportunities, until it came to a sudden resolution. He had to stop Zoha. Find her, before she slipped out of his hands forever. Do whatever it took to bring her back home.

"Give me your cell phone," he said to Mumtaz.

"What?"

He grabbed her roughly by her arm, dragging her toward the front door. "Give me your phone."

"Iqbal, for God's sake . . ."

He snatched the purse—Zoha's purse, which he'd bought for her in a shop in Colaba years ago—from her hand and rifled through it. He pocketed her cell phone and then opened the front door. "You're staying with Ammi until I get home," he grunted.

"Hussein is waiting for me, Iqbal. Don't be crazy. He'll be worried."

But they were already out in the hallway, Iqbal's fingers boring into her arm. "You should've thought of that sooner. Before you poked your dirty nose into my business."

"I had no idea what Zoha was planning, Iqbal. Allah ki kasaam. Swear on God."

Iqbal flinched. "Don't. Don't say Allah's name. I don't like to hear His name in your vile mouth."

A few minutes later, he was racing down the five flights of stairs. His knee was throbbing still but he barely noticed it now. He was thinking of the startled look in his niece's and mother's eyes when he had barged in with Mumtaz and locked her in Ammi's bedroom. He had given his mother a quick kiss on the forehead and said, "I'll explain later. But no matter how much she shouts, don't let Mumtaz out of the room. Understand?" He was out in the hallway before the old lady had time to nod.

And now he was running out of the building and into the busy, noisy street, his eyes frantically searching for his waiting cab, his heart screaming a prayer: Please let the taxi still be here.

He found the cab driver leaning against his vehicle, yawning and stretching mightily. "Kya, sahib," he began. "Just two minutes, you said. I was beginning to think you had vamoosed with my money."

Iqbal shook his head impatiently. "Big change of plans," he said as he got in. "We're going to the airport. Bhaisahib, I beg you, drive like the wind. My whole life is in your hands."

25

I t took them twenty minutes to make their way from the
entrance of the airport to the terminal. The gray minivan
inched along the narrow lanes of the airport, locked in a
massive traffic jam. Taxi drivers honked their horns for no apparent reason, chauffeurs in private cars lowered their windows
and cussed at the other drivers. "You see?" Adish said to no one
in particular. "This is why I wanted to leave early."

When their vehicle finally reached its destination, they all
gasped at the sight that greeted them. It seemed as if the entire
city had turned up at the airport. Thousands of people stood
straining against the metal barricades, held back by a few police officers. It looked like a scene at a rock concert. Most of
these men and women were simply here to see their relatives
off, but the general pandemonium slowed down the movement
of the travelers themselves, who were trying to make their way
into the building, ramming their baggage carts into the carts
of those who stood in their way. Tempers flared, eyes glared.
Nobody, it seemed, knew if there was a queue to stand in or if
the law of the jungle applied. "So here it is, amchi Mumbai," Laleh said, her voice heavy with irony. " 'India Shining.' The next
global power. And we can't even organize one friggin' airport.
What a joke."

"You said 'frigging,' Mom," Farhad pointed out in that sleepy, deliberate manner of his.

Adish beat a smaller car in the race to claim an open spot near the curb. "Go grab some carts," he ordered his son. "We can't stop here for long." Kavita hopped out of the vehicle after Farhad. Adish exited, also, after muttering a terse, "Wait here," to the other two passengers.

After they'd unloaded the suitcases into the carts, Adish tossed the car keys to Farhad. "Go park," he said. "I'm going in with them. Wait for me near the entrance, okay? And remember, this will take time. So don't wander away."

Adish did his best to keep the three women and their trolleys together, shepherding them toward the main doors where a big sign declared TICKETED PASSENGERS ONLY. Rather than stand in line, they moved forward with the general flow of the crowd, as if riding a wave. At long last, it was their turn to show their tickets to the two tired-looking constables at the entrance. "You, sir?" the younger one said to Adish.

He pulled out a typed note from his shirt pocket. "VIP pass," he said. "From the airport manager's office." He had sent his peon this morning to pick up the pass from the manager, whom he knew from having done some renovations at the airport a few years ago.

The constable made as if to peer at the note but then saw the wall of people pressing in from behind and gave up. He waved Adish through.

"Well, that was fun," Adish said to the three women as he caught up with them. "Now let's get your bags checked in." Nishta, he saw, had lowered her veil again. Smart, he thought. No point in taking chances. He took hold of the cart Nishta was rolling and smiled. "I'll wheel this for you," he said. "I imagine it's hard to see with that thing on."

He accompanied them to the end of the baggage check-in line and then looked at Laleh. "I guess this is where we say goodbye," he murmured. "I don't think they'll let me escort you much further, even with the pass."

She took his hand. "You don't have to go yet, do you? This line's going to take forever to move, by the looks of it."

He smiled at her. "I'll wait," he said.

Laleh was right. Forty-five minutes passed and there were still five people ahead of them in line. Nishta began to cough and Adish's hand itched to fling the blasted veil over her head. He remembered what he'd always heard about the high rates of TB among veiled women. "Would you like something to drink?" he said. "There's a refreshment stall just a short ways from here."

"A Mangola," she gasped.

"I'll be back in a jiffy."

He hurried down the large room, his eyes scanning the faces of the people he passed. He was halfway near the cold drinks stall when he realized what he was doing—searching the room for Iqbal. He laughed at himself. Relax, he thought. He glanced at his watch. Iqbal was probably still at his trustees' meeting. By the time he reached home, it would all be over. Adish felt his body slacken and give up the tension that he realized he had been holding in.

It was at the very moment, as he felt himself relax, that Adish spotted Iqbal.

26

No, no, no, no, no, Adish thought. Not Iqbal. Not here. Not now. This couldn't be happening. Not after all the trouble they had gone to. But even while his mind was reeling from the shock of Iqbal's unexpected, unfortunate appearance, he was also calculating the significance of Iqbal's presence. If Iqbal could convince someone—an airline official or a police officer—that his wife was leaving the country without his permission, that she had snuck out of his home like a thief, there was no telling what could happen. This was India, after all, where a husband's accusation of his wife's infidelity still carried a lot of weight. Throw in an additional accusation—that she'd stolen money from his mother, say—and that could seal Nishta's fate. At the very least, Iqbal could hold things up, have them detain Nishta, delay her until the flight took off without her. Which meant that Laleh and Kavita would be faced with a terrible decision—whether to stay behind or go. They would be pulled between two friends, both needy, both in their own ways dying. It wouldn't be fair for them to have to choose. Not to mention what this would do to poor Nishta.

No. It couldn't be. Iqbal shouldn't be here. Besides, what was he doing inside the airport, anyway? How had he managed to sneak past the guards at the TICKETED PASSENGERS ONLY sign?

Sure, Adish had made his way in, but he had a legitimate pass. He had official permission to be here, unlike that white-garbed pipsqueak who was flitting around the airport frantically, pushing people out of his way, almost stumbling now, tripping over himself in his haste to find his wife, dodging the airport carts heading toward him, each of them carrying at least two massive suitcases. Adish found himself moving, weaving and bobbing as Iqbal did, trying to stay out of his line of sight, so that he was engaged in a kind of dance with a partner half a ballroom away. He noticed how disheveled Iqbal's hair was, the mud-streaked pajama bottoms, the patch of dirt across his face, as if he had run into something or fallen on his way here. As he noticed Iqbal's frantic, anxious expression, Adish fought against an involuntary stab of pity. Pity was self-defeating. He had learned this lesson the hard way on the playground when he was in third grade. He had been on the verge of defeating the fastest boy in his class in a race when he had noticed the boy's teary, stricken face as Adish had rushed past him. And in the remaining seconds, Adish had felt his feet slow down as he realized that the race meant much more to the other boy than it would ever mean to him. He felt the other boy zoom past him and when he looked up, there he was at the finish line, sneering at Adish, his young face twisted in a look of cruel, triumphant ecstasy. Adish had felt a sharp sense of regret.

Now he saw that Iqbal's darting eyes found their target. Across the enormous room, Iqbal had spotted Laleh and Kavita and was now looking for his wife. Another second and he spotted her. Having checked her bag in first, Nishta had left the queue and stood waiting on the sidelines, clutching her ticket and passport, ready to head toward customs as soon as the other two were done checking their bags. "Zoha," Iqbal called but his words were eaten up in the noise of the bustling terminal, so that only Adish, who was now a few meters away from him, heard him. Adish was moving fast now, as if he were on a soccer field, ready to intercept, to foul, to tackle, to do whatever he had to do to keep Iqbal from the goal. He was ready to use his body, his tall, powerful frame, to block Iqbal's way, to keep the three women out of his sight, to buy them the few precious minutes they needed to get through the check-in process. Because once they disappeared toward customs, he knew they would be out of reach, out of sight, untouchable. All they needed was another three, four, five minutes.

"Hey," Adish said, coming around a pillar and planting himself in front of Iqbal, so that the latter had to reel back to keep from colliding with him. Adish realized he was panting slightly and forced himself to take a breath. "What are you doing here?"

Iqbal's face showed his disdain. "You lying bastard," he said. "I'll deal with you later." He tried to step around Adish but he blocked his path again. "Get out of my way," Iqbal said through clenched teeth. "I won't ask again."

Adish mustered up a laugh he did not feel. "Or else, what? What are you going to do?" he taunted. All he could do now was stall and distract Iqbal, buying Nishta and the others a few precious moments.

Iqbal turned on him fiercely, his eyes bright with hate. "You're beneath contempt," he said. "A liar. A home-breaker. Turning my wife and sister against me." He spat at Adish's feet.

Until that moment, Adish's anger had been manufactured, just a delaying tactic. But the accusation of being a home-wrecker stung, precisely because it resonated with Adish's own doubts about what he had done. "Don't ever do that again," he said through clenched teeth.

Iqbal craned his neck to look past Adish and across the room to where the women were. "Just move out of my way," he said, shoving Adish in the chest.

The world slowed down, became a movie shot in slow motion. Adish saw the scene clearly: two men, one scrawny, the other plump but muscular, standing under the fluorescent lights of a large terminal, glowering at each other; a passerby pulling a black hard-top suitcase while yelling to his lagging wife to keep up; a pack of teenagers in blue jeans hooting and hollering and running into the other passengers; a tired-looking police officer dressed in his drab khaki uniform, walking past them, aimlessly tapping his baton on his thigh. Sound, too, seemed to have become muffled, long-drawn, distorted, a record playing at the wrong speed—the elongated wail of an infant; the metallic sound of the walker being used by an old man as it clicked on the tiled floor; the sound of Iqbal's voice as he yelled, "Zo-haaaaa!" And now, Adish turned his head, slowly, still in slow-mo, caught in this frozen river called time, and he watched as Laleh, still standing at the airline counter, turned her head to her left and he imagined he saw her eyes widen as she spotted Iqbal and then he saw her turn toward the other two, saw them spin around, saw Kavita's slowly raised hand and pointed finger as she gestured toward where he and Iqbal were locked in their strange, slow, shuffling dance.

It was up to him. He had promised Laleh he would see this through. He would see this through. If only this stupid bastard had not showed up at the airport. How lighthearted their drive here had been once Nishta had gotten into the car. The relief that they'd felt, the giddy, surreal delight that their crazy plan had actually worked, was suddenly in danger of being undone by this fool.

Iqbal was saying something now as he pushed Adish's shoulder, and Adish forced himself to shake off the slow, lethargic feeling that had come over him. "You can't win," Iqbal said. "Know why? Because Allah, praise be to Him, guided me here. I caught my traitorous sister red-handed."

"Did you hurt Mumtaz? If you hurt her, I swear . . ."

Adish saw the flame leap into Iqbal's eyes. "Now you're going to tell me how to treat my own sister, chootia?" A faint spray of spit accompanied Iqbal's words. "I'd rather kill myself than harm Mumtaz." He made a dismissive gesture. "Now move."

Suddenly, Adish knew how to end this standoff. He looked at Iqbal with new eyes, the way in which a lion assesses the distance between himself and his prey. Nishta would leave India. It was as good as done. He could—he would—destroy Iqbal. Still, he hesitated. Because the price for destroying Iqbal was high. And Adish alone would pay it, not Laleh, not this time. In cutting off Iqbal at the knees, he would also be severing the last, tenuous link to his past.

His eyes were cold as he faced Iqbal. "I'll ask you once—get out of here." There was a new authority in his voice.

Iqbal looked at him incredulously. "I'm the one who should leave? No, *you* move out of *my* way." And he pushed Adish roughly in the chest again.

Adish's hand shot out and covered Iqbal's. They stayed locked in that position for a second, and then, still looking into Iqbal's eyes, Adish yelled, "Police!" His voice sounded strange even to his own ears. "Help. Terrorist. This man has a weapon. Help." He gripped the stunned Iqbal with both arms.

"What?" Iqbal managed. "You lying . . ." He struggled to get out of Adish's grip, but a burly man in a suit came running over to help Adish. A woman scooped up her toddler and ran shrieking away from the commotion. An older man waved his wooden cane in the air and yelled, "Police. Where are the damn police?"

And then a deafening whistle sounded, and two officers—

and then four, and then six—came rushing over. They threw Iqbal to the ground and kicked him a few times. Adish turned his eyes away as Iqbal moaned. He looked over quickly to see Laleh hurrying down the hallway, hustling the other two in front of her. He felt a second's relief—and then he turned his attention back to the chaotic scene in front of him. In the din, he heard his cell phone ring in his shirt pocket but he ignored it. It was either Laleh, trying to find out what the commotion was about, or Farhad, who was getting impatient outside.

The chief inspector was pulling Iqbal up to his feet, yanking him up by his kurta. "So, madarchot," he panted, "what do you have? A revolver?"

"I have nothing," Iqbal cried and received a sharp slap to his face. "Frisk him," the inspector said to his deputy.

As the inspector stepped back, Adish pulled himself up to his full height and put his hand on the inspector's shoulder. "Inspector sahib," he whispered urgently. "I think there's been a mistake. I thought the bugger had a knife."

The inspector's face flushed with anger. "False accusation is a criminal offense," he said sharply.

"Sorry, honest mistake." He was about to say more but before he could speak Iqbal's voice reached them. "This bastard has kidnapped my wife. He's the criminal, not me."

Adish saw the inspector's eyes narrow and he gritted his teeth. He hated Iqbal for his doggedness just then. "This man just threatened me," he said to the inspector, hearing the theatrical quality in his own voice. "I think a night in the lockup would do him some good."

The inspector looked at him skeptically. "On what charge?"

Adish thought quickly. "How did he get in here? Ask him if he has a permit. This is a major security breach." He put his hand in his pocket and pulled out the typed note. "Whereas me, I'm

here to see my wife off. To America. I have special permission
to be here from the airport manager, who is a personal friend
of mine." He looked into the inspector's mean, yellow eyes and
saw reflected there the information he was transmitting—I'm
an important, influential man who could get you transferred or
promoted, while this nondescript Islamic fellow with the long
beard is a nobody. All that was not said—I live in an apartment
at Cuffe Parade worth a few million rupees, while you live in
a chawl; I am rich enough to offer bribes, while you are poor
enough to accept them; my son will someday study at any university in the world that he wishes to, while yours will struggle
to finish his bachelor's degree from a Marathi-medium college;
I can alter your destiny with a single phone call, while you can
spend your entire life trying to alter yours—was more important than what was said. The inspector looked away first, and
Adish knew he'd hit his mark.

Just then, the deputy spoke. "No weapon found, sir."

"Then what are you holding him for?"—a man in his forties
who had witnessed the whole affair addressed the group of policemen gathered around Iqbal.

The inspector spun around. "Who are you?" he said. "What
relation to this man?"

"I'm nobody," the stranger said. "I don't even know this man.
I'm just a passenger. But I witnessed you roughing up this man
for no reason."

The inspector glared at the man. "A passenger, eh? Here to
catch a plane, is it?" His mouth twisted in a snarl. "Then go.
Catch your bloody plane. Unless you want to be arrested for
aiding a terrorist."

"But—" the stranger protested.

"Gentleman, I'm asking properly one more time. Please go."

The man scowled at Adish and then walked away. But his

intervention had rattled the inspector, who turned toward Iqbal. "Okay, chalo, let's see your bloody ticket," the inspector said.

Iqbal was silent.

"No ticket? How about permission slip?"

"I have nothing," Iqbal said sullenly. "But I—"

"No ticket, no nothing, and still you got in?" With a swift movement, the inspector surreptitiously but savagely stomped on his foot. Adish winced as Iqbal let out a soft cry. "Saala, troublemaker," the inspector said. "How the hell did you sneak in here? What terrorist activity were you planning, you chootia?"

"I was planning nothing . . ." Iqbal started but seeing the look on the inspector's face, he fell silent, having finally acknowledged the futility of his situation. The inspector spoke into that silence. "Chalo, take him away to the chowki. Hold him until I get there."

Adish was scanning the room for any sign of Laleh as they handcuffed Iqbal. "I'll get you for this, Adish," Iqbal spat out, a moment before he was jerked back by the deputy.

"Iqbal," Adish said quietly. "Just shut up. For your own sake, I'm telling you to shut up." He turned again to the inspector and motioned for him to walk a few paces with him. "Listen," he said. "This fellow is basically harmless. He's just a bit confused. I don't want you to rough him up, okay? Don't touch him. Just keep him overnight. Let him cool down. Which station are you taking him to?"

The inspector told him. "It's the nearest one, sir," he added.

"Okay. I'll stop by there in the morning. Or I'll send my peon. Release him then, would you?"

"No problem, sir."

Adish eyed the man's name plate. "You're a good man, Inspector Manmohan. My peon will come to the chowki tomorrow with a small envelope for you. What time should I send him?"

The inspector looked away. "My shift starts at three o'clock, sir," he mumbled.

"Okay. I'll send Jogesh at that time. Thanks for your help."

He dialed Laleh's cell as soon as he had walked away from the inspector. "What happened?" she asked immediately.

"Iqbal showed up."

"I know. I saw him. But then there were too many people and I couldn't see. Did you two get into a fight or something?"

He smiled mirthlessly. A dull ache had started in his heart and was spreading through him. "Something like that."

"Are you okay? Did he hurt you?"

"That pipsqueak?" He forced a bravado into his voice that he didn't feel. For Laleh's sake. He didn't want her to worry.

"Where is he now?"

"Gone." He would tell her more after she reached America. Or maybe he never would. His behavior hadn't been exactly honorable. He felt a bitter, metallic taste in his mouth.

"What do you mean, gone?"

"Lal. Forget about it. Just enjoy your time with your friends. Everything's fine. Taken care of. Now go. Enjoy yourself. Tell Nishta sorry about the Mangola. Maybe I'll buy her a drink in the U.S. next year."

She made a soft, choking sound. "I miss you already. How can this be?"

He smiled. "It's easy when you're married to someone as dazzling as me." But he didn't feel dazzling. He felt—what?— cheap . . . dishonest . . . corrupt. All of the above. Tears threatened him. "Bye, janu," he said hastily. "I'd better go check on Farhad. He's been standing outside for a long time."

But he didn't wander outside. Instead, he dialed Mumtaz's

number, his heart sinking with each second that the phone went unanswered. What had Iqbal done to her? But then he remembered what Iqbal had said about not harming his sister and, to his surprise, he realized that he believed him. After everything that had happened between them, he trusted Iqbal.

Adish sat on one of the blue plastic chairs and held his head in his hands. Terrorist. He had called Iqbal a terrorist. How he had despised those politicians, both Indian and foreign, who had exploited the tragedy of 9/11 for cheap political gain. How he had railed against the Indian government when it had rewritten the laws so that it was easier to label political opponents with that dreaded word, so that it was easier for the police to trap and snare political prisoners in the iron net of antiterrorist activities. And how effortlessly he had done the same convenient thing, had taken advantage of Iqbal's long beard, his mullah-like attire. How easily he had exploited the reflexive dislike and fear that many Indians had for Islam. He had counted on the inspector's own prejudices, had used the inspector's visceral distrust of Muslims to play off against Iqbal's otherness. The Parsi as middle-man, as trickster, as the cool, suave, immoral asshole who played one party against the other. How was he different from the bastard who had molested Mumtaz, who had taken advantage of her minority status as a Muslim?

Maybe Laleh had been right about him all along. She alone had sensed that his moral center had the firmness of pudding. What had she said to him that day in the bedroom? That everything mattered. Maybe it did. Maybe the lie he had told decades ago, the easy manner in which he had colluded with his father-in-law, had set him on a course that had brought him here, to the betrayal of a man he had once considered a brother. But if everything mattered, what about the other parts of his life? He had been honest in his business dealings, quite an accomplishment in this goddamn corrupt country. He had never cheated on his wife, had been a loving and attentive father to his children, a kind and generous employer. Did all of that count for nothing?

He heard the self-justification of his thoughts, heard the whiny, bargaining quality, and his face contorted with self-disgust. The fact that you don't cheat on your taxes justifies what you just did? he mocked himself. Getting a man thrown in jail because he was unlucky enough to be born a Muslim? What is your quarrel with Iqbal, after all? But then he remembered looking in the rearview mirror just as Nishta had flung back her veil and how she'd blinked her eyes at the sudden rush of light and he felt a lump in his throat. He did have a quarrel with Iqbal. It was his treatment of Nishta. He had had Iqbal jailed so that she could be free. Wasn't that the way of the world, the constant lesson of history, the one unchanging rule—that with every new world order the old guard had to be killed, imprisoned, banished, exiled? He shook his head, knowing that he wasn't making too much sense.

"Excuse me." It was the old man with the cane, who had called for the police.

Adish looked up, startled. "Yes?"

The overall affect of the man was one of buttoned-down neatness. He had a white, well-trimmed beard, round glasses that reflected the glare of the overhead lights, and wore a dark, well-pressed Nehru jacket. "I just wanted to congratulate you," the man said with a slight accent. Many years abroad, Adish guessed. "What you did was heroic."

Adish's face flushed. "It turned out to be nothing," he mumbled. "My mistake." He felt trapped in his seat with the elderly man standing in front of him.

The old man's glasses flashed as he shook his head sharply. "Can't be too careful," he said. "These people are spreading like a cancer all across the world. Have to be crushed before they take over."

Adish felt nauseous as it occurred to him that the man was talking to him as a fellow sympathizer, as someone he could confide his hateful ideology in. "Excuse me," he said pointedly, but the man spoke over him. "You're a Parsi, correct?" he asked and Adish nodded warily.

The man smiled. "A model community, the Parsis. Adaptable. Wish the other minorities took after you. But the Muslims and Christians . . ." He made a disgusted sound and then looked over his left shoulder. "I see my son is calling for me. Good evening."

Adish watched as the stranger moved away briskly. He rose to his feet and took a few steps toward the man. "He was my friend," he called out. "He had no weapon." The old man turned around, his mouth slightly open, as if he might say something. But he merely nodded and resumed walking.

He would try and make amends, of course, Adish thought, as he made his way toward the exit. Maybe he would go to the jail tomorrow instead of sending Jogesh. He wouldn't speak to Iqbal, not tomorrow. But maybe over the next few weeks he could check in on him. He would stop by the shop where Iqbal worked. Iqbal would be angry at first, violently angry, even. But he would win him over. He could offer him a job in his businesses, or if that didn't interest Iqbal, he could . . .

"Bullshit." He said the word out loud, drawing a glare from a matronly woman walking past him. Stop lying to yourself, he said. None of this would come to pass. He would spring Iqbal out of jail tomorrow, for sure. But after that, their association would end—unless Iqbal came to his door seeking revenge. And somehow, he doubted that would come to pass. Because the scene at the airport had made one thing clear—that he, Adish, could always crush Iqbal, could use the very fact of Iqbal's Muslimness against him. A night in jail would simply reinforce this message. No, there would be no righting this situation. He and Iqbal would go back to where they were before Armaiti had called with her sad news, would return to their earlier positions, occupying different parts of the city, their fates never intersecting. This time, Mr. Fixit would lie dormant.

He walked out through the open doors, happy to leave the tired, recycled air of the terminal behind him. Out of the corner of his eye he saw Inspector Manmohan, but the man was checking the tickets of one of the passengers and didn't see him. He dialed his cell phone and let it ring but Farhad didn't answer. Adish knew that it would be hard for the boy to hear his phone amid the din of honking cars and the chatter of the crowd that swelled outside the airport. He looked around desperately at the thousands of faces around him wondering how he'd ever find his son in this crowd when he saw Farhad's smiling face approaching him. He felt something swell in his heart, felt a moist tenderness for his beautiful, untainted son. "There you are," he said and hugged him as if they'd been apart for years rather than hours.

"Okay, Dad, easy," Farhad muttered uncomfortably. "Did Mom leave?"

He looked at his watch. "They will be boarding soon."

"So everything went fine? No problems with the bags?" And before Adish could answer, Farhad added, "I liked Nishta auntie. She's sweet."

"Isn't she?" he said distractedly. Maybe they could visit Nishta in America next year, he was thinking. Richard had said something about contacting an attorney to figure out how to keep her in the country permanently. What was that expression? Once you save a life, you are responsible for it. He just hoped that they had indeed saved Nishta's life, that he wasn't deluding himself into thinking so.

"Want me to get the car? I had to park pretty far away."

Adish put his arm around his son's shoulders. "No," he said. "I want to walk. Let's walk together."

27

Laleh chewed on her lower lip as she hung up from the phone call with Adish, not liking the rote, hollow way in which he had answered her questions about Iqbal's unexpected appearance and his sudden disappearance. Something unpleasant must've happened with Iqbal—he hadn't left the airport simply because Adish had said please, she thought wryly. She would find out more when they next talked on the phone. The more pressing task was to calm Nishta down.

"I can't believe he was here," Nishta kept saying. "And that he left? Without me? I know Iqbal—he'll make sure I don't board this plane."

"Nishta," Kavita said, snapping her fingers. "Look at me. We'll preboard, okay, if that makes you feel better? Nobody's going to keep you back now. Do you think Adish would let him hurt you?"

"I don't understand," Nishta said, shaking her head. "How he found out."

Kavita sighed. "Look. His meeting probably ended early and he saw your note. We lost so much time in the damn traffic at the airport, remember?"

Nishta looked wild-eyed. "But what about Mumtaz? Do you think he . . . ?"

"I don't understand," Nishta said, shaking her head. "He must've gone home early. But why? Why didn't he go to his meeting?"

"What does it matter?" Kavita said. "Maybe the meeting was short. We lost so much time in the damn traffic at the airport. If it hadn't been for that, he wouldn't have even—"

"I didn't tell you this," Nishta interrupted. "I did something really stupid. I left Iqbal a note."

"You did what?" Laleh said.

Nishta looked miserable. "I wrote him a note this morning. Telling him I wasn't coming back. I felt like I owed him that much, you know?"

"You told him you weren't returning? Forever?" Laleh couldn't keep the disbelief out of her voice. "After all the elaborate planning we did?"

"I did. I'm so sorry, Laleh. I really wasn't thinking."

Laleh bit down on her tongue. She could see that Nishta was on the verge of hysteria. Nothing to be gained by chastising her now. She would have to squeeze in a call to Adish before they took off, alerting him to what had happened. "It's okay," she said. "No use crying over—"

"But what about Mumtaz?" Nishta looked wild-eyed. "Do you think he . . ."

"Mumtaz is fine," Laleh said in a pacifying tone. "She's okay."

"I want to phone her. To make sure."

Laleh took a deep breath. "Adish said Mumtaz is safe," she lied. "She left before Iqbal got home and saw your note."

She watched as disbelief wrestled with hope on Nishta's face. "Really?" she said finally. "Adish said that?"

Laleh forced herself to look Nishta in the eye. "Yes."

"Thank God. Thank God."

Kavita put her arm around Nishta's shoulders and the two

women wandered around the lounge, Kavita speaking quietly but firmly. After a few minutes, she managed to coax a wan smile out of Nishta.

Laleh moved to a corner of the large room and dialed Adish's number. The phone rang several times before it went into voice-mail. "Hey," she said, raising her voice so that she could be heard over the din. "Got some bad news, I'm afraid. Turns out Nishta left a note for Iqbal in which she told him she's not returning to India. Pretty crazy, huh? Anyway, that's probably why he came to the airport. I just want you to be careful, okay, janu? Alert the kids, also. No telling what he might do. . . ." Out of the cor-ner of her eye she saw the other two headed toward her. "Okay, 'bye for now. I love you."

She hung up and watched as Nishta and Kavita walked across the room. She felt a spurt of anger at Nishta for having endan-gered her family with a stupid, impulsive gesture, but shook it off. She would not start the trip by being resentful of her friend. Besides, it was hard to stay angry with someone as broken and hurt as Nishta. She had changed, perhaps forever, Laleh realized. There was a nervousness, a skittishness about her that was new. Well, new to me, she corrected herself. The poor girl has prob-ably lived like this for years now. Laleh felt a pang of sadness at the thought of leaving Nishta behind when they left America in three weeks. How in the world would she manage? And with Richard preoccupied with taking care of Armaiti, how much could they expect him to do for her? She knew that Nishta was planning on helping with Armaiti's care, that she would tempo-rarily live with her. But later . . . after Armaiti . . . Lal shook her head. They would simply have to stay involved in her life. Nishta would be fine. Look at what she'd already achieved. Despite all his faults, Laleh knew that leaving Iqbal hadn't been easy for Nishta. But she'd done it. Don't be fooled by the nervous tics and the abrupt manner, Laleh told herself. She remembered that in college Nishta had had more stamina, more physical strength, than any of them. She recalled the set of her mouth the morning she'd come to college and announced that her mother had threatened to commit suicide if she married a Muslim. "What did you say?" they had asked breathlessly. And Nishta had looked at the three of them with cold, clear eyes and said, "I told her her life was her own business. Just like my life was my own. And I am going to marry Iqbal."

Remembering that long-ago incident now, Laleh felt a sour feeling in her stomach. What kind of a mother says such an awful thing to her child? she wondered. But the memory also kindled hope in her. What kind of a daughter—especially an Indian daughter, brought up to respect her parents, to believe that duty came before love, to be self-sacrificing, selfless, to always put the needs of others ahead of her own, could have given such an answer? Only one who was tough as nails, who knew the dictates of her heart as clearly as Nishta obviously did. She'll be fine, Laleh thought. She'll not just survive, she'll thrive.

She smiled as Nishta and Kavita reached her. "Seems like I'm destined to lose all my friends to America," she grumbled good-naturedly. "First Armaiti, now you."

Nishta took Laleh's hand and, in a completely unselfconscious gesture, held it up to her mouth and kissed it. "You'll always have me, my Lal," she said. She held on to Laleh for another moment before letting her go. "I need to go to the loo," she said. "Don't leave without me, accha?"

Kavita grinned. "Yeah, right. After what we've been through."

They watched as Nishta crossed the lounge and disappeared into the bathroom. Laleh said, "Let's sit. I'm exhausted."

Kavita nodded. "You look awful."

Laleh grimaced. "Thanks, Ka. You're so good for my mo-rale."

"You know what I mean, yaar."

Laleh sighed. "This business with Iqbal has wiped me out. Adish was really vague on the phone, but I know something hap-pened between him and Iqbal." She shifted in her seat so that she could look at Kavita. "Tell me we did the right thing. With Nishta, I mean."

Kavita stared straight ahead. "I think we did the only thing we could," she said after a while. "I mean, leaving Nishta to her fate would've been a betrayal of . . . everything."

"That's what I keep telling myself. But I must say, seeing Iqbal at the airport freaked me out."

They were quiet for a moment. Then, "Ka," Laleh said, not bothering to disguise the ache in her voice. "What happened? I mean, to Iqbal? To us? How did we end up on opposite sides?"

Kavita smiled, and there was a world of sadness and hard-won wisdom in that smile. "What's the clarifying principle here, you mean? Remember how we used to try and solve all political ar-guments by asking that question, Lal? It's amazing how we were ever stupid enough to think there was a single answer. Because there isn't one. What happened to Iqbal? Life happened. In all its banality, brutality, cruelty, unfairness. But also in its beauty, pleasures, and delights. Life happened."

Laleh opened her mouth to argue, to protest that Kavita's answer was too easy, not sufficiently critical of the social forces that ground human beings into the dust, when a figure moving toward them caught her eye.

The shaking started as soon as Nishta went into the bathroom. She bunched up her robe and lowered herself on the commode, waiting for the sensation to pass, but her hands fluttered like butterfly wings and her bones felt as cold as the moon. It was as though her very skeleton was rattling. Seeing Iqbal appear at the airport and then disappear had unnerved her. Even now, she could not believe that she was actually free, that she was getting away with this. Surely something will still go wrong, she thought. Surely, at this very moment, he is talking to the police, convincing them to come looking for her. But then she remembered that Adish was at the airport, too, and she felt a little better. Besides, if something were to happen, if Iqbal were to create a scene, surely it would've happened by now.

Why had she been stupid enough to leave Iqbal a note? A dangerous pity had made her do so, the thought of him coming to an empty house and no explanation too bleak for her to bear. When she'd spotted Iqbal at the airport, her first thought was that Mumtaz had betrayed her after all. But already she knew better. Sweet, guileless Mumtaz. How could she have been suspicious of Mumtaz, of all people? If anything, she had betrayed Mumtaz. Would she ever understand? How would she react when she found out that her sister-in-law had flown forever, that she was never returning to her cage? She hoped Mumtaz would heed her advice and never confess her role to Iqbal.

Nishta looked down at her hands and for an instant imagined that she saw claws instead of fingers. Was she really this strong? This tough? To deceive not just her husband, but the woman who had been a younger sister to her, who had risked her relations with her entire family, to help her? To use Armaiti's illness as a ladder with which to climb out of the dark pit her life had become? Could a woman, a human being, turn her back on so much, give up everything that once belonged to her and that she once belonged to—husband, parents, in-laws, home, city, country—and still be called human? Or was there another category for people like her, would she suddenly sprout fangs and horns, would she be consigned to a new category of beast, another species—rudderless, rootless, homeless, stateless? How many metamorphoses must she still go through? First Nishta, then Zoha, and still it wasn't enough? Was her evolution still unfinished? Who else must she become? Who else would she become?

She shivered again. But just once. She realized she had been holding her bladder and now she let go and peed. And as she peed, she felt warmth seep back into her body. As the shaking stopped, it felt as if her body, its true shape, was being returned to her. This is the last time I'll be peeing on Indian soil, she thought, suddenly, implausibly, and the realization was accompanied by a sadness sharp as glass and an excitement bright as a diamond. Yes, it would be hard, building a new life in a new place. Who knew if she would succeed, who knew whether she would ultimately regret what she was throwing away? But one thing she knew for certain: it would be her life. The failures, the regrets, the successes, the joys—they would be her own. It would be her name on her life, from now on.

She flushed the toilet and came out and rubbed her hands vigorously at the cracked porcelain sink. She had her hand on the outer door of the restroom, ready to rejoin Kavita and La-leh, when she remembered something. She turned around and went back in toward the stalls.

"Life happened," Kavita concluded and Laleh opened her mouth to argue, to protest that Kavita's answer was too easy, not sufficiently critical of the social forces that ground human beings into the dust, when a figure moving toward them caught her eye.

It was Nishta. She was wearing a red T-shirt and blue denim pants. The outfit was poorly tailored and Laleh noticed that Nishta's soft belly jiggled through the thin cloth of the T-shirt as she moved. But what took Laleh's breath away was Nishta's hair. It fell like a thick, dark waterfall down her face until it stopped, at her upper back. Even as she watched, Nishta was reaching up to gather her hair into a ponytail. There was something unfamiliar—and heartbreakingly familiar—about the gesture.

Beside her, she heard Kavita breathe a soft "Oh my."

Both of them rose involuntarily as Nishta reached them. Laleh cocked her head, a bemused look on her face. "No more burkha?" she said.

"No more burkha," Nishta answered. Her voice was expressionless but her face looked as if it were made of liquid wax, melting and freezing and melting again from multiple, contradictory emotions.

"How do you feel?"

Nishta thought for a moment. "Naked . . . exposed . . . scared. And free."

Laleh smiled deeply, looking into Nishta's eyes. "What'd you do with it?"

Nishta's eyes shone. "I dumped it. Into a dustbin in the bathroom."

The dustbin of history, Laleh thought. Some things deserved to be relegated to the dustbin of history.

A half hour later they are boarding the plane. They are traveling business class—Adish had bought Nishta's ticket, refusing to hear about Mumtaz paying for it. They settle into their seats and almost immediately, it seems, the stewardess offers them a drink. Kavita orders a gin and tonic—earlier, she has confessed to being an uneasy flyer, a fact that Nishta finds oddly gratifying—while the other two sip on orange juice.

They hear and feel the rumble of the plane's engines. Laleh tries Adish's cell phone one more time but there is no answer. Nishta longs to borrow the phone, wanting to check in on Mumtaz, but something makes her hesitate. She is afraid of what she might find out. So she tells herself that she has to start practicing letting go right now, from inside this giant steel beehive, from this place that is already both India and not-India. She looks out the small window into the blackness of the night outside, and realizes she has already begun her new life. Her body will simply have to catch up with its new reality, her brain will have to learn to selectively remember and not remember.

Beside her, Laleh glances at her wristwatch. "Half-hour late, already," she mutters. "Guess we're on Bombay time."

Kavita speaks as she chews on a piece of ice. "I don't care. Just as long as we make up the time. I'm so anxious to see Armaiti, I could fly this plane myself."

"She coming to the airport?"

"Can't say. Diane said it would all depend on how she feels." Kavita has been talking to Diane almost daily the past two weeks.

The plane's doors slam shut a few minutes later. Nishta experiments with the buttons on her seat, raises and lowers the leg rest. She thinks of Armaiti waiting for them at the other end of this journey, willing them toward her, across oceans and mountains, reeling them in like a kite. She contemplates for a second how much lovelier this trip would be if they were going to America for a happy occasion—Diane getting married, say—but then yanks her mind back from its path of sentimentality and wistfulness. She is suddenly, profoundly, tearfully grateful to Armaiti for the invitation, for thinking of them, *her*, for wanting them, *her*, the gift of them, as her dying wish. It is enough that Armaiti is waiting for them at the other end. It is enough that she is still alive.

Already she is feeling herself become a nomad, a vagabond, a ghost occupying a no-man's-land. I could live here forever, she thinks, on this giant ship in the sky. The cold synthetic air, the impersonal buttons and lights, the regimented routine of eat-drink-sleep, the anonymous feeling of sharing a flying house with hundreds of strangers, it all agrees with her, she discovers. She tells herself to remember this feeling, the ease with which she is slipping into a new fate. It is evidence of her toughness, a toughness that she will need to wear like a bulletproof vest in the months to come.

The sound of the engines rises to a shriek-like pitch. The screen in front of her features a pretty woman telling her about floatation devices and oxygen masks. Nishta stifles a laugh. Where were you and your safety instructions during my married life? she asks the woman on the screen. The past few weeks? That's when I needed rescuing.

But she was, wasn't she? Rescued, that is. Whisked away from her life, from this city of a million memories that is now receding furiously behind her as the jet tears down the runway, as if the plane wants to escape the past as much as she does. Lifted, she was, like a teacup, and placed into this flying saucer. She grimaces at the pun.

They are climbing now, into the night sky, and the lights of Bombay look like a weak constellation of stars. She wants to blow them a kiss—or, more precisely, she wants to blow them out, suck in her breath, make a wish, and then blow out those lights, as she trades the known world in for the unknown.

She looks down until the thick cloud cover snuffs out every light below. Bombay, the city where she was loved and where she loved, is no more. She looks out for another moment and then leans back in her seat. She takes Laleh's hand in hers.

I am here, she thinks. We are here. We are all here.

Acknowledgments

Deep gratitude and thanks to the following, who light my path every day:

Noshir and Homai Umrigar, Eustathea Kavouras, Gulshan and Rointon Andhyarujina, Roshni and Dhunji Dastur, Judy and Kershasp Pundole, Diana Bilimoria, Kim Conidi, Barb Guthrie, Barb Miller, Noreen Chambers, Perveen Freeland, Hutokshi Rustomfram, Anne Reid, Wendy Langenderfer, Arkady and Natasha Lerner, Cyndi Howard, and Barb Hipsman.

A blown kiss to those who have left this world, but not my heart:

Ketty, Jeroo and Jamshed Umrigar, Harriet Kavouras, and Mani Chandaru.

Hugs and kitty kisses to Kulfi and Baklava, for curling in my lap and keeping me company on days when the writing was slow.

For the children in my life—Feroza Freeland, Anna Lerner, Bini Iranpur, Sara, Abbey, and Elizabeth Florian, Madison, Thomas, and Quinton Likosar, and Maime and Josie Blados—you reassure me that the world will remain a beautiful place in your capable hands.

This book benefited greatly from the input of Dr. David Peereboom, oncologist at the Cleveland Clinic's Brain Tumor and Neuro-Oncology Center. Thanks to Phillip Canuto for introducing me to Dr. Peereboom.

Thank you, Sarah Willis, for reading the book in manuscript form. Thank you, "Pen Gals," for reminding me that writing is holy work. Thanks to Luis Alberto Urrea, whose definition of "the trembling ones" inspires my work.

A special thanks to Claire Wachtel, Marly Rusoff, Michael Morrison, and Jonathan Burnham who make everything possible. A shout-out to the folks at HarperCollins, for their talent and hard work. Thanks to my colleagues at Case Western Reserve University, whose brilliance, good humor, and camaraderie I cherish.